WHEN WE DANCED ON WATER

WHEN
WE
DANCED
ON
WATER

ALSO BY EVAN FALLENBERG

Light Fell

WHEN
WE
DANCED
ON
WATER

A Novel

Evan Fallenberg

HARPER ⬤ PERENNIAL

NEW YORK • LONDON • TORONTO • SYDNEY • NEW DELHI • AUCKLAND

HARPER ● PERENNIAL

HarperCollins books may be purchased for educational, business, or sales promo-
tional use. For information please write: Special Markets Department, Harper-
Collins Publishers, 10 East 53rd Street, New York, NY 10022.

FIRST EDITION

Designed by Justin Dodd

Library of Congress Cataloging-in-Publication Data
Fallenberg, Evan, 1961-
 When we danced on water : a novel / Evan Fallenberg. -- First edition.
 pages cm
 ISBN 978-0-06-203332-1 (pbk.)
 1. Choreographers—Fiction. 2. Older men—Fiction. 3. Waitresses—Fiction.
4. Middle-aged women—Fiction. 5. Tel Aviv (Israel)—Fiction. I. Title.
 PS3606.A43W48 2011
 813'.6—dc22 2010053600

11 12 13 14 15 OV/RRD 10 9 8 7 6 5 4 3 2 1

For Hagai and Micha, more than ever

ACKNOWLEDGMENTS

I wish to express my deepest gratitude to the following, all of whom took an active role in helping me create this book: Abby Frucht, Mary Domenico, Mary Grimm, Jenni Tsafrir, Joan Leegant, Kathy Jacobi and George Eltman, for reading the manuscript at various stages and providing excellent suggestions; Ayelet Hadar, for sharing her love and knowledge of Vermeer, and a theory all her own; Miriam Wrobel, for immeasurable help with all things concerning ballet, choreography and Denmark; Peter Koeppe in Berlin, the late Lui Beilin in Copenhagen and Terry Goodman Lipman in Jerusalem, for deepening my familiarity with my characters and their milieux; Jill Horowitz, for hospitality and the Sophie Calle exhibit that changed everything; Carolyn Starman Hessel, for ongoing encouragement and advice over excellent food; agents Deborah Harris and Robert Guinsler, for knowing when to say no and when to say yes; Rakesh Satyal, for unparalleled editorial acumen; Vermont College of Fine Arts and the MacDowell Colony, for the space to create; Rosalie Fallenberg, for behind-the-scenes assistance; and, especially, Yariv, Yonina, Micha and Hagai, my four reasons why.

WHEN
WE
DANCED
ON
WATER

WHEN
WE
DANCED
ON
WATER

H e said, "Where's Rona."
She said, "Who's Rona."

These were, in fact, their first words, though neither would have remembered them even a week later, had anyone asked. And the issue of Rona was never solved, since there had never been a Rona. Maybe she was Nora, or Nola, or Ola, or Ora; he was always getting it wrong. But she had brought his coffee the way he liked it—strong, one sugar, hot foamed milk on the side, along with a glass of water with ice and a slice of lemon—and so that morning when *she* had appeared at his table, this new she, he was already missing someone he had never really cared for beyond his cup of coffee.

Their encounter took place in a Tel Aviv coffee bar so small that it cannot be called a restaurant and barely even a café. When disassembled at the end of the day, chairs piled on tables and stools upturned on the bar, it squeezes into an area no bigger than a closet. But this coffee bar is in an old shopping arcade, once newfangled and popular, that stands near Ibn Gabirol and King Saul streets, occupying a niche, an alcove, that most people run past to get to the medical center at the back, the cosmetician, the sex shop, or the ballet studio in the

basement. Regulars come here to swap complaints with Yossi, the proprietor, while enjoying the brew from his excellent Italian coffee machine, but others notice nothing more than the fake tulips budding from tiny vases on each table as they whip by.

"Where's Rona?" he asked, tilting his head back and fixing a watery gaze on her disheveled face.

"Who's Rona?" she asked, startled not by the question but by his eyes, one blue, the other green. They made her feel that the floor was gently tilting.

"Never mind," he said, and he gave her instructions on how to prepare his order.

Teo stops for coffee late in the morning on the days he now comes to supervise, advise, or merely watch the dancers of the Tel Aviv Ballet; he no longer teaches. After he has unlocked the studio doors, turned on the lights, aired the place (there is always a below-ground mustiness one gets used to in minutes), he checks his desk for mail or messages left for him by the ballet company administrator, then heads upstairs for coffee with a pile of paperwork and dance magazines in hand. Within just a few days Vivi knows to have Yossi start preparing the coffee the minute she sees Teo pass by on his way downstairs, so that his order will be ready by the time he reemerges.

When Vivi leaves the coffee bar she never takes the short, direct route home. First, in nearly any weather, she steps outside the shopping arcade, parks herself on the nearest bench—a slatted wooden affair that the Tel Aviv municipality occasionally paints green—and smokes one of the three daily cigarettes she allows herself. She stretches her legs out as far as they will go, wriggles her toes, watches passersby and birds, and enjoys each deep inhalation of her Winstons. When she has had her fill of smoking and looking, she rises slowly, as if with regret, and chooses a direction. Sometimes she will walk to the right because the woman who just walked by was wearing a beautiful pair of shoes, and sometimes she will walk to the left because there are a few clouds in that direction. There are days when she closes her eyes and spins around, then chooses left or right, and days when she stands waiting for a sign, any sign, and does not move until that sign appears. It always does, though once it took a full five minutes, during which a little boy stopped to ask if she were lost.

Then she begins her perambulations, wending her way from street to street in concentric, uneven circles. She walks eastward down Kaplan Street past the peaked-roof houses with flowerboxes built by the Templars, toward Azrieli Center, where she bends her head backward to stare at the edge of the triangular tower as it spikes

the sky. She walks north to the open emptiness of Rabin Square. She walks west under ficus trees dangling vines like moss to the shade of the Royal Poincianas at Masaryk Square. And mostly she walks south, where Tel Aviv really happens.

She has what she calls her Theme Walks, still capricious but with a motif. So there is Scent Walk, where she picks up on the smells of coffee and steamed milk, falafel and shaved lamb's meat, hyssop seasoning and roasting cashews and coriander and chicken on a spit and even certain people, leaning into their wakes as they pass; there is Foliage Walk, for noticing and naming the great many flowering plants she encounters; there are Jewish Walks, mostly at holiday times, when she counts Stars of David and synagogues and Orthodox passersby and Chabad emissaries and old men selling skullcaps on overturned orange crates. She has Graffiti Walks and Merchandise Walks and Architecture Walks and People Walks. Her most frequent are Baby Walks, featuring soft, cuddly babies of every color and size and women with bellies in various stages of pregnancy. On bad days she has Ugly Walks: dog shit on the sidewalk, people spitting, honking cars, the junkies and pimps near the old Central Bus Station. No matter what kind of walk she is having, though, she is aware of the stunning, relentless blue sky and green leaves nearly all year round. She wanders past old stores—Zion the Tailor, Madame Julie's Institute of Beauty, a hardware store offering "Hebrew labor"—and shiny new places, their names written in English only. She cuts through parking lots and apartment buildings and hotels in order to reach backstreets, she emerges at the seashore and traverses beach after beach, each with its own crowd and style. There are people she waves at along her way—some whom she knows, some just because they seem pleasant—and at times she stops to exchange a word about the weather or the traffic or a cute baby or an elegant dress. She talks

more to women than to men, since the men usually misinterpret her intentions, but children get more of her attention than anyone else. She walks like this for an hour, sometimes two, until finally she has had her fill of the city and can go in peace and silence to her apartment.

This ritual began years earlier, in a different country and climate, and continued quite naturally, almost compulsively, after her dramatic return to Israel. Mostly, in the twenty years that have passed since then, she has not missed a day, whether she has just finished work in a bicycle repair shop, a nursery school, a pastry shop, a library—after all her jobs, no matter whether she spends her days on her feet or at a desk, she walks, clears her mind and fills it up again, tries to observe but not to think or even feel. Her footsteps grow slower as she approaches home; she smiles less. There will be no messages on the answering machine save those from her worried mother, Leah; there will be breakfast dishes to wash and rumpled sheets either to stretch taut or nap on, there will be walls taunting her loneliness and framed photographs flaunting other people's happiness and her own, long ago.

Maybe her flatmate, Pincho, will be home and awake, maybe not. She likes finding him there, a genial, patient presence, a good listener, someone who, like Vivi herself, has few plans outside work and welcomes time-consuming disruptions, always ready for a new project, an adventure. She loves, too, his perfect, effortless male beauty, the way every feature seems expertly crafted. After nearly two years sharing a flat, that beauty still catches her under the rib cage, tingles in her fingers and toes. She wipes her face of all interest or attentiveness but secretly she watches every movement and gesture: the way his pale gray eyes grow luminous with excitement; the way his smile spreads slowly, evenly, across his face until no corner of it remains

untouched; the nervous thrum of his fingers when about to meet a member of his family; and the tightening of his countenance—eyes that narrow, lips that purse, all of this puzzling to Vivi—when he realizes that a man or a woman has taken notice of his looks and is wooing him.

She lets herself into the apartment and knows at once she is alone there. Pincho's door is ajar, the flat is fresh with open windows and cross breezes. His favorite mug and another—one neither she nor he drinks from—stand drying on the countertop. She peers into the waste bin and sees tissues, the glint of a shiny packet farther down. She assumes it is a condom but she closes the lid before she can tell for sure. She glances about the kitchen, uncertain what to do now or for the next bundle of hours that stand before her like a dark thicket of pines.

T he spotlights are blue and gold, the air around him speckled with floating gems that sparkle and shimmer like bubbles in his wake. Dark figures—his fellow dancers—crowd the stage, but they are silent and still, and, like the enraptured audience, focused completely, solely, on him. Indeed, he feels himself to be the source of all the air and light and energy in the great theater, as if he had sucked it away from everyone and everything else, gathered it in from every corner of the cavernous hall. His feet effortlessly negotiate a complicated routine but his body simply twirls, spinning evenly under a powdery trail of stars. He neither tires nor dizzies. His arms levitate to shoulder height and bob there on waves of air.

A man in full dress uniform joins him onstage, barely visible at the edge of a gold spotlight. He continues to spin as the expressionless man sidles closer, stealing into the arc of his dance. The man presents him with a rose, whose scent reaches him and catches a ride on a twirl. He still watches the stars but is also, always, aware of the intruder just beyond his vision.

The uniformed man raises a gloved hand and the dancer halts, his back to the officer. The spotlights dim and the stars flicker and fade. He can feel the officer close behind, the man's breath on his neck. Quite suddenly the officer rams the rose, now thick and hard,

inside him from behind. It penetrates and pierces, and he feels the thorny, leafy flower climb higher and higher in his body, snaking past his heart and through his lungs until it rises through his throat and pries open his mouth, wider and wider, climbing all the while so that his head swings back on his hinged neck and the rose pushes upward past his gaping mouth, growing and smothering and growing and smothering until the tips of the petals tickle the ebony sky.

Teo awakens before dawn, more stiff and sore than usual. With difficulty he closes his mouth by cracking his jaw sideways. He catches a sidelong glimpse of Nelly in her nightdress standing at the edge of the bed as she gently lifts his head, with its thick and unruly mane of white hair, and slides under it the freshly plumped pillow. He stares up at the ceiling as he catches his breath and regains his bearings. After a minute he asks quietly, in Polish, "Was I . . . moaning again?"

Nelly, patient and stoic as an old dog, nods. She turns and walks silently from the room, but Teo can hear her morning sounds from the kitchen and knows she will return soon with a cup of steaming tea and a glazed-glass bowl of sugar cubes and two butter cookies on a china plate. It is too early for the tiny single rose in the porcelain bud vase or the linen napkin; those will arrive with breakfast, precisely at seven. He knows the night-darkened sky keeps Nelly from breaking routine, that as a creature of habit she will refuse to alter their schedule a whit until it has become perfectly clear that these early mornings of fear and pain have in fact *become* their routine; that each day, before morning's official arrival, he will awaken parched and cheerless and contorted and that she, his faithful housekeeper for twenty-five years, will bring him tea and comfort on a tray.

He does not tell her of his nightly dream; their intimacy, though recently expanded due to his increasing frailty, has always been minimal. In fact, apart from discussing the weekly letters he receives from

his sister, Margot, they talk little beyond the technicalities of their mutual existence: the daily menu, the weekly schedule, the rare visit. When he was younger, healthier, still choreographing, she kept the house silent and guest-free to enable his creativity, and managed the household with a bare minimum of questions in spite of her faltering, primitive Hebrew, a terrible handicap with shopkeepers and handymen. Even now that he no longer creates and few people come to call, their cloistered existence renounces change, their quietude turns its back to noise and life.

A tall eucalyptus tree in the garden strums its soft, drooping leaves against the bedroom window. It is too early for the birds, those that did not travel south to the Nile Delta or the Red Sea; only an occasional car horn in the distance reminds him he is in the heart of Tel Aviv. As the sky lightens he can tell it will be cold, colder than yesterday, that they will probably skip their afternoon stroll today, too.

Nelly enters with his predawn repast, a small surprise: hot milk it is, with a touch of rum and sugar. She places the tray on his nightstand and helps slide him into a sitting position. The smell of camphor reaches his nose. "Nelly," he asks, "is your tooth hurting again?" She lowers her eyes, embarrassed to be caught. "Really, Nelly, this is absurd. You do not need to be with me every second of the day, I can manage by myself. If you put it off any longer you will find yourself terribly ill." She stands at his bedside as he lectures her between tiny sips of hot milk. "Make an appointment for this afternoon. Promise me you will go today."

The camphor scent hovers above him even after Nelly has silently removed his tray to the kitchen.

A little makeup," Teo says on a windy morning three weeks later as Vivi approaches his table, the table that is always his first choice: not too close to the bar and the noise from the coffee machine, not in the farthest row of tables jutting into the shopping arcade.

"What?" she says, startled. Until now barely a word has passed between them.

"A little makeup wouldn't kill you," he continues. "A light foundation. A touch of rouge. You have fine features, but who can see them?"

She finishes placing his order in front of him. The coffee cup clatters in its saucer.

Her chin rises slightly before she speaks, but her hand flutters nervously as she curls a stray wisp of hair behind her ear. "Save it for your ballerinas," she says about to reel away from him.

"Wait . . . ah, I've forgotten your name—"

"Vivi."

"Vivi? Unusual. What is it short for?"

With polite impatience she says, "I started life as Varda. Terrible name. I've been Vivi since I was a kid."

"But Varda is Rose. And what could be lovelier than that? My mother was Rosa."

"That's nice," she says, stifling a frown, "but I have to—"

"Your boss tells me you're an artist," he says in a rush, as if his words were hands trying to encircle her.

She shifts her weight to one foot, no longer poised to run. "I'm a waitress," she says flatly.

He ignores her response and her tone and asks cheerfully, "What sort of art do you do?"

"What sort of . . . ?" She sighs in exasperation, trapped. "I paint. I embroider. I make collages," she says, bending back a finger as she lists each addition. "I whittle, I sculpt. I photograph. I sketch, I bead, I weave. I do video art. And right now I'm learning glassblowing. That's not the whole list, but you get the picture."

"Well," he says, leaning back in his chair as if having been blasted backward, "that's . . . how shall I put it? Impressive."

She smiles for the first time, not sweetly. "Then why don't you seem impressed?" she asks.

"It's just that . . . I have spent my entire life in one art form: dance. Oh, dance certainly incorporates a lot of other arts, but really, when you come down to it, I've taken a very narrow path while yours is . . . as broad as can be imagined. In fact, I cannot imagine it."

She glances around as if hoping to find customers needing her, but in fact, his is the only occupied table. She turns her full attention to their conversation. "From your tone I'd say you're not impressed, you're actually quite critical."

He laughs like an old man, dry and doleful. "Am I truly that transparent?"

"To me, yes," she says. "I'm pretty good at reading people."

"Add that to the list of your arts," he says.

"Let me guess: you believe that a person can only be good at one art, the one he throws himself into wholly. Which makes someone like me—"

"A dabbler."

"Not serious. Someone who wastes time and potential."

"Vivi," he says as if affirming the fact of her name, "I never would have said this, but since you seem to crave honesty then yes, with that kind of breadth you can never really be sublimely good at anything."

"Sublimely good," she repeats. "That's beautiful. I wouldn't actually mind being sublimely good if it weren't for the downside." She places one hand on the tabletop and leans closer in to his face. "With breadth you get variety. You get excitement. Fun. You never get bored."

He purses his lips and gestures to the chair across from him, inviting her to sit. She glances at Yossi, who is reading a newspaper behind the bar, then pulls out the chair and sits.

"You know," he says, "I studied with Balanchine in the early fifties, when he was just making his mark. Do you know who Balanchine was?"

"A great choreographer," she says.

"The greatest. Beyond the dances, he created modern ballet itself. But he was not just looking to create the perfect dance or the perfect dancer, he was in search of no less than the truth. His quest seemed almost like a religion at times. Did you know that Mr. Balanchine frowned on his dancers marrying? He expected them to stay married to the ballet forever. I suppose that was a leftover from Imperial Russia, but still you would be surprised how many of his dancers did just that. He was profoundly disappointed when one of them let a romance get the best of her, and much worse when they got pregnant.

Ballet is a way of life that leaves little room for anything else. But any art is like that, if you take it seriously enough."

She is shaping a response, but he is suddenly eager to share something and so she remains silent, attentive.

"Those Russians!" he says with a smile of disarming charm. "They were peerless. I had an adagio class with Pierre Vladimiroff—he was a principal with Diaghilev and was the great Pavlova's last partner— and Madame Danilova's variations class, about dancing the classics. These were the classics, but she made them so fresh that everything seemed new. I had a class, too, with Mr. B. himself, a class in precision. We spent hours on the exact fifth position, on transition steps like the pas de bourrée. Those teachers demanded perfection, nothing less. It was glorious. But it was his choreography that defined his true greatness. He burned off all the lyric romanticism so that what remained was chunks of music and pure movement that he heaped one on top of the other. He used constantly changing rhythms, he pushed his dancers beyond the confines of the music. And this was all new, new, new! Can you imagine? He was changing the very way we look at the human body and how it moves! Do you see? These are not achievements that come from dabbling. Only from complete and utter devotion."

He is nearly out of breath, and flushed with excitement. His eyes are shining.

Although she is fully aware that she is being upbraided, it feels to Vivi like a privilege of sorts to hear these stories firsthand. Still, she cannot resist asking what she needs to know. "What about the price?" she says.

He folds his hands over his heart and frowns, but he does not avert his gaze. "Which one?" he asks.

"Well, for starters, not raising a family. Losing contact with friends who are not part of your art. Shunning every other form of creativity

in your life. I like to believe that what you call dabbling is enriching in a different way. Fuller maybe," she says, not sure how far she can push this, but on a roll. "And don't different arts inform one another? There are lots of interdisciplinary artists these days, after all."

"Bah!" he says, nearly spitting. "Excuses. Young people who don't know how to commit themselves to anything. 'Interdisciplinary' is just another word for taking the easy way out."

She glances sideways, into the shopping arcade. Slowly and without rancor she says, "It must be wonderful to be so sure of yourself. I've never been that sure about anything."

He eyes her differently, really looking at her. He suddenly sees it, the scrim pulled over her lovely features. He had thought all she needed was makeup, but now he sees it is much, much more than that. Sometime, somewhere, a light inside her extinguished and altered her. Before he can fully formulate the thought he asks, "Was it a man? Was it a man who stole that from you?"

"Stole . . . ?" Her jaw drops and her eyes water as if she has been slapped. "Why did you ask me that?" she says, her voice shaky.

"Something about you does not add up," he says. "I've been observing you these past few weeks. You act . . . as if you've experienced a great loss."

She rises quickly from her chair, nearly toppling sideways. "You have no right—"

He grabs her wrist, pulls her in toward him, his firm and bony grip a surprise. His face is so close she can smell his old man's breath. "Use it," he says sharply. "Exploit it for your own needs. As long as you let it fester without making use of it, he'll always have you under his power. I know." He releases her hand and leans back in his chair.

Stunned, Vivi makes her way to the bar, wordless and tearful.

On her next day off, a quiet Sabbath morning, Vivi sits down at the computer she rarely uses with a cup of tepid instant coffee in one hand, a cigarette in the other, and crumbs from an aging croissant on her face. She looks up Teo on the Internet and finds him everywhere: in interviews, news items, quoted, critiqued, though much of the material is not new. She reads this on a Who's Who in Dance site:

Teodor (Teo) Levin, dancer and choreographer, b. Warsaw, Poland, 22 February 1922. Studied and performed under Harald Lander at the Royal Danish Ballet, and George Balanchine at the School of American Ballet. Founded the Israel Dance Theater (1948), later the Tel Aviv Ballet. Choreography includes *Point Blank* (1953), *The Wanderers* (1957, for the San Francisco Ballet), *Dolly Suite* (1960, for Ballet de Monte Carlo), *Pas de Deux sans Amour* (1964, San Francisco Ballet) and *Obsession* (1981). Awards and honors: RDB Excellence in Choreography (for *Dolly Suite*, 1961), Order of the White Eagle (Poland, 1980), IDA Outstanding Choreographer (1981), Israel Prime Minister's Award for Artistic Achievement (1991), Israel Prize for Life Achievement (1995).

Vivi does a quick calculation and is shocked to realize that he will turn eighty-five in just a few months. He still has a full head of white hair coiffed into a stiff mane, a flat stomach, muscled arms and legs. Only his sagging old man's bottom, the way it curves under and tilts his pelvis like the skeleton he will soon become, gives him away.

The worn, secondhand leather chair squeaks as she leans back and takes a final drag on her cigarette. She gazes up through the thin cloud of smoke hovering about her head and tries to imagine him younger, young. Was he as handsome as Pincho back then? Was he remote, a man devoted in his entirety to his art? Or, perhaps, could they have become friends?

Vivi chortles, breaking the silence in the apartment. Friends? One could not be friends with so self-absorbed a person! And yet, through her umbrage and anger at his prying question, she felt oddly satisfied. He had pushed his way through a door long since locked and the rush of fresh air was sobering.

Vivi tightens the sash on her bathrobe and plods noiselessly through the flat. She had heard Pincho come in just as the first fingers of light pulled back the fading night sky. More nights than not he returns from Indigo, the gay dance club where he works, with someone he has met. Often she hears them enter the flat, shushing each other, giggling. There are thuds and moans, splashes of water, the flushing of toilets, then all goes quiet. These men never seem to stay the night, or even the few hours into morning. So she assumes that Pincho pushes them out. After all, who wouldn't want to sleep curled up beside him?

Now he is sleeping behind the closed door at the end of the hallway. She is careful to tiptoe around the apartment, close cupboard doors softly, refrain from putting on music, even though she knows

nothing will keep him from sleeping soundly. In the home of her childhood, quietly populated by two busy parents and a studious brother, there was never an uproar, but in his house, with six younger brothers and sisters and a mother who spearheaded efforts against the Israeli withdrawal from the Gaza Strip and lives the Disengagement and the loss of the family home like a second skin, one learned to sleep anywhere and through anything.

Vivi washes her face, piles dishes in the sink, and dresses for the glassblowing workshop she will be taking part in in just an hour. This has become her latest passion, one in a long, long list that began with ballet and swimming when she was a little girl, and has metamorphosed through photography, pottery, embroidery, music (ukulele, cello, voice), poetry, painting, sculpting . . . she has art supplies and equipment in every drawer and cupboard, mostly crusted or broken, mostly long since abandoned. This will be her third glassblowing workshop and she feels she is beginning to find her way in this sleek, brittle art. She hopes it will enable her to express the pent-up feelings, the longing (for what?), the beautiful swirls of light and color that tease her and urge her to create.

She is slipping her feet into a scuffed pair of pink Crocs when the phone rings. This early in the day, on a Saturday no less, it can be only one person.

"This will have to be short, Mother, I'm on my way out the door," Vivi says in a low voice somewhere between a whisper and a growl. Her lack of a greeting has nothing to do with the fact that she is in a hurry; their conversations are seamless, they pick up and leave off as if part of one, ongoing lifetime mother-daughter dialogue.

"Glassblowing, I know," says Leah, her voice pitched low to match Vivi's even though her husband has been dead for years and there is no one in her home but she. "Any interesting people in the group?"

Vivi sidles up to the full-length mirror by the front door. She has pulled her hair into its usual top-head ponytail, a fountain of hair that leaves a spray of loose strands cascading in all directions. Over a pair of jeans and a long-sleeve coffee-colored camisole she has thrown a hand-knitted sweater she picked up in the Jaffa flea market, which she hopes will somehow pull together all the different hues in which she has carelessly wrapped herself. She stands sideways, trying to crush her belly and breasts inward while uncurling stooped shoulders. She gives up quickly and reverts to a slouch. "You mean men, don't you, Mother?"

"That would be nice, of course," Leah says with a sigh. "But even a good new friend would be pleasant, don't you think?"

"Pleasant," Vivi repeats.

"Vivi, you're not getting any younger—"

"I'm well aware of that, Mother."

"Well it's time—"

"Time for what? And according to whom?"

"It's just time, that's all. To get started with your life."

"Mother, I'm not doing this now," she says, her voice rising. "My life started forty-two years ago. Okay, I don't have a degree and I don't have a family, but my life's pretty much in the middle and it's filled with all kinds of . . . stuff, whatever it looks like to you."

"Vivi, don't get excited, I'm on your side."

"Of course you are, Mother. Who could doubt it?"

"Why don't you take a day off and come up to Haifa? We'll go to the Mane-Katz Museum and then we'll have lunch down at the boardwalk, on the beach."

Vivi cuts off the conversation with her mother when she sees Pincho stumble out of his room, shirtless and in boxer shorts. His beauty twists itself around her heart, as always, but when he flings his arms

around her and rests his head on her shoulder he has the slightly stale smell of every man, any man, fresh out of bed.

"Hi, sweetie," she says, patting his back. "Make you a cup of coffee?"

He nods into her neck.

She holds him for a minute longer, then parks him at the tiny kitchen table and busies herself with the electric kettle and his favorite mug. She puts two leftover pastries from the coffee bar on a plate and brings it all to the table, where she finds him sleeping, his curls spilling over the wooden tabletop.

She leans over, pecks his cheek. "Drink up, the coffee will do you good," she says.

He pulls himself up, wraps his hands around the mug, takes a sip, opens his eyes.

"Rough night?" she asks.

He nods. "Huge crowd. Lots of requests. I was on my feet the whole time." His voice is thick with slumber.

"And everybody was hitting on you," she says, and as usual with this line of questioning he ignores her. She has seen him in his DJ booth, earphones on and off his head, messing with the equipment, happy to be above it all, literally, in the smoky, writhing, throbbing cave that is Indigo. She has also seen him—from her perch at the bar, where she can sit unnoticed—constantly approached, constantly discussed by the men around her. But despite her best efforts, she cannot get him to talk about this with her. She has a feeling it has something to do with his upbringing, and she wants to be the one he can confide in since he has told none of his family or friends about himself. But so far he remains silent.

His face is hanging over the mug now, enshrouded in curls, and she cannot get a read on his expression.

"I'm going off to glassblowing, remember?" she says.

He nods.

"Let's have dinner together, okay? I'll pick up some stuff on the way home."

"I'll be here," he says.

She is about to give him a hug from behind when something—the slope of his bare back, a mole she has never noticed, the thickness of his neck—reminds her of Martin, and she stops, steps away, and flees the apartment.

Teo is writing a letter on heavy paper the color of sand. He uses a thick pen he does not like; it bleeds dark blue onto the page if left in place for even a second too long, but since it is relatively easy for him to grasp he has little choice. He has written the date and "Dear Margot" at the top. Soon the rest of the page will be filled with his tiny, precise handwriting, perfectly straight row upon perfectly straight row marching across the paper like troops on a march across the desert. A Polish dictionary lies open at his side.

There was a long period of time, maybe sixty years depending on how you figure it, with one or two significant exceptions, that Teo did not think about his early years as a dancer, when every minute in the studio brought the promise of a great career, a career of the most immense dimensions imaginable. At first, during the war, he forced himself to forget how close he had come, realizing that to save himself, his sanity, he would need to distance himself from those cruel memories. Then forgetfulness became habit, or perhaps it was the fact that his life was busy, filled to the last second with teaching and choreographing and events and worries so that when he tumbled into bed each evening for four hours of restorative slumber he was so spent that he could barely make it through even a few pages of the ballet journals that piled

up on the nightstand; certainly there was no time for reflection, for reminiscing, for wondering how different things would have been without a war.

So now, as he approaches his eighty-fifth birthday, he is surprised to discover himself visiting the past more and more. There he is, dancing with that charming partner of his, a freckle-faced girl who stayed her whole life at the Royal Danish Ballet, all the way into retirement; he cannot recall her name, only that her own mother, an Austrian, had been a dancer in Vienna. There he is, too, lifting his dear Sofie high in the air on a warm summer evening, her thin skirt fluttering in his face. There he is again during his first winter in Copenhagen, performing in *The Nutcracker* along with the whole student body of the ballet school on the old stage at the Royal Theater. And here he is in a Bournonville ballet, *The Konservatoriet*, on stage at the Berlin Staatsoper on a beautiful, ominous Friday evening in 1939, so young and unaware. It is this dance he visits most often now, after having expunged it, he thought, from his memory over half a century ago.

He can hum the music in his old man's quivering voice, but he prefers it in his head, where it lives on in violins and reedy winds. If he imagines it in rehearsal he can remember every step of his three-minute solo as if he had danced it only yesterday, but he knows, too, that one time, onstage in Berlin, he had not danced it as he had learned it; this much he knows but cannot recreate, could not recreate it even a moment after he had finished dancing it. While dancing he had felt blind to the stage and audience, deaf to the music. He had let his body do what it needed to do, free to expand and contract in space, to soar and spin. So, accordingly, when he tries to remember the way he danced it on stage, he cannot hear the music or feel his feet or get a sense of the audience.

He is embryonic, momentarily cut off from the world around him. The three most important minutes of his life, the ones that determined his fate and future, are the three to which he cannot gain access, ever.

Dear Margot,

 Your last letter amused us greatly. Nelly and I agreed that your eye for the smallest detail brings a priceless richness and humor to your stories. We could not help but admire the mice of the convent for their tenacity and sheer cleverness, but woe to the hapless exterminator! And the postulant with such notions of God and the world, how lively you made her questions sound! We could picture the young woman in question so clearly and accurately. Please do continue to regale us with even the tiniest details of your life.

 We are underoccupied here, or at least I am underoccupied so causing our Nelly to work harder than ever. I still spend several days a week in the studio—in fact, my time there has been unusually productive lately, as the Tel Aviv municipality has commissioned a restaging of one of my ballets and I am serving as an advisor—but this "extra" work causes Nelly to worry about me incessantly, can you imagine? Turning eighty-five is not something I am looking forward to, in spite of all your exhortations to the contrary, but I suppose the alternative is still worse . . .

His hand aches too much to continue. With difficulty he caps the pen and places it next to the paper, planning to finish the letter in the late afternoon or perhaps even tomorrow. What does it matter? His

news will not change, Margot will still be where she is another day and then another after that and so on until she dies; so what is the hurry?

His mind flits and wanders. To a snippet of ballet, an appointment later in the week, his mother's face. There is no longer any logic to the meanderings of his mind's eye. It crosses decades and continents without pause. Still, he is surprised when it settles on the girl from the coffee shop. Vivi: this name he can recall. That look on her face—the shock, the dismay, the mortification—comes to him in intimate detail. What had possessed him to speak so frankly and upset her?

There they are again, the first two chords of his solo. He is dancing it in the old Bournonville studio at the top of the Royal Theater, oblivious to the noise of the busy square below him. The half-moon windows near the floor remind him of the jellied candies covered with sugar that he and his mother would buy from a street vendor just outside the Saski Park in Warsaw. The bust of Auguste Bournonville looks down at him as he poses to begin: tendu croisé, arms in third position.

They are dancing the pas d'ecole. A Danish boy, Niels, has finished partnering the andante maestoso and first allegretto with that half-Austrian girl—what *is* her name?—who is now dancing a short andante solo. Teo will dance the second allegretto with her, moving her deftly to the corps de ballet posed along the back wall in preparation for his own solo, the moderato and final allegretto.

The music is fast and frilly. His dancing, too, is frilly, but still it sparkles. If only he had danced it thus, in Berlin. Pirouette, pirouette, chassé, grand jeté. Repeat to the left. A series of grand jetés to the back of the stage, where he brushes up against clusters of his fellow dancers, knocking into them if he overshoots. A skipping run so fast

he can feel the breeze he is making. High, turning leaps ending in arabesques. A masculine dance full of height and sharp lines, the role that of a student at the Paris Conservatory dancing to impress his teachers.

And impress them he does, far beyond what is prudent.

I'm wondering," Vivi says one morning as she places his water and coffee in front of him, more careful than usual not to spill on his pile of paperwork, "if you could let me come and watch you teach sometime."

At once, Teo frowns, feeling put upon, and so does she, angry with herself for expecting a favor from this man. "You see, I'm doing this glassblowing workshop—"

"Yes, glassblowing, I remember," he says, interrupting her. "I'd been thinking you'd given it up since you're often mooning around here with a camera."

"You know me," she says. "A little of everything." She breathes in sharply to steady herself, then says, with clarity, her voice a bit louder now and defiant, "I'm doing this glassblowing workshop, and I'd like to watch your dancers. To try and capture their movement in glass."

His gaze floats out toward the shopping arcade but lands on nothing. When he looks up at her his blue-green eyes seem glassy with fever, his complexion sallow. She wonders if she should ask about his health.

"That's impossible," he says at last.

"I didn't think you'd agree, but—"

"I'm not talking about a visit. You're welcome to visit whenever you like. I'm talking about capturing the movement of a dancer."

"Oh," she says.

"People keep trying it, but it cannot be done. Oh, something or other will come out of it, something even rather pretty. But it won't be dance, that's for certain."

"I didn't say, I mean I want to capture——"

"It's ethereal, you know," he says, brightening. "Dance is fleeting, it exists in a moment. Once you capture it, it is no longer dance."

"But . . . you're willing for me to come. To try."

"Willing, yes. But I have a price."

She crosses her arms, listens.

"You have to sit down here, across from me, for five minutes and tell me about yourself."

She laughs. "That's ridiculous," she says, but she pulls out the chair and falls into it. "What do you want to know?"

"Anything. Everything. Whatever comes to mind." He moves his pile of papers to the side.

"Well," she says with a coy smile, "I'm an artist. But of course you know that already."

"Not that I've had the privilege of seeing any of your artwork yet, but all right, that will serve as our point of departure."

"I waitress to pay the bills. But I've had lots of other jobs. Which won't surprise you. I live with a gorgeous gay man. He comes from one of those right-wing religious families that had to be pulled out of their homes in the Gaza Strip during the Disengagement. I'd fix you up but——"

Teo scowls, he stares into Vivi's eyes. "What makes you think . . . ? Not all male dancers are gay," he says.

"Of course not. I just thought . . . never mind, sorry, back to your question: I was born in Haifa and came to Tel Aviv when I returned—when I was twenty-one or twenty-two."

"Never lived abroad?" he asks, picking up on her self-correction.

"I did, after the army," she says, diverting her attention to a toothpick she has plucked from the table. "In Berlin."

"Berlin," he repeats, coughing lightly. He spits into a crumpled tissue.

"I don't really want to talk about that," she says. "I didn't love it there, that city wasn't for me."

"So you returned to Israel to begin your adult life."

"You could say that. But it didn't really begin, not for a long time."

"Why not?"

"I was . . . damaged. It's not a period I like to . . ."

He is looking intently into her face, but his eyes carry kindness and understanding, so she answers.

"I left a man there, in Berlin. When I came back to Haifa I just couldn't . . . I wasn't going anywhere. I didn't go out to work, I wasn't studying. I barely left the house for months. At some point I started dating. Dating! I don't think you can call it that exactly. My mother, who's a real pusher, got the mothers of all the nice religious boys in Haifa to ask me out. There was no telling her I wasn't interested, I was simply forced to accept. So I made a game out of scaring them off."

"How? You're hardly frightening."

"I became a predator," she says, looking down at her knees. "I used them, devoured them. I made a name for myself. Haifa is really just a great big village. Soon, everyone knew. The nice boys and their mothers disappeared but there was a line around the block of bad boys waiting for me."

"I'm sorry. To hear that."

"Yeah, well," she says, taking a deep breath. "After that I came to Tel Aviv and started over. No men, lots of jobs. It suits me."

"No men? I thought you said you'd started over."

"Not on that account. It's easier without them. Without you."

"Ah yes, ease. I see that's quite important to you."

"Are you going to give me another lecture now? How I should have stuck to one art and one man?"

"No lectures. I certainly don't have all the answers. Funny though, my fate was also determined by a man in Berlin. And when I finally made it to Israel, I shut down as well."

"So . . . you've never . . . been in love . . . ?"

He takes so long to answer, and his expression is so blank, that he appears not to have heard the question. But after a spell, he responds. "I suppose I have," he says. "Twice. Neither of them in the last sixty years. I've kept away from love. Devoted myself to my art."

"At least you have something to show for it," she says.

"Yes. Something. I do have something to show for it. But there is a lot missing, too. A lot I failed to accomplish."

"Vivi!" Yossi shouts from behind the bar. Vivi rises from her chair, her eyes still on Teo.

"So, you really don't mind if I come watch you teach?" she asks.

"I'm afraid I don't teach anymore," he says. "But the company will be performing one of my own ballets soon and I'm working with them in an advisory capacity. I invite you to attend a rehearsal."

"Okay, then I'll come by on Friday afternoon when I finish work."

He nods and puts his hands on the pile of papers, then watches her as she moves away from him.

It is raining lightly as Vivi walks to work early Friday morning. She will be staying later than usual, since Yossi has plans to head north to the Galilee on his motorcycle around noon, but she is happy for the diversion. She is both eager and reticent about the ballet class she will observe later in the afternoon, her first in more than thirty years.

She pauses at a newly renovated apartment building with a curved Bauhaus verandah and porthole windows, and puts one hand on the low, pale yellow wall surrounding the property. The other she stretches out to her side, then lifts her leg into an arabesque, bringing it around to the side before planting it in what she thinks she remembers is third position. She curves her arms into a wide loop, and remains in that position for a moment, feeling her muscles stretch and bend under her skin.

The ballet teachers of her childhood in Haifa in the early 1970s were all elegant, fading refugees, European *ladies* whose Hebrew was soaked through and bloated by heavy accents—Polish, Czech, or, like her mother's, Hungarian—and speckled with French. She had had three such teachers, all with tight black buns pulled severely from their faces. They all clucked and shook their heads with her mother, a hopeless case this little Vivi. *Avec charme,* they would call out to her;

Slowly, gracefully, they would remind her; but Vivi's heavy limbs always seemed to betray her, finding the floor far more quickly than she had intended. Her meaty leg would land with a thud, provoking nervous giggles from the other girls, that flock of startled doves. Even Madame Irma, the Polish ballet teacher, had tried once to help her find the "airy lightness" that filled her bones, but Vivi could not help but think of the thick marrow her uncle Tibor sucked from the soup chicken at the Sabbath table.

It was not merely anatomy, she knows now, that separated her from the other girls in leotards and ballet slippers, a tiny, heartless regiment lined up at the barre, primping in the mirror at every occasion.

"Glissade, assemblé, glissade, assemblé, glissade, assemblé, pause. Now left!" Madame Irma's voice exploded in Vivi's ears, the sharp clap of her hands like gunshots in the small studio. Silk and satin flowed from her mouth when talking to parents, but alone with the girls in the studio her voice was all metal. "Glissade, assemblé, glissade, assemblé, glissade, assemblé, bras bas!"

"Stop, stop!" Madame shouted. Mademoiselle Rena, Irma's spinster sister, lifted her hands from the piano; the room fell silent. The girls cowered together, all except Sharona, who knew Madame Irma would never shout at her. She was the star of the class; her father was the mayor's right-hand man.

"Sharona," Madame Irma said in a tone of mock sweetness, "would you show Vivi our short, simple routine from the beginning, please? Vivi dear, watch Sharona's every move and commit it to heart." Mademoiselle Rena played and Sharona danced and Vivi knew every move as though it were the path she followed each morning to school. When her turn came to perform, Madame Irma shook her head at the piano, so Vivi was forced to perform in silence. Glis-

sade, assemblé, glissade, assemblé, somehow her arms and legs could not grasp what her brain was telling her. Should she plié? When should her leg shoot to the right? She knew her arms should rise to second position, but when exactly? On her second assemblé she tumbled sideways, falling onto her shoulder. Through her tears, through the noise of the girls laughing, she could see herself in this studio, lying in a puddle of light dumped there by a tired late-afternoon autumn sun. Madame's foot tapped impatiently near her head. "Girls!" she shouted, not soon enough. The tittering ceased immediately. "Vivi, you'll never be able to perform in our recital if you can't remember which movement is which. Go home and practice, practice, practice. I don't want to see you here again until you know this routine perfectly!"

Maybe, she muses now, it was an actual disability, a chemical imbalance. Maybe the wiring between her brain and her legs was faulty, little jolts of electricity that could not make the leap from one nerve-ending to the next. Chronic immobilia, they could call it, or physiological discordancia. She should not have been expected to dance like the other girls, perhaps not even permitted to try. If only they had known about her disability they could have exempted her, or taken special measures on her behalf like they do nowadays for dyslexic students sitting for matriculation exams. They could have given her her own dance at the recital so she would not have had to keep time with the other girls. Or, she thinks, they could have told her that ballet was simply not for her, that the "pleasure" of taking part was not worth the torture of humiliation, the sacrifice of self-esteem.

Later that day she was going to observe, not take part in, a ballet class. Would he make her feel like that all over again? She cannot be

sure either way; with him she feels off-balance, teetering between his concern and his indifference.

She notices that a little girl has been watching her from an upstairs window in the Bauhaus building. She waves and the little girl disappears.

Margot has been using the same stationery for the entire fifty-five years of their correspondence, so her letters, some six hundred in all, form remarkably uniform stacks in the antique roll-top desk next to his bed. The handwriting on the oldest among them, written shortly after a traumatic and unplanned meeting in 1947—their first in nearly a decade—was almost identical to the last, though the later letters retain the scent of soap and candles he has come to associate with his sister.

These three neat stacks of identical sheets of paper are the first thing Teo notices each morning, and they comfort him, evidence of his longest relationship. He and his sister write to one another about their everyday existence, and he craves the keen and precise observations Margot makes of her quiet, contained world. He is certain he would recognize Sister Beatrice by her triple chins, Sister Agnes by her winking left eye, Sister Anne by the way her ears turn red when she is angry. And the convent cats, as quiet and contained as their surroundings. And the caretakers, first Josep and then Josep Junior, one family of Polish peasants maintaining the convent for nearly seventy years. How little that world has changed from year to year, from season to season.

There was once a break in the letters, a rupture swallowed up by time, by the envelopes that began to reach him again sometime later. He looks for the gap in the orderly piles of letters, guesses it must be somewhere in the second stack, but of course there is no evidence. It came after a brief reunion in Warsaw in the early 1980s. Both Teo and Margot were out of their element, the elegant hotel at which they met felt natural to neither of them, and their conversation was awkward and distant. Without ever mentioning it, each resolved never to meet again, preferring instead their glorious epistolary relationship. Several times Teo has mentioned the possibility of publishing their correspondence, that scholars and even the general public would find their letters engaging and perhaps important on several levels, but his sister, in her calm, powerful manner, much like a subtle force of nature—a persistent wind that bends trees, rushing water that carves holes in rocks—was adamant about this: not now, not after their deaths, not ever; it would be unseemly and improper, and it was the one thing that could cause her, with enormous sadness and regret, to refrain from communicating with him ever again. So since neither of them could bear this possibility, the idea has always, after being mentioned, been dropped immediately.

Teo keeps copies of his own side of their correspondence in satchels bound with ribbon stashed on a high shelf in his bedroom. They are less accessible to him than Margot's letters, but he feels the need to revisit them far less often. Still, lately he has been drawn more and more to both sides of their correspondence, their combined half century of letters: to the elegant, prewar Polish by which they stand loyally, to the chunk of history to which they give witness, to the sheer volume of it all; and to their ability, so lost in the world now, to suggest so much, to tuck meanings into words, to crouch emotions

behind mellifluous phrasing, to crunch a mountain of feelings into a mound of pure gold, without ever using an explicit, naked word. They are masters of inference, experts of the long, sly wink.

There were letters from his side, he remembers, that described and detailed the dances he was creating better than he had done anywhere else, letters from which choreographers and dancers alike would profit greatly. There were letters from her side on the role of the convent in modern life that would serve the Church and its adherents brilliantly, if only one Church scholar were given permission to read them. World events march through their letters as if their correspondence were an immense stage in a theater with only two seats. Teo and Margot observe, they comment. Sometimes they rage, sometimes they weep; occasionally they disagree, but always courteously. On the rare occasion they are in open conflict, both are miserable and seek to resolve their differences quickly.

More than anything, they are respectful of one another. Although they held forth on theological issues in the mid–1950s and again thirty-five years later, Teo has never questioned Margot's abandonment of Judaism in favor of Catholicism and life in a convent. Margot has never asked her brother about the war. She has noted, with wry amusement, that their collective contribution to populating the world has been abysmal, "and we should both be chided for that," but nothing more. In the late 1950s, when it seemed that a virulent strain of anti-Semitism was about to swallow Poland whole, they argued about the Polish national character. On the other hand, they mostly agree about Israel's two periods of intifada and the need for territorial compromise, though Teo surprised even himself with a few comments that bordered on national pride.

He picks up the uncomfortable pen again and wraps his hand around it.

I have been thinking lately about Mother. I have been wondering if she wanted to marry Father or whether she felt obligated, when her sister Anna died in childbirth and left him so bereft. Was it her family who decided she should marry Oskar, or was it her own decision? She always seemed headstrong to me, soft but stubborn—much like you! She had a way of getting Father to agree to her every whim without ever raising her voice or crying or pleading. I remember her almost as a pampered daughter to Father, do you, too? After all she was quite a bit younger, and of course gay and frivolous compared to his serious nature.

He remembers how he and Mother would sit apart from the nannies and their charges at the park, how they went to puppet shows, the public library, the vegetable market, the train station, their favorite spot on a bank of the Vistula River—wherever young Teodor would be entertained, wherever he would find sights and sounds of interest. She sat by quietly as he hopped after a passing butterfly or rolled down a grassy hill. She spied as he imitated a trotting dog or a fat nanny chasing her charge, not in jest but as a way of learning their bodies, their movement. He was very nearly speechless, rarely asked questions, preferring to construct his own truth from his own kaleidoscopic imagination. Neither he nor his mother was ever, ever bored together and their daytime world was solid and complete.

On the very day that the American stock market plummeted, pulling the European bourses along for the ride, Rosa gave birth to a girl, Margot. Small and pinched, Margot did not elicit the nurses' loving attention as her brother had seven and a half years earlier. She was red and unlovely compared to the other babies, and though tinier than the rest she could squeal and wail like the most robust.

Teodor had been expecting a playmate, a fan and a foil to keep him interested on long, dreary winter afternoons, and so he was profoundly disappointed when this wrinkled, good-for-nothing baby took up permanent residence in their house. She could neither walk nor talk, she knew no songs, and Nanny would not let him dress her up for skits or games. She was often rheumy, or feverish, or chilled, so Rosa would cancel their afternoon outings, condemning Teodor to the confines of the small apartment. Worst of all, baby Margot had a deformity that both frightened and intrigued him: one eyelid did not fully open, so she constantly gave the impression of peering out at the world from a secret hiding place.

When Margot was still an infant, even before her first birthday, she was hospitalized for several months with complications following ill-advised and unsuccessful surgery on her damaged eyelid. Rosa ran frantically back and forth to the hospital, leaving Teodor with the nanny for longer and longer stretches. Oskar tried to compensate, taking his son to the park and the puppet theater, but he lacked his wife's gaiety and her infinite patience, and so father and son often returned from their excursions ill-tempered and offended with one another.

It was a sympathetic neighbor, Mrs. Zabrinski, who first suggested that the Levins enroll Teodor at the ballet school that stood just one block down on Szara Street. He could, she reasoned, reach the school on his own, or at the very least with the help of his nanny. He was naturally graceful and would certainly have no trouble executing any movement demanded of him. And, she gently hinted, ballet lessons would provide him with much needed discipline, respect for authority, and a framework for the strange leaps and twirls he was always performing as he walked down the street. Teodor was a boy who could never simply walk from one place to the next by placing

one foot in front of the other, a trait Mrs. Zabrinski suggested would brand him as odd by the children in school, and cause him to suffer.

So subtle was her suggestion that Rosa almost missed it.

"He . . . he . . ." she stammered, "do you think he is really, I mean, do you think there's something wrong with him?"

"No dear, not at all. He's just high-spirited and very clever and full of energy." Mrs. Zabrinski had brought four boys of her own to manhood and knew the pitfalls. "Take my word for it, ballet will do him a world of good."

And so, in the spring of his eighth year, Teodor began to dance.

Those early years of dancing, Teodor recalls, were sweet years of discovery, years of blissfully losing himself to the beautiful world of movement. He found himself there, knew just who he was and what he wanted. At first it was the thrill of being better than everyone else, and so effortlessly, but after a while it became the thrill of pushing the limits of his body, the sheer physicality of stretching that much farther, reaching that much higher, turning that much faster. And feeling so strong and stuffed with muscles that seemed to burgeon under every inch of his skin.

But finally, ultimately, in the years that followed, the excitement of creativity surpassed all the other elements. Teodor was progressing rapidly beyond what he was being taught, inventing new steps and feeling the music course through him, shooting through his blood to every extremity like mercury, until his body had no choice but to move and move and move, always something new and completely his own. He began to feel as though his body were a comet; each time he danced he pushed past another planet, another star, another galaxy. He felt he brought light and color to where nothing had existed before, spinning faster, leaping higher, his body creating new hinges and pivots and axles. He had no patience for anything but

dance, and searched wearily for someone who could understand; he wanted to find another human being who knew how it felt to have the stars cheer him on each time he stepped into ballet slippers, how the planets shook themselves out of their slumber and the galaxies flicked their sparkling tails and the sun shot great bolts of heat and light through the cold universe each time he pirouetted across the floor. He had moved beyond conceit and pride to the humility of a great and endless discovery, but found no one with whom to share it.

And he was only fourteen years old.

Once Vivi has wiped down the tables and the bar and stacked all the chairs, she locks up and steps into the empty shopping arcade. Normally she loves walking home at this hour on a Friday afternoon, when the citizens of Tel Aviv have finished their leisurely brunches and are resting before an evening of fun or prayer. But today she walks deeper into the arcade and down a flight of stairs to the door of the Tel Aviv Ballet company studio. She takes a deep breath and pushes it open.

Inside, the air is thick and musty. She walks forward, past a darkened office or two, until she reaches the studio itself, a large, spacious, well-lit room with three mirrored walls. At the entrance she finds an easel with the day's schedule posted. She sees that the dancers had a class in the morning, then a break, and since twelve o'clock they have been rehearsing Teo's ballet *Obsession*.

Teo is sitting on a chair in the middle of the studio with his back to her, his thick white hair more of a mess than usual. He is surrounded by more than a dozen sweat-stained young dancers. No one appears to be having a very good time.

"We're in rehearsal, sweetheart," a male dancer calls out to her.

She waits for Teo to explain but he is engrossed in conversation with one of the female dancers, whose forearm he is holding and tapping vigorously.

"I'm . . . he's . . ." Vivi sputters. She is at a loss to explain her presence there, uncertain even how to address her coffee-shop customer, but she draws herself in and says with a nod of her head, "I'm his guest."

Teo turns his whole body around in his chair, bows stiffly in her direction, and says, "Welcome."

She seats herself on a stool in the corner, her coat folded on her lap, and watches.

"All right, boys and girls," Teo says. "Let's try it once again. Lighter. Firmer. With precision, everyone. Pre-ci-sion. Mrs. Nudel," he calls out to the air, "back to the beginning of that section, please."

A heavy-set platinum blonde at the piano licks her fingers, turns the music back several pages, and begins to play. Vivi winces as the dancers throw themselves into bone-crunching positions. Teo is dissatisfied and stops them almost at once.

A terrible silence falls on the room as the dancers wait and Teo sits slumped in his chair, his head bent. They begin to throw worried looks to one another, and Vivi herself wonders if something hasn't happened to him.

Then suddenly his head rises, his back straightens, and he is all at once on his feet, as though he has floated there. Slowly he rotates his body so that his back is now to his dancers, his face turned toward Vivi. His arms spread grandly to the sides, his chest expands, his legs pivot. Everything about him is taut and lean and sculpted, his shoulders beautifully squared. He no longer seems his age, or even old at all. Vivi shifts in her seat, uncomfortable at how aroused she is by this man who could be her grandfather. His muscles are remarkably firm, his stomach flat, and there is no way to describe him as anything but sexy. After a long moment taking him in, fully, she wills her gaze to drop to the floor.

"Épaulement," he cries. "Épaulement. Épaulement. Épaulement. Épaulement. Shall I say it a few more times? Will it help?" He drops the pose, turns back to them. "You are beautiful, talented dancers," he tells them. "You have mastered these complicated steps in a very short period of time and will dance them at the gala in less than two weeks from now. Your ballet master has trained you impeccably. But without these touches you may as well be doing aerobics. In this particular ballet, which is about the very nature of obsession itself, one of the obsessions explored is that of art, in this case dance. This ballet must reek of obsession, which the viewer understands through precision. What did Monsieur Balanchine used to say about precision?" he asks in a way that makes it sound like a rhetorical question.

The male dancer who had first noticed Vivi answers him. " 'If it is not precise it falls to pieces,' " he quotes, clearly not for the first time.

" 'Nobody criticizes the sun or moon or the earth for being precise, and that is why they have life,' " Teo adds. He spends the next twenty minutes moving from dancer to dancer, making individual suggestions and demonstrating, as far as his ancient body will allow, what he wants from them. Vivi watches as their muscles extend and they reshape themselves, responding to their teacher's instructions and pushing to their limits. When they try the dance again they are focused and precise and serious, and the results are discernibly different. She can feel it, and she sees by the expressions on their faces that they can, too. She watches as toes and fingers curl as they should and a lift that fails several times suddenly rises to miraculous perfection and the timing of a double pirouette is halved to fit the music. She is riveted, sweating along with these beautiful, lithe creatures in constant, frantic motion, their bodies often split vertically, down the spine, the right side moving against the left. She recognizes patterns: a pas de deux full of off-balance extensions and surprising shifts of

weight reappears in a larger group of dancers; movements are reversed, inverted, performed upside down or with new rhythms; they expand into complex shapes or contract to the simplest gestures. The dancers twist and bend and collapse, and she breathes with them, feeling the floor as it slides around beneath them. When it is over she suppresses the urge to run to each and every dancer and to Mrs. Nudel and embrace them.

She smiles at them as they file out alone or in pairs. After the last of them has left she rises from her seat and approaches Teo, who is toweling dry his upper body.

"It was breathtaking," she says.

"My breath was certainly taken," he says, "but not in the way you mean. I find this both invigorating and exhausting." He disappears for a moment behind a partition and reemerges with a bottle of cold water and two glasses. He passes the glasses to her, but when he begins to pour his hand wobbles and water spills on the floor.

"May I?" she says, offering to switch roles so that she can pour.

He ignores her, glaring at his own hand until it is perfectly still. Then he pours for them both without spilling another drop. When both glasses are full he raises his eyes to meet hers, flashing her a blue-green look of defiance.

"So, mademoiselle," he says as she places a chair near his own, "did you find what you came looking for?"

"I think I got more than I came looking for," she says.

"Tell me."

"Well, certainly for my glassblowing I saw some wonderful, fluid lines I hope I can use. But it was just a pleasure watching them, and watching you teach them."

"A pleasure?" he asks, his eyebrows raised. "That's not a word that gets used here very much." He pulls his chair closer to hers. Once

again, his ageless good looks and the fierce intelligence in his mismatched eyes draw her attention momentarily away from his words. "Young lady, do you have any idea whatsoever what it takes to be truly outstanding at something? I mean, original, creative, inspiring: the best. Can you even begin to conceive what that means?"

She sighs heavily, avoids the intensity of his gaze for a moment, then meets it again. "Look," she says, "I know what you see when you look at me is a waitress. Somebody who just has to manage to get your coffee on the table while it's still hot. But can you even conceive that that's not all I am? That maybe I'm an artist, too, but a different kind?"

"What does that mean, a different kind?" he asks, now irritated. "All artists—true artists—know that their art must become their passion." He settles back in his chair.

"But there's so much out there," she says. "So many ways to create. I don't like cutting off my options."

"Ah, but then you cut off your chances of creating something important. You're only left with mediocrity, and mediocrity is the true enemy."

She frowns.

"Mark my words, my dear: mediocrity is the true evil, in all its banality. I have always pushed myself and my dancers to strive for the best. *Ad astra*, reach for the stars, I always tell them. Otherwise what is the point? If you don't seize opportunities and take risks you get to my age with too many questions and too few answers. In life you regret what you have *not* tried, not what you have tried and failed. You know," he says after sipping water from his glass, "when I arrived in Israel the place was a wasteland in terms of dance. Classical ballet was the ugly stepsister of modern in this country, did you know that? All that awful German expressionist nonsense, all those

ridiculous methods, they all got dumped on this country and grew like weeds, long after they had died in Germany! Classical ballet was too bourgeois for a new country, the hearty pioneers wanted to leave their good manners back home in Europe. No more ties and hats and suits. No more 'please' and 'thank you.' They wanted to work up a good healthy sweat here in the Near East. Well, we sweated, too, my dancers and me. We worked so hard, almost as hard as Balanchine's dancers back in New York. Because we were building something, too, something new and exciting. And while the pioneers sneered at us, despised us even, the people who were not afraid of beauty and art and grace and form, those people loved us, loved what we were try-ing to bring to this country. If I hadn't pursued it, devoted my life to it, there would still be no classical ballet in Israel. In the end, the best of my students—the ones who understood the devotion necessary to succeed—have actually reached the stars. These were the dancers who knew mediocrity would never do, not in ballet, and now they are dancing in Copenhagen and New York and London and Paris and San Francisco and Monte Carlo."

"And you yourself have never done anything mediocre?" she asks.

"Not until old age brought me down," he says dryly.

"While I was sitting here watching you, watching them," she says, pursuing a different agenda, "I started thinking about my own cre-ative process. When I get an idea in mind, something new I want to work on, it feels like a tickle, a kind of tingling in my nose and the back of my head. I don't know if that makes sense, and I've never tried to describe it before, but that's what it's like."

He nods.

"When that happens, I know I have to pursue it. I get really caught up in whatever it is. But somewhere along the line, I lose my sense of purpose. I start telling myself it doesn't matter if I finish the project

because nobody really cares. That even I don't care. And that's when I rush ahead and just complete it, and put it away. I keep doing that, I've been doing that for, well, too many years now. I guess that leads to the mediocrity you're talking about. But I can't even worry about creating something mediocre, I'm left behind at the frustration stage. I want to learn how to carry through. And I'm hoping if you can tell me how you do it then somehow I'll learn."

"Vivi," he says, and she starts, unaccustomed as she is to hearing him use her name, "I will tell you how I work, how I create. But let's get this clear from the start: it's not the work methods that really count, it's the seriousness of purpose. Things only matter in life because we invest meaning in them. Does the world really need another ballet? No. That is, until you create that ballet and cause the world to realize that it was actually lacking something that only this ballet can provide. But that cannot happen until you convince yourself that what you are doing is good and necessary. Or perhaps you never ask yourself that question, and there are many artists who don't. They simply create and send their creation out into the world without worrying the issue. One way or the other, it cannot be a preoccupation or it will paralyze you. It has paralyzed you."

"Yes, it has," she says.

"My own creative process always begins with the music," he says. "Sometimes I had music foisted on me, something someone was requesting. That's less pleasurable than finding one's own perfect score. I have probably gone through thousands of scores in my life looking for music that begs me to create a ballet for it. Much of it, most of it in fact, is danceable. But it rarely possesses the mix I crave."

"Which is?" she asks.

"Certainly hard to describe. A lovely melody, interesting rhythms and syncopations, variety, a certain emotional statement, but then

something else. An element that speaks to me on another level entirely. I know it when I see it, I feel it immediately but it isn't something . . . usual."

"Go on. Please," she says.

He gathers himself, calls in various parts of himself to help answer. There is an intake of breath, a rise in posture, his hands flutter and his eyes narrow, all conspiring to turn what they already know into an answer. Both he and she understand this is not an answer he is usually willing to give. Then, in a whisper, he says, "Color."

She leans in close and cocks her head to catch his feathery words as they float forward so lightly from his mouth. "Excuse me?" she says.

"And heat," he says.

"Color and heat?" she asks. "Reminds me of the Dead Sea . . ."

"Color and heat," he repeats, ignoring her, his eyes now closed. "When I listen to music, some music, I see it. See the music, I mean, I see it in colors and varying degrees of hot and cold. Sometimes it turns into shapes, but most often not . . . I . . ."

"Are you looking at them now?" she asks.

His eyes open. "There is no music in my head now. Just noise."

"So, once you've found the music, what happens then?" she asks.

"I devour it. I read the score, listen to it if I can obtain a good recording, or ask my pianist to play it for me. I let it seep into my brain, my heart, my legs. After a while, not long at all really, I start to feel it in my body, as though I have absorbed it into my blood-stream. That is when the movements become almost inevitable. The phrase I hear translates into a very specific movement. Which is not to say it doesn't change; it certainly does, once I begin working with the dancers. The ideas are set by the time I hold my first rehearsal. The changes are usually only variations, not alterations, or perhaps

adaptations would be a better word, since you are adapting what you thought would work to the strengths and weaknesses of your dancers."

"And so you walk them through it?"

"Yes, it's quite tedious, I'm afraid. The pianist keeps playing those same bars over and over, the dancers—I keep sending them back again and again until I get what I was looking for, or a close approximation at least. No, that's not true: I push them to achieve what I want but I listen to what they say. I watch for what their bodies are saying. I correct myself."

"I still don't understand, though, this business of color and heat."

"They are a manifestation of something else, something ancient . . ." he says. He seems about to float away from her, into his own memories, but suddenly he returns, looking eager to make her understand. He speaks slowly, with great deliberation. "I was born with a rare and precious gift, in fact I have never found another soul with such a gift, never read a word about this . . . phenomenon. Maybe there is information today, I don't know. Do you know what perfect pitch is?"

"More or less," she says.

"To a person with perfect pitch each note is an entity. A thing. Unalterable. It has weight, and a shape. It exists in space. Well, I was born with perfect pitch of movement."

"Perfect pitch of movement," she says, trying out the phrase.

"From earliest childhood all my sensual experiences filtered through me into movement. I was very nonverbal. I didn't really speak properly until nearly the age of five because what I absorbed, all the sights and smells and sounds and tastes, came back to me as gesture. I translated, as it were, all of my experience into my own language of movement. For example, walking once with my mother

49

along the Vistula River when I was a very small child, no more than three or four, we saw a group of workers slowly rolling an enormous cement sewage pipe, big enough for a man to stand in, toward the embankment. I can still feel the roll of my shoulders, the curve of my neck, the turn of my hands." His eyes shut and his body approximates the description. "The rolling of that pipe will always and only be that series of movements, that precise combination."

"Can you give me another example?"

His eyes open. He shakes his head. He cannot—or will not.

"And when did you lose it, that language?" she asks.

He gazes evenly at her. "I did not lose it. It was cut out of me. Those are war stories," he says with artificial nonchalance.

"I'm not afraid of those," she says. "I grew up on them."

He looks at her as if he is weighing several possibilities. Then he surprises them both by answering. "It was mid-morning," he says blankly, "on my nineteenth birthday. The sky was white with clouds, or one single huge cloud like a blanket. Everything around me was still, so still it didn't seem like I was in a city at all. I could have been anywhere: a village, a farm. I was drinking a cup of tea but in my head I was dancing, as usual. Only a year and a half had passed since . . . I'd been forced to stop dancing but I'd danced that dance in my head already a thousand times. When I could, in my confined quarters, I even danced it for real. But then one day, my nineteenth birthday, I just couldn't bear it anymore. Those memories and those desires, all those years of dancing, of working so incredibly hard, they all just seemed like smoke, like mist. Like nothing. I suddenly didn't want the reality or the dream of it, I was sick of longing for something I realized I would never have again. So I let it go. I stood up and poured my tea down the drain and with it, all those years of ambition and longing. It deadened me for a long time, years in fact, but eventually

that act helped me save myself. I was able to return to life as someone else, wanting different things and eventually attaining them."

Vivi nods. "So you traded one dream for another."

"One life for another," he says. They are quiet together for a while, like old friends who feel no need to fill up silences.

"You know," he says, "I'm actually glad you came here today."

"Why is that?"

"I don't know, really. Maybe because you're a witness. Someone to share . . . ideas and memories with. Pleasant to talk to."

"That's nice, I like that. And I'm hoping some of your creative energy will rub off on me."

"Have you given some thought to what I said that time? About not letting people who have hurt you have power over you? About using your hurt and your anger in your art?"

She turns her attention to the mirrored walls, where she spies an old man in a chair and a woman of indeterminate middle age leaning her elbows on splayed knees. She tries to gather her resolve, the defenses she has constructed and reinforced over twenty years, but she can muster no feeling at all. She says, "I've thought about it," but that is all she can bear to tell him. It isn't fair, she knows; he has told her private things about himself while she is holding back.

The magic of the rehearsal has evaporated. She feels trapped, and deprived of air. "I'm sorry, it's late," she says lamely, and in no time she is out on the dark street greedily gulping down night air and heading nowhere, especially not home.

She walks, mumbling to herself, for nearly an hour, till she begins to tire. Only when she steps in front of a taxi and is nearly plowed down does she realize that she has ambled in a roundabout manner all the way to Jaffa. Her stride is slower now, but determined still. She climbs up stairs into the Old City, past the stacked-stone houses and over the Wishing Bridge to the little park, where she makes her way to one particular bench as if this whole walk had been planned for this very purpose. Suddenly fatigued and lonely, Vivi breathes deeply to stave off sadness. She lights a cigarette and calms herself by looking out at the night-blackened sea, then toward the sparkling towers and bright, bustling streets of Tel Aviv. Her mind fills with memories she has not allowed to visit her for years and years. She sits with them, her stories, her history, on a bench in a park in Old Jaffa, and for once she does not run away.

His name was Martin. She had met him during her military service in army intelligence at an outpost just south of the Dead Sea, where she monitored radio broadcasts from Jordan, a job she was able to land thanks to her serious study of Arabic and the Middle East.

She was surprised to find she adored the desert heat, the feeling of wading through electricity. She loved the muted colors and jagged textures, the lack of gentility. There was no polish here, no artifice.

Scorpions stung and plants pricked; everything alive was engaged in a fierce battle for the paltry food and water the desert had to offer. As often as possible Vivi tagged along after guides from the field school at Ein Gedi to learn more.

That was where, at the beginning of her second year at the Dead Sea, she met Martin, a volunteer from Germany. Tall and sedate, Martin worked mornings picking dates and studied in a Hebrew-language *ulpan* with other volunteers in the afternoons. Already after a single month in Israel he could hold a short and simple conversation, even if he consistently reversed the masculine and feminine pronouns and verb forms.

"In Europe the sky is never this color," he told Vivi in Hebrew on their first mutual excursion. "And certainly we don't have creatures like those," he said, pointing to a dry and cracked lizard making its way slowly past them. Switching to English he asked how to say "dinosaur" in Hebrew.

"They do look like dinosaurs in miniature," Vivi said, laughing. She made polite conversation, curious about a man who had put his medical studies on hold to spend a year doing onerous physical labor under a malevolent sun, but at the same time she could not escape the thought of her mother's inevitable disapproval for associating with a German.

Vivi and Martin met again the following weekend and after that Vivi found herself thinking about him during the week, hoping the tall, friendly German would not miss a trek. On their third outing he asked her to meet him at the Ein Gedi spa, right on the Dead Sea, the next afternoon.

He jogged up to the spa, bright red and puffing, five minutes after the appointed hour. "I'm so sorry," he said, hands on his knees, trying to catch his breath. "The usual shuttle from the kibbutz wasn't

running, so I jogged down here." She motioned to a stone bench and they sat together while he settled back to normal and drank from her water bottle. When he had recovered he said, "It's nice to see you for once not in uniform."

Vivi smiled but did not look him in the eye. In the spa they tried out the hot and cold mineral baths and the solarium. On plastic lounge chairs she stole glances at his smooth lankiness, his flat stomach, his muscled thighs. She watched as he dozed lightly, fatigued from the early start to his day, the hard work, the run to the spa. He awakened suddenly, caught her staring, and smiled, first with caution and then with abandon.

"Mud," he said mockingly stern, practically shouting, "we need mud!" In one swift motion he pulled her from the lounge chair and led her in a jog out the back of the spa and down to the Dead Sea itself. He thrust both hands into a trough of mud on the pebbly beach and grabbed Vivi's shoulders, smearing downward toward her hands. His grip was strong and the mud was warm; the feeling was so sensual that Vivi could feel her whole body responding. She wondered if he noticed her erect nipples, then realized he could not possibly miss them. Martin covered her in the black mud, rubbed her back, her legs, high up on the inside of her thighs. Another second and she would have to make him stop but how wonderful it felt, as he applied more just above the top of her bathing suit, to her neck—which he massaged—and then, with gentle motions of his fingers, to her cheeks and forehead and finally a daub on her nose. He stood back to observe his work.

"A black goddess you are, the Queen of Sheba," he said, clearly pleased with himself. "Now my turn. Make me the *King* of Sheba."

She was timid at first and coated him with huge handfuls of mud to create a barrier between his body and her hands. The mud slid

downward, dripped to his scanty bathing trunks. She stood close behind him at first, reaching to his shoulders and the nape of his neck, then moved a step away to coat his back and the backs of his legs. He stood silent and still. She gathered more mud from the trough and came around to his front side. His erection nearly reached her stomach, she had to stand away from him and lean into his body to continue smearing his face, his chest, his stomach. When it was time to squat down to finish the fronts of his legs she considered stopping, having him smear himself. But she was embarrassed to acknowledge the problem, and more than a little curious. She squatted low, daubed the tops of his feet, his shins, his knees, did everything to avoid his shiny black bathing suit, though she felt a terrible urge to pass her hand over it, lightly, lightly, no more than a breeze. Instead she stood too quickly, swooning. He caught her.

"Are you all right?" he asked. There was a catch in his voice.

"Fine," she said without conviction. "It's the sun, or maybe the smell of all these minerals." He pulled her closer and she could feel the mingling heat from his mud-covered body and her own, perhaps even the cloth of his bulging trunks just below her navel, she was not sure. She breathed deeply, hoping for composure, waiting for logic and sanity to kick in. He breathed with her.

After a moment she leaned away from him and he let go, cautiously, testing to make sure she would not fall. She took in a deep breath, let it out, and said, "Let's go wash off in the water."

Vivi tried to stay away from Martin after that, skipped the next desert trek and the one following, but all she could think about was his soft voice, his tender attention, his warm and lovely body. By the time he phoned, after the second missed outing, she was ready for him.

It was a chore to keep their relationship a secret from her fellow soldiers, less so from her mother. She was no longer in Leah's orbit. When she came home for Shabbat every other weekend her parents knew she could not answer their questions, was forbidden from giving even the slightest details of her work in the army, and so, by extension, they refrained from asking her about her life at all. Vivi volunteered little, kept them informed about her high school friends and mentioned her two best army girlfriends and even a boy or two; Leah was most attentive then, though Vivi assured her they were only friends. In the meantime she and Martin hiked Thursday afternoons or Friday mornings whether there was an organized group going or not, and Vivi hitchhiked to Kibbutz Ein Gedi to see Martin every evening she could. Often she stayed over, sleeping with Martin on a small mattress in a gardener's shed to which he had the keys, slipping back to her base before dawn. She loved to drift off to sleep in his arms in their tiny self-contained world, loved to wake up with her head on his chest, rising and falling with his measured breaths. She had never felt so much at peace, and the guilt she felt vanished entirely from the moment she saw him until the moment they parted.

By Passover Vivi and Martin had been together for half a year. He had told her eight times that he loved her; she had refrained more times than that from telling him that she loved him in return. Her friends at the base knew Martin, his friends at Ein Gedi knew her. Martin was intrigued by Jewish tradition and Vivi was desperate to invite him to her house for the Seder meal, but she knew the obstacles were overwhelming. Instead she volunteered to spend the holiday on the base and planned to sneak Martin in for the Seder; there

would be only a slim crew and they all knew him, so she was sure nobody would mind. Her mother was devastated that she would not be joining them, had offered to call her commanding officer to argue for her release. In the end Leah acquiesced and sent Vivi a package of Passover supplies.

On the morning after the holiday, as the soldiers returned to the base, Vivi was summoned to the office of the commander, an affable captain named Hezi.

"Close the door behind you," he said without looking up as she stepped into his office. He was sitting at the head of his T-shaped table under a photograph of Israel's current president, Chaim Herzog.

"I understand that you have a boyfriend, a gentile kibbutz volunteer from Germany, and that he spent the Seder night with you here on the base."

Vivi was too shocked to respond, did not even nod or indicate in any fashion that she had heard what Hezi was saying.

"That's grounds for court-martial, you could have breached the security of this entire base, or worse. You've been a good soldier and excellent at your job so I'll spare you a dishonorable discharge. Still, you leave me no choice but to use my authority as base commander and sentence you immediately to twenty-one days in prison, the bare minimum for such an infraction. Incidentally, the guard on duty that night will also be going to jail, for letting you talk him into allowing your friend onto the base."

Vivi burst out crying, but Hezi was unsympathetic. He let her cry herself out, nonchalantly completing some paperwork as she sobbed. When she had finished crying she realized she would be forced to tell her parents where she was and why she would not be coming home. The thought frightened her beyond measure. Terrified, she appealed to Hezi.

"I'm sorry this will get you into trouble at home, but you should be glad I'm not going to make this any worse than it is. I can't believe a girl as smart as you could do something so incredibly stupid." He leaned back in his chair. "Anyway, maybe you'll be surprised, maybe they'll be more understanding than you think."

With that, Vivi began to cry again, harder than last time. Hezi called to her through her tears. "Vivi." He tried again, louder and with less patience. "Vivi, pull yourself together and get yourself organized. I've contacted military police and they'll be here soon to pick you up. Get yourself ready."

On her way out of the office he called to her from his desk. "I just want you to know," he said evenly, "that when you come back it'll be fine between us. No hard feelings either way, I hope."

Vivi fled the office in tears.

Late that evening, the events of her long and traumatic day just barely behind her, Vivi sat to write a letter from the large cell she shared with five other female soldiers. The others were asleep, so Vivi wrote in a corner, where orange light from the hall shone weakly in a small square.

Dear Mother and Father,

I am writing to you from Prison 400, the prison for women soldiers at Zrifin. I was sentenced to three weeks and brought here this morning. How ironic that this should happen on the second day of Passover, our celebration of freedom.

I am here because I invited a friend, a Christian kib-

butz volunteer from Germany, to the Seder on our base, thus
violating regulations and breaching security. You probably
understand that Martin is more than just a friend, and I am
certain this will cause you more grief than my imprison-
ment.

 We are allowed visitors every afternoon between six and
seven o'clock. I will understand if you do not wish to see me
under these circumstances, but I hope nonetheless that you will
see fit to write to me.

 I remain, as always, your loving daughter,
 Vivi

Sealing the letter she felt surprisingly strong, as if a burden had been
lifted and she had recovered her energy. She sat to write another.

Dear Martin,

 I am in prison for breaking the rules and breaching
security. I realize now that I never should have invited you to
the Seder at our base, but I'm not sorry you got your wish and
enjoyed yourself so much. It really was a special evening.

 I am certain when you read this you will feel terribly guilty,
but please don't. The decision was mine and the action was my
responsibility. Besides, the girls here are nice and I'll only be
here for twenty more days.

 The only bad part is not being able to see you. I miss you
already. From this safe distance I can tell you the truth: I love
you, too.

 Please wait for me with patience,
 Vivi

Three days later Martin showed up at prison, disheveled and in tears. The trip had taken most of the day, nearly making him too late for a visit. Vivi comforted him, held his hands under the careful stares of several guards. She wondered if they thought of her like the girls she would glimpse at the Haifa port whenever a big ship docked, on the arm of a beefy Scandinavian or a boisterous American.

Vivi begged Martin to return to the kibbutz, but he rented a cheap room in Tel Aviv and came back the next day and the next to sit with her for the allotted hour. There was no response from her parents. Martin returned to Ein Gedi but rented a room again the next weekend and visited Vivi on Friday, Saturday and Sunday. At first his attentions were awkward, but the longer he stayed, the more grateful for his company she became. By the third and last week of her imprisonment she was dependent on his visits.

Four days before her release her parents arrived during the visiting hours. Vivi was startled to find them waiting for her, and even more apprehensive that Martin was due to show up at any minute. She sat facing Leah and Amatzia on brown plastic chairs. No one spoke, and Vivi kept one eye on the door at all times.

Finally Amatzia looked at his daughter. "I'm sure you understand how disappointed we are. About this *goy*," he said, sputtering, unable to continue. Leah pursed and gnawed her lips but said nothing. Vivi shifted uncomfortably in her seat, crossed and uncrossed her legs. Would Martin comprehend, would he leave when he realized they had come? Vivi was not quite sure she did not prefer a confrontation.

At ten minutes past the hour, with little said and Vivi hoping that somehow Martin had miraculously gotten stuck in traffic or lost in

Tel Aviv, the door creaked open and he burst into the room. His hair was freshly washed, wet even. He wore jeans and a creased cotton shirt, and sandals on his feet. Vivi felt a rush of love as he entered, and a huge smile blossomed on his face before he realized she was sitting with her parents.

A look of stupefaction and horror rose to Leah's face the moment she understood that this was Martin, the Martin who had stolen her daughter and sent her to prison. The Martin who, no doubt—it was there in their cozy smiles, in the heat they radiated, for everyone to see—was sleeping with her daughter, her precious Varda, her delicate rose. In one glance, Leah took in the whole picture, the six months of friendship and passion, before either Martin or Vivi, or poor Amatzia with his back to the door, could react. In that instant, Leah was out of her seat and at the door, her hands reaching for Martin's neck.

She threw herself at him. Martin, caught off guard, reeled backward and hit the door with Leah barreling into him. "Swine," she shouted in Hebrew. "Pig! You vile filthy German goy, you barbarian!" She pushed herself far enough away from him to swing her fists at him. Martin let her hit him, protecting only his face. When she scratched him he caught her wrists and tried talking to her.

"Mrs. Berger," he pleaded in Hebrew, "please . . ."

A guard pulled Leah off Martin. She continued screaming, and Amatzia was shouting, and the guards blew whistles and in the midst of it all, as the visitors were pushed from the room, Vivi and Martin stood silent, gazing at one another. But Martin disappeared from her vision, was removed from the room with all the other guests, before they could utter a single word to one another. Several of the other prisoners shouted at Vivi since her guests were the cause of the ruckus, but she did not care. On the way back to her cell she felt as though she had just solved a riddle, found the missing piece in a

puzzle, but did not yet know what it was. She felt very still at the core of her being.

After her release from prison, Vivi returned to her base. She was efficient and capable as ever, but watchful now, guarded. She wondered who had informed on her. She no longer socialized with her fellow soldiers and spent as much time with Martin as possible. Her incarceration began to feel like a rite of passage, a solo trek into the desert from which she had emerged purified and silent. On weekends she returned only rarely to her parents' house in Haifa. No one ever mentioned Martin or prison.

In June Martin returned to Germany for summer courses and Vivi spent the last two months of her army service planning a dramatic escape from Israel as soon as possible after her release. Her army service ended the week before Rosh Hashanah. She went to synagogue with her parents and prayed for a good year.

Martin had sent her a ticket that would remove her to Germany during the ten days of repentance before Yom Kippur. She was relieved to think she would be gone by then, could not face the Kol Nidre service in which she would be asking God to cancel the oaths she had made during the past year just before flying to Berlin to live with her uncircumcised German Christian boyfriend in what had been, only forty years earlier, the all-time capital of Jew hatred.

On a Tuesday morning in mid-September, Vivi emptied her bank account, then returned home to pack a medium suitcase and a long, squat duffel bag full of clothing and shoes and—at the last minute, on her way out the door—a prayer book, left a note on the dining room table, and caught a bus to the airport. She was airborne before her parents even knew she was gone.

It is Sabbath dark outside, but Teo has no way of knowing so in his underground studio. Nelly will have prepared a good, special meal for them this evening, as if she were a regular Jewish housewife, with wine and challah bread and chicken soup, but he does not think about returning home, not yet. He sits, depleted, looking around the studio as though he has only just seen it for the first time. He catches sight of himself in the mirrors, first on one wall and then the next. He has spent a lifetime looking at himself in mirrors, but now, instead of his turnout or musculature or the angle of his head, it is his face that he notices. It is pinched, sagging, timeworn. Colorless. Even his brilliant eyes, blue and green, cannot salvage it. His shoulders sag and he sits hunched and humpbacked, something he has never, ever allowed himself to do—in front of another living soul, or even alone.

So he was right. The girl has been damaged by a man. How badly, he cannot say. Nor is he sure he wants to know. Why should he get involved in the sad, stale story of a woman half his age? Why, he asks himself, is he preoccupied with her at all? What about her makes him care? Still, he wonders if he has pushed too hard; some souls can take it, learn from it, but others are merely crushed. He has had dancers of all persuasions, seen them flourish or fail under his withering criticism. But he understands that what is good for a professional dancer

may not be good for a fragile creature who has never, he sees clearly now, banished her demons to find fulfillment.

How can he tell her, without telling her, that he, too, was nearly crushed by a man? That his life took a turn, veered off to a new and less promising track, though as far as that is concerned he realizes one can never say which was better unless one has lived them both—and that is impossible. He has found success, he reasons, is recognized in his field, lauded even. And yet, this was not the path he had started out on. If only he had listened to the warnings, had stayed away from that performance in Berlin. And if in Berlin, if only he had not danced quite the way he did. But he was there. And he danced, spectacularly. So the rest unfolded as it had.

An image of himself suddenly crosses his mind. He was fourteen at the time, the war still three long years into the future, and he stood gazing into a mirror that threw back a reflection of himself and Valentina Ahmalitova at her elegant home in Warsaw. Teodor was not nervous in the least. In spite of her social position as wife of a Belgian diplomat, and her reputation as a former prima ballerina with the Ballets Russes, Madame Valentina was warm with him from the start. "Oh," she exclaimed as she scrutinized his face just after he stepped into her home, "my first lover also had one green eye and one blue. I've always found that absolutely fascinating, and a sign of greatness." In fact, he was testing her as much as she was testing him. He wanted to know what she knew, what she could teach him. He danced a little for her, a small, flashy routine, and she asked Teodor to do a few specific steps for her. And then they talked. Or at least Teodor did. He was so full of dance, so crammed full of ideas and thoughts and so appreciative of the fact that Madame Valentina understood much more than his last teacher had. He talked and talked, told her everything that was in his head about dance, and when he

had finished Madame Valentina told him to report to her every day after school, that she would continue his training at no charge—she did not need money, she said, gesturing to the tall, arched windows of the magnificent studio that overlooked an English garden in the courtyard—but that Teodor would have to remain fully devoted to his art, would have to be willing to work very, very hard. She said she would give him some instruction but that mainly she would help him move what was in his head out into his body. They began the next afternoon.

"I danced for Diaghilev," she told him with pride. "I partnered Nijinsky." Teodor knew just barely enough about these legends of ballet to be impressed, but it was not until Madame showed him photographs, then pushed and pulled his body to emulate the great Nijinsky, that true comprehension began to awaken in him. "The arms," she exclaimed, "look at their extraordinary lightness, Teodor, how they are suspended in air. Do not lift them from your shoulders; the power of your arms comes from your back." At this point Madame would lift her own arms, gazing off to a far wall, oblivious to Teodor. When her gaze returned to him it often seemed as though she did not recall they were in the midst of a lesson, did not, in fact, recognize him for a long and confusing minute.

Often she would disappear into the library, reemerging with large and heavy art books filled with glossy reproductions. "Look, Teodor," she would say, "look at Michaelangelo. Look at Raphael. This beautiful flow of lines, this grace, they are not achieved by avoiding strain, they are attained by *incorporating* the pain and struggle." She would turn her full attention to Teodor, staring, gravely serious, into his eyes. "Do not run away, embrace the suffering."

"No!" she would shout as he stood poised to dance, "not at all like that. You do not dance from your *legs*," she would say scornfully, as

if he had suggested they perform a polka. "You dance from *here*." She grabbed his pelvis tight with both hands so close to his penis that he blushed furiously. Noticing his embarrassment she cocked her head at him, squinting an eye. "Beautiful boy, you cannot be shy about using your body. This, Nijinsky understood only too well," and she was silent again, lost in a private reverie.

The months passed, and though Madame Valentina could still be provoked to outbursts, she clearly enjoyed Teodor's progress. He could tell she thought he danced well, very well, and she kept him for longer and longer hours in the studio. She worked on his hands, his face, his neck. Hours and hours on his toes, his heels. "Nijinsky did not press his weight on his big toe, he used his entire foot to grip the floor." She called Teodor a Petersburg dancer, her highest compliment, as he perfected long, high, suspended leaps and fiery pirouettes.

On a spring Sunday, nearly a year after she had begun teaching him, Madame asked Teodor to bring his parents for tea. In the studio, alone with Madame, Teodor felt only the awed respect of pupil with teacher, but in society he knew she was an aristocrat, descended from a long line of White Russian nobility with connections to the royal family, and married to an international dignitary. He in turn took it upon himself to ensure his parents would appear in their finest clothing and behave with the best of manners. He badgered them for days, his instructions insufferable, until finally his father threatened to cancel the entire appointment.

That Sunday, little Margot deposited at Mrs. Zabrinski's, the Levins arrived precisely at the appointed hour. The butler greeted them and ushered them into the receiving room, a small, circular chamber of singularly sedate elegance. Madame entered immediately.

"My dear *famille* Levin, how good of you to come." She spoke to them in her usual mix of French, Russian and Polish, which Teodor understood completely but which confused his parents terribly. "Please join me for tea and biscuits."

Oskar and Rosa, cowed by her formidable presence and the resplendent room, nodded.

When they were comfortably seated and had been served by the maid, Madame placed her teacup on the low table in front of them and leaned back in her chair.

"Mr. Levin, Mrs. Levin, you must already know about your son's enormous talent, and I hope you are proud of him. Teodor has a rare gift and I am grateful for the chance to help him realize it."

Rosa gazed at Teodor and smiled. Oskar thanked Madame for her time and trouble. "And please allow us to present you with this token of our gratitude for all you have done."

Rosa started, late to Oskar's cue. She fished a parcel from her handbag and placed it on the low table in front of Madame. "We have heard from Teodor that you and your husband are collectors of clocks, and we hope this small addition will suit you."

"*Simplement magnifique*," Madame exclaimed when she had disengaged the gold satin bow and wrapping paper from the clock. "Bertrand will also be thrilled."

A silence fell on the small group. Madame looked from Rosa to Oskar to Teodor, then back to the clock. "Ah, my dears, such a lovely gift in such ugly times. I have begun to worry so about what is facing us in Europe." She stood and moved to the courtyard doors and spoke to the silent garden beyond. "I have clear memories of the revolution in my country. Precisely twenty years ago it was when my family lost everything we had not managed to spirit out of Russia or hide. My parents never recovered from the shock, and both died far

too young from worry." She turned to face the room. "What are you doing to prepare yourselves?" she asked. "What are you doing so as not to be caught unawares?"

Teodor and Rosa turned to Oskar, who was staring at Madame. No one stirred and no one spoke.

"You are Jews," Madame said, "and surely you are aware of what is happening in Germany right now. I can vouch for the Poles, they like the Jews even less than the Germans. So what are you doing to protect yourselves?"

Oskar cleared his throat but did not speak.

"I see," said Madame, as her gaze dropped to the floor.

She returned to her armchair and sat facing the Levin family.

"Then let me help you start. Get Teodor out of Poland. A dear friend from my Ballets Russes days is now teaching at the school of the Royal Danish Ballet. I would like to recommend Teodor for study there, both because he has the potential to become a star dancer and because the Danes treat their Jews far better than the Poles or the Germans, or most other Europeans. It will take a bit of wrangling, since the ballet school is open only to Danes, but my friend is quite resourceful and will surely manage to arrange matters. Teodor will be safe there, and free to develop his talent." She stopped talking and watched the small family before her. "And I am willing to undertake the entire cost of his education."

"Oh Madame, what an amazing, generous offer—"

"Yes, as my wife says, amazing and generous. But we cannot possibly accept such a large gift. We are already indebted to you for everything you have given Teodor but could not think of imposing . . ."

"Mr. Levin, I have no children. I lead a comfortable life. And I am an artist, a dancer who looks at your son and recognizes greatness. I do not wish to offend you by offering help, but you may well need

your resources to reestablish yourselves abroad one day soon, and a ballet education might seem terribly frivolous to you then. Teodor is fifteen, the only time life allows for taking chances and exploring the limits of what we can do. He will work hard, harder and more focused than he has ever done. He will learn about music and movement and he will learn even more about what he can and cannot accomplish in life. I beg you to give him this chance."

Oskar shook his head slowly from side to side, thinking. Teodor sat in prudent, hopeful silence. Rosa interjected. "Perhaps we could talk about it at home?" she asked, looking first to her husband, then to Madame.

"Of course, dear. Discuss between yourselves. But I must be in touch with my friend in Copenhagen soon if we wish to enroll Teodor for the upcoming school year."

"Thank you, Madame, thank you so much," Rosa said excitedly. "We'll talk it over tonight." She glanced at their gift clock on the table. It had cost them the equivalent of their maid's yearly wages, and she was now especially glad she had pushed Oskar to such extravagance. With a last look around she thanked Madame again and the family took its leave.

Months later, on the night before Teodor's departure, Rosa threw a grand party. Two brothers—a flautist and a violinist—were hired to accompany a neighbor, Mrs. Oestriker, on the piano. Oskar spent most of the day stringing colored lights across the salon, crisscrossing the wires and checking to see that all the bulbs lit up when plugged in. Rosa had devoted a week to baking her finest pastries, had spent a small fortune on exotic ingredients: coconut, butterscotch, white chocolate, dark rum. She pulled silver trays from every corner of the

house and set Maria, the maid, to polishing them all, even twice and thrice, until their shine dazzled. On Saturday evening the trays were heavy with sweetmeats and Maria stood at attention in her starched uniform while Rosa and Oskar greeted the guests by the front door, she in an evening gown, a small string of pearls and diamonds around her neck and a tiny red rose tucked behind one ear, he in his most elegant suit, his shoes burnished to a black-mirrored glow. Rosa sparkled and laughed, she listened and chatted, and only once during the party did Teodor catch her glancing in his direction, a look of wistful resignation spread across her face like moonlight.

Madame Valentina stopped briefly at the party, en route to a diplomatic ball. She did not remove her stole, but chatted amiably with the hosts in the foyer. Before leaving she asked Teodor to step outside with her.

"There are still so many things to teach you, my young friend," she said with a sigh. "And I fear I do not even know what they are. The Danes will teach you what they know to do well, the charming arm poses, the excellent stage manners, the fine passés and the superb pantomime. But this I must remind you: dance, always, with intelligence, by making your body interesting to look at whenever you are being watched. I'm not talking about a particular gesture or the angle of a line, the details we've spent so much time on. I'm talking about the whole of you, your body as a whole. Whatever anyone does to your style, remember to dance with intelligence, with your body and your mind and your soul. I know you can do this, Teodor. I know you will." She cradled his face in her gloved hands and descended to the car. She did not look up at Teodor as the chauffeur closed the door behind her and drove off.

The next morning before dawn, Rosa was a wreck. She had gathered her hair too hastily into an untidy chignon, and now wisps

slipped away and fell across her face. Her eyes were bloodshot and her face looked lined and tired as Teodor had rarely seen it. She busied herself with breakfast, and with sandwiches and fruit for the trip; she could barely stand to look at Teodor, for fear of bursting into tears. When it came time for them to leave she hugged Teodor hard, then pushed him away, speechless and sobbing, and he left the house with his father in silence.

But Teodor was fifteen years old and off on his first big adventure. He could not be morose for long, too excited about the journey and what lay ahead. He had only ever been to the Tatry Mountains and to the countryside, never as far north as the Baltic Sea, in fact had never crossed the border from Poland into another country, where people spoke a language he had never heard and could scarcely imagine. He tried puckering his mouth and creating the sounds of Danish, but had no idea where to begin.

They sat in the first-class section of the train, far from the Poles guzzling beer with their breakfasts. On the way out of town, on a bridge over the Vistula, Teodor caught a quick glimpse of the riverbank where his mother would take him to play, but he let it fall back with the rest of Warsaw. Soon they were roaring across flat, open fields of potatoes, wheat and mustard. They passed shimmering rivers and peasants on horseback. They skirted grazing cows and huge bales of hay and sagging castles, stopping in tiny towns with walls and ramparts from another age. Oskar told Teodor of a great kingdom that had once had its capital here, but Teodor's mind skittered with the scenery and soon Oskar fell silent.

From the moment they alighted from the train, Teodor felt he was in a new country, and in fact he was; despite its geographical location in the north of Poland, Danzig was a German city with German laws and customs. Teodor, however, knew nothing of the laws or customs,

he knew only that the air was different here, saturated with sea smells: salt, fish, a soupy thickness that never descended on landlocked Warsaw. The roofs were different here, ornate and frivolous, and there were flowerpots in every window of every building. After a meal of fish and potatoes, they strolled the waterfront, pausing to admire the great stone gates of the city and an enormous medieval loading crane. Teodor persuaded his father to buy a necklace of Baltic amber for Rosa, and before retiring they enjoyed a hot chocolate topped with a cone of whipped cream in the lobby of their hotel. Neither father nor son slept well, whether from the strange sounds—ships' bells and sailors' yells—or fear of what lay ahead, or just sheer excitement.

They rose early, ate a small breakfast in the dining room, and packed in silence. Both felt keenly the absence of Rosa, who always maintained a happy chatter that was their comfort and pleasure. The day passed slowly. Finally, mid-afternoon, still well in advance of departure, Oskar hired a taxi to bring them to the port.

From far off they glimpsed the SS *Frederik VIII*, a vessel Teodor had imagined as a simple fishing boat with perhaps a few other passengers but which was in fact long and sleek and as tall as their apartment building in Warsaw. Who, he wondered now, were all these people traveling, like him, from Danzig to Copenhagen? He looked to his father's face to see if he, too, was in awe. "I've booked you a second-class room with a young man from Stettin. He's continuing on to America."

"America?"

"Your ship sails from Copenhagen to America, Teodor. But don't worry, they'll make sure you get off in Denmark." He laughed, watching Teodor's wide-eyed astonishment.

By the time they reached the great ship, loading was well under way and the scene was of controlled chaos. There were people and

parcels scattered everywhere, boys selling newspapers and cigars, sailors carrying kit bags. Families seemed to be traveling with entire households, and several times in line to board arguments broke out between irate porters and departing passengers with regard to the sheer bulk of belongings set to enter the ship. Teodor and Oskar did not speak; they stood, nearly shoulder to shoulder, quiet and self-contained, each observing the scene and thinking private, very different thoughts.

Oskar fished an envelope from his breast pocket.

"There's money here for you, and your ticket and identification papers, as well as a letter from the Danish folks inviting you to the school there." He brought a handkerchief from another pocket and daubed at the beads of sweat on his brow. Teodor wondered whether he, too, would lose his hair young, grow stout, and sweat when it was not hot. Adulthood did not seem all that wonderful.

"There's also a letter from me in there, just a few bits of things I was thinking. I did not quite know how to say them so I wrote them down for you. I hope my handwriting is legible." He had begun to sniffle, and now applied the handkerchief to his nose. "Anyway, good luck my boy. We're expecting great things from you, but do not stay away from home too long. Remember your home is always here, in Poland."

"Yes, Father, I'll remember," Teodor said, shifting weight from foot to foot. Oskar hugged Teodor tightly, crying lightly now. Teodor longed to bolt for the gangplank but he held on to his father. He did not wish to see his face.

Oskar pushed him away. "Go on, get on the ship. And write us as soon as you get settled with the Sonnenfeld family. They sound like good people, I'm sure you will do fine with them."

Teodor lifted his heavy suitcase and struggled with it up the gangplank. He found a spot and moved to the railing to wave good-bye to

his father. At eight o'clock the ship sailed, and Teodor waved until he could no longer distinguish his father from the hotel behind him.

Benno, his cabin mate from Stettin, was a Communist. Teodor had only a vague idea what that meant, but did not wish to seem stupid in the eyes of this young man fully six years his senior. "I'm an artist," he told Teodor, "and I'm going to America for freedom. It's the only place you can be a Communist and an artist and be free, and probably rich, at least after a few years. And anyway, it's no good being a Jew in Europe anymore, they don't let us breathe. In the USA I'll be able to breathe."

He talked endlessly about himself and asked nothing about Teodor, even why he was sailing to Copenhagen and not, like him and most everyone else on this ship, to the New World. At dinner, however, they were seated with a wealthy Jewish couple from Stettin, in whose circles Benno clearly did not move, and so, outclassed, he grew silent. The couple's daughter looked to be about Teodor's age. He guessed, by her carefully braided and ribboned hair, her fussy clothing and her pout, that she was terribly spoiled.

"You'll see," Mr. Steinberg was telling the table, "Herr Hitler will not stop with Germany, Germany is only his starting point for European conquest. He has grand plans." He pointed his fork at Teodor. "And wherever Hitler goes he'll make trouble for Jews, you wait and see." Mrs. Steinberg gently lowered her husband's outstretched arm and everyone continued eating.

"Why are you traveling alone, dear?" Mrs. Steinberg asked Teodor.

Teodor placed his fork on his plate and quickly swallowed the food in his mouth. "I'm going to study ballet in Copenhagen," he told them simply.

Mr. Steinberg nearly exploded. "Ballet!" he shouted, drawing the attention of several tables nearby, and a stern reprimand from Mrs. Steinberg. "The world in an economic downturn, Hitler making trouble for everyone, especially Jews, and you are going to learn to turn pirouettes? And your parents are allowing this?"

Teodor had no idea how to defend himself. His love of ballet, his adoring mother and his talent had created just one path in life, one clearly marked path he had never had cause to question. But he did not need to provide Mr. Steinberg with an answer; his daughter was pleased to oblige. "Father, listen to you! If a person is not a doctor or a businessman you think he is loafing about wasting his time. What about art, and creativity? What about beauty?"

"Ach, *Liebchen*, that's for women. Men need to set the world on its course!"

"Or muck it up, more likely," Mrs. Steinberg said with a smile at Teodor. He was grateful for the intervention, but perplexed nonetheless, and the meal passed uncomfortably for him. Later, in the cabin, as they lay in their bunks, he asked Benno for his opinion.

"The guy's an old fart, if you ask me, lots of wind."

"But what he was saying, you know, about art. I've never really thought about it, I've always just danced . . ."

"Well," Benno said slowly, "you must admit that dancing isn't like art, not really. You do it and it's gone, it's all over. When I paint something it's my statement, and it's there forever. Unless of course I destroy it. But no matter what you do, your dance is over the minute you've danced it."

Teodor thought about this for a while, but when he was ready to answer, or perhaps ask another question that lay a bit further on in his line of reasoning, he realized that Benno was breathing the soft and steady breaths of sleep. Filled with energy and feeling quite dis-

quieted, he stood up from his berth and let himself out of the cabin. There were few people milling about, and Teodor climbed two flights up and went out to the starboard deck, where a strong cool wind caught him and tossed him about, and from there he climbed another level higher, to a secluded observation deck at the rear of the boat, pointing back in the darkness at Poland. He tried to imagine his new life, but too many images flew about in his brain; too many languages and faces already, a huge, noisy confusion. He stood at the railing, gazing first down at the wake of the great ship, then up at the stars. Out here, things were simpler, and his mind let go of the images, and quieted. Here there were only wind and stars and water. And a barre, he suddenly realized: he was holding a cold, white, metallic barre, and so he slipped off his shoes and began to stretch and bend, to lift and pose. And, after a few minutes and a glance about to make sure he was alone, he let go of the barre and danced, really danced, the deck his stage and the wind his music and the stars his audience. He flew from corner to corner, in great leaps and turns, higher and longer than he had ever soared. He grew warmer, and it seemed to him the stars shone more brightly the longer he danced. He had broken a sweat by the time he stopped, but had no clue how long he had been dancing. After bowing a grand révérence, first to the wind and then to the stars, he slid down the stairs and returned to his cabin.

He sat up abruptly in the morning. Benno was still sleeping, but Teodor leapt from his berth; the ship was quiet, which meant they had docked for a short stop in Trelleborg, and Teodor wished to catch this first glimpse of a new country, a new land. Up on deck, however, what he could see of Sweden proved to be a disappointment. Ships and low houses under a thin sun. Nothing shimmered as he had hoped it would. He was idly watching two brawny Swedish dock-

workers unload crates of potatoes when he remembered his father's letter, and walked quickly back to his cabin.

It consisted of one short page on lined paper, snippets of practical advice his father wished to impart to him. Teodor lit the lamp over his bed and, to Benno's snores, read: "Follow the customs of your hosts, even if they are strange or primitive in your opinion." "Be flexible where you can, but do nothing contrary to the principles upon which you have been raised." There was no listing of those principles, and Teodor wondered what they were. "Be polite with strangers but not overly friendly." And in a smaller handwriting, at the bottom of the page: "Let no person touch you untowardly. Your body is your private kingdom and let no person violate that right." In fact, "person" had replaced the word "man," which had been heavily scribbled over but which was easily discernible by flipping over the page and glancing at the indentations of the pen. Benno stirred and muttered something. Teodor folded his father's letter neatly and tucked it inside the envelope.

They remain seated: she on a bench in a park in Old Jaffa, he in a chair in his basement studio on Ibn Gabirol Street in Tel Aviv. They talk to no one, only themselves.

Briefly, Vivi thinks of Pincho. He will not be worried about her absence, since he goes to his parents' home every other Sabbath, dons a skullcap, and becomes the Pinhas of his boyhood. He will stand praying in the synagogue between his bearded father and his younger brothers. He will bow his head as first his father, then his mother, recite blessings on him and his siblings before the Sabbath meal. He will sing songs with them at the table, only occasionally letting his thoughts wander to the simmering, shimmering, half-naked bodies pulsating on the dance floor at Indigo.

She thinks of Teo, too. He has probably collected his belongings, gone home to a hot and savory Sabbath meal. What would it be like, she wonders, to sit across the table from him during a languorous meal, good wine warming their veins? She shakes her head and turns back to her memories.

● ● ●

Briefly, Teo thinks of Nelly. She will be terrified that something has happened to him. The incessant ringing of the office phone is certainly Nelly dialing the only number she ever uses. The Sabbath candles in their heavy silver holders will be melting down, the soup cooling in its pot. He is her entire life. It has been more than twenty-five years since he was in Warsaw to receive a prize and found her there, orphaned and unmarried and destitute, living hand to mouth in the flat her family had occupied across the hall from his own. He brought her to Israel then so he could look after her—a debt of gratitude repaid—but instead she has spent a quarter century looking after him. She has made no friends and rarely leaves the apartment except to shop for food and other necessities. Although he has assured her that he will provide for her forever, long after he is gone, he understands she has no raison d'être beyond caring for him. And still, he cannot rise to answer the phone.

He thinks of Vivi, too. She is probably on her way to meet friends for an evening of dancing, drinking, talking. Briefly he envisions her meeting a man in a bar, the brisk walk back to her apartment. He shakes his head and turns back to his memories.

Martin's hair, when she had last seen him, was thick and wavy and sandy brown. Had he brushed it downward instead of curling the ends behind his ears, it would have reached halfway to his shoulders. Now, however, it was cut close to the scalp and shockingly blond. A bigger surprise still was his face, once obscured by a thin, wispy beard and now smooth-shaven. How round and open it was. He looked slightly stuffed and padded, though he did not seem to have gained weight in his body.

Martin lived in a second-floor flat of what had once been a grand mansion—now subdivided and rented to negligent students—near the Grunewald train station in the British sector of West Berlin. An old wrought-iron gate gave way to a shabby, untended garden. Various entrances to the separate apartments had been knocked through the outer walls, giving the entire structure the look of a large mouth missing teeth in several crucial places. The apartment was tiny, but the high ceiling and a verandah, which afforded views of leafy, healthy old trees in the garden, gave Vivi a sense of space that the room did not.

In the first days following her arrival in Berlin Martin took time from work and university to show her the city, introduce her to friends. Berlin seemed to be filled with students; in some neigh-

borhoods nobody appeared to be older than twenty-five. Many, like Martin, had come to West Berlin from other parts of Germany for its special status as an occupied city, meaning that Berlin residents were not required to serve in the German army. He brought Vivi to the local greengrocer, to the bank, to the post office. He invited her to all the popular hangouts: Die Ruine, Café Einstein, Terzo Mondo, and especially to Zweiblfisch, an easy train ride away, where the intellectuals debated anything and everything all night, to dawn. Vivi clung to Martin, awed and fearful, worried how she would manage on her own when Martin returned to his schedule. He taught her words she would need to know and was generally solicitous and quite glad to have her with him. They made love often, though at Vivi's insistence it was usually in the dark.

Before leaving Israel Vivi had had trouble picturing her life in Berlin, what she would spend her days doing, but had been generally excited to be in Europe, with so much culture and history lying around like a field studded with precious gems waiting to be collected. What she had not counted on, however, was the isolation of Berlin, a city—not even a city but a half city—that was a geographical dead-end, a cul-de-sac. Whereas in Israel she had sometimes felt hemmed in by troubled borders too close for comfort, here in Berlin she felt absolutely threatened, and had frequent nightmares in which she was constantly, accidentally, stepping across the border into East Germany and getting shot or beaten or imprisoned.

As a foreigner with no official status, Vivi was forbidden from working or studying, so after a month of settling in to Martin's routines, after recovering from her initial shock and fear, she began to explore Berlin. She walked the Tiergarten, the Charlotten-Schlossgarten, the Zoologischer Garten, the Fritz-Schloss Park. She walked the grand boulevards and the small side streets. She visited the mu-

seums, the churches, the concert halls. She spent one whole week in the newly remodeled KaDeWe department store, a day on each floor testing perfumes, sampling cheeses, watching television broadcasts in the electronics section. Even halved it was a huge city, but she walked Berlin tirelessly, in ever-expanding concentric circles. On sunny days she prowled the parks and on rainy ones the museums or the shops. Mostly, on these long days of rambling energy, she spoke to no one, other than a quick request for coffee in a café or a ticket at a museum. Sometimes, however, she was approached, usually by men. They talked of the weather or commented on her brisk walk, all the while a smile on their rosy-cheeked faces. But their eyes would always drop downward, stopping at her chest, her hips. She quickly learned to cut off these aimless conversations before their eyes could wander.

In the evenings she was eager for conversation, real human interaction, and wished to recount the events of her day to Martin. Martin, fatigued from medical studies and a day job in a hospital lab, wished for study time in the evenings, hoping to dispense with conversation over dinner. Vivi found this intolerable, and looked for ways to provoke his anger in order to coax him into talking to her.

"I spent the day in the portrait gallery of the National Museum today," she told him. "All those pale inbred aristocrats. I thought they were so *ugly*. Then afterward, on the street outside, I kept running into them. They're all over the place, haven't changed a bit!"

Martin grinned but did not look up from his books.

Vivi made a great, noisy show of scraping and stacking the glass dishes. "Then I stopped back in KaDeWe for a pair of socks and wound up buying four sweaters and a new winter coat."

"Hmmm," he said absentmindedly.

"Then I had sex with the bear keeper and one of the bears at the Tiergarten Zoo."

"Which did you prefer?" he asked, without looking up.

She threw a dishtowel at him.

"Martin," she screamed. "I'm bored and miserable!"

Martin slipped a bookmark between the pages and closed his book. He stood, stretched and approached Vivi, taking her into his arms so that her cheek pressed against his chest. "I know, darling, I know. Tomorrow night I'll take you out dancing, or to a film. Would you like to see a film?"

She listened to his voice as it reached her both from his mouth and from the deep rumble in his chest. She put her arms around his middle. "I miss you," she said softly.

Despite the tremendous size of the city, even just her half, Vivi had exhausted the museums and parks of West Berlin in a matter of weeks. The weather turned cold; her lips chapped and her skin grew dry. Her concentric circles shrank and she stayed closer to home, but still she spent hours outside the house every day.

Vivi found herself drawn eastward, toward the wall and the city that lay beyond. Through November and December her outings always started off the same way, with a ride on the 129 bus to Potsdamerstrasse or Friedrichstrasse, both close to the wall. Some days she would walk the wall north, to where the Reichstag sat on the river, other days south and eastward through Kreuzberg, where once again she met the River Spree. Always, she kept to the wall for as long as she could before a biting wind or a freezing snowfall pushed her home. Often she would choose a spot and simply stare up at the wall, learning its structure, imagining scaling it, wondering if there were a Vivi standing just across from her on the other side contemplating all the same things. At night she was full of questions.

"When exactly was it built?" she would ask Martin, who was sprawled on the mattress reading a medical textbook.

"*Neunzehnhunderteinundsechzig.*" He could never come up with numbers quickly in any language but German and had long since abandoned Hebrew for English as their mode of communication.

Vivi paused to calculate. "*Sheeshim v'echad.* That's 1961. So what was happening until then? I mean, from the end of the war, did people just move back and forth or what?"

"Aaarrghhh," said Martin, slamming shut his textbook. Vivi was certain she had derailed him and he would be angry. "I hate studying all these diseases, I learn the symptoms and start to imagine I have them." He stood up from the bed and yawned, then turned his attention to Vivi. "What were you asking me?"

"About the wall. About Berlin before the wall."

"Ja, there were checkpoints and you needed an *Interzonenpass* to get around. It was far easier for Westerners to pass to the East than vice versa. The East Berliners wanted the exotic fruits we had in the markets, the women wanted seamless stockings. That's why the Soviets built the wall."

Vivi thought about the KaDeWe department store, how close and tantalizing it must have seemed to the Germans east of the wall, and yet how impossibly distant. Like a high window to a blue sky in a prison cell.

"The signs," she said to Martin. "There are so many different signs and I'm always trying to understand them: '*Verursacht durch die Schandsperre,*'" she quoted.

"'This now dead-end street,'" he translated, "'is the result of the barrier of shame.'"

"Ah," she said. "And, '*Sektoren-Grenze in Gawässer Mitte,*' what does that one mean?"

Martin smiled. "That the border is in the middle of the lake or canal or river."

"Oh yes," she says, "I've seen buoys floating in the water marked GDR or FRG. It's absurd!"

"It's absurd, yes, but it's the only logical solution for now."

She had heard him debate this at length at Zweiblfisch many times and had no desire to hear his arguments again. She had more questions, she was bubbling over with questions about the wall, but Martin had crossed the room and was pulling her to him. He wrapped her inside himself, hugged her with heavy arms.

One morning well into January, as she stood gazing upward at a corner in the wall where Kommandantenstrasse met Springerstrasse, a tiny man appeared at her elbow from nowhere. "*Fünfundvierzig tausend*," he said.

Vivi was too startled and too curious to be afraid. She knew he had said a number but she could not figure which one, nor what it had to do with anything.

"Forty-five thousand," he repeated in English. "The wall is made up of forty-five thousand of these segments, each one 3.6 meters tall and 1.2 meters wide. They've been rebuilt and refurbished four times, most recently in 1975. It seems they'll be here for a very long time."

"What are they made of?" she asked, immediately at ease with this dwarf. In fact he looked quite powerful, in spite of his size, but she felt she could trust him.

"They're concrete slabs between steel girders and concrete posts, with concrete sewage pipes on the top," he said in precise, rehearsed English. "The new segments put up in the last few years are supposed to be more resistant than ever to breakthroughs."

She sized him up, trying to guess his age. "Can you tell me what it was like before they built the wall?" she asked.

"Certainly," he said quickly, "for a hot chocolate with whipped cream in the café over there."

Vivi did not glance over her shoulder to where he was pointing. "Lead the way," she said, "it's a deal."

Peter, he was called, or Hans-Peter if you insisted. He had been raised in Leipzig but had come to Berlin in the summer of 1961, when rumors of plans to seal off the West from the East were rife. He had tried to convince his aging mother to come with him but she insisted he go alone, and so he crossed quite undramatically into West Berlin and never saw her again. He told Vivi he had been twenty years old when he had crossed over, so she figured he was in his mid-forties by now.

"Lucky for me I wasn't born any earlier than I was," he said, a whipped cream mustache foaming on his upper lip, "or the Nazis would have experimented on me for sure." He looked down into his cup and Vivi thought he might start to cry. There was a teaspoon next to his mug but Peter preferred stirring his cocoa with his finger and sucking off the cream and the chocolate. Vivi found him highly amusing, and safe, like a grown-up child.

"What is it like in the East?" she asked, taking a sip of her own hot chocolate.

"Well I don't know anymore firsthand, of course, but I have a pretty good idea. Lots of parades and marches, power shortages, speeches. No good television—I love television!—no pineapples, no fancy clothes or sports cars. Lots of rationing." He shrugged his shoulders, as if to inform her he had said all there was to say about

East Germany. She waited for more but Peter was busy with the bun she had ordered.

With a mouthful of bread Peter said, "You walk a lot around here, along the wall, I've seen you. This area is my territory. Every once in a while someone manages to escape from the East into West Berlin and I am always hoping he'll drop down the wall right in my sector. I've had a few, two actually, a chap from Berlin and another from a tiny village near Leipzig. He spoke the same dialect as me, even knew my mother's little newsstand. He's married now, living in Spandau." Peter drained his mug and licked the chocolatey rim. "I can show you around the neighborhood if you like."

Vivi paid and the two were out in the street. The sun had come out and suddenly the ice and snow shone brightly in the light, blinding her. Peter seemed unaffected.

That day he showed her one small street in his territory, one small street that she might have happened past a dozen times and never noticed, for it was unremarkable in every way: a short and narrow lane of insignificant buildings that dead-ended at the wall. But Peter brought the street alive for the entirety of its seven-hundred-year existence. He told of princes who had slept or dueled there, merchants who had prospered and failed, a patrician family who had used their roof garden for several suicide jumps stretched over three generations. He told of East Germans who had plunged from the wall to the street, a single bullet through the neck. And he told of Jews, Jews tortured or beaten or chased.

Vivi was riveted. She stayed with Peter in the street until she could no longer feel her fingers or toes. She met him the next day, and the next. She learned his likes and dislikes, and took pains to pack lunches he might enjoy, since she could not afford to invite him for hot chocolate and buns every day of the week.

Peter showed her the real Berlin and its ghost. He pointed out where the jazz clubs had flourished, where prostitutes and pimps had gathered. Together they stood at the site of Europe's first traffic light, in Potsdamer Platz, or they trekked paths that pursued and frightened Berliners had used to stay clear of the marauding Soviets at the end of the war. Peter taught Vivi to see Berlin in layers, like a woman with countless rustling petticoats, each concealing secrets large and small. He was clearly both in love with and appalled by his adopted city.

This was the parallel Berlin she had sensed was still there, in the shadow of modern, cosmopolitan Berlin, the one she had felt haunted by from her first days in the city. The Berlin that coughed up Jews for the slaughter, the Berlin that harbored train stations to ship the unwanted to concentration camps, the Berlin that had been sectored off differently from the way it was now, between Jews and Aryans. But this parallel Berlin was visible only to those who searched her out with diligence.

Vivi stayed out longer and longer hours with Peter, often returning after dark, when Martin was already at home. "The dwarf again?" he asked when she blew in with the cold air late, later than he, for the third time that week. She was surprised to find him reading a newspaper instead of a textbook or medical journal. Something was bubbling on the stove.

"Peter, yes," she said, removing her coat and hat and gloves and scarf, scattering them as she moved quickly around the room. "Today we went out to the prison at Spandau, where they're keeping Rudolf Hess. Peter told me the whole inside story. Fascinating."

"I'm so glad you've found both an occupation for yourself and a friend to share your days with," he said with a sarcastic lilt, his voice growing louder as he spoke. "Why not bring this Peter home

for a meal sometime?" He glanced over his newspaper to catch her reaction.

"I'd love to, but he won't come," she said, shrugging her shoulders. She had suggested dinner at their place on several occasions to Peter, but he changed the subject each time.

Vivi lifted the lid of the pot on the stove. Chili, the only dish Martin could make with constant success. "Martin, did you know that Hess is the only prisoner left in Spandau, in that whole huge complex?"

"Frankly no and I don't care. Why are you so obsessed with all our ugliest characters, and that damned hideous wall? If I'd studied in Hamburg or Heidelberg, you could have become obsessed with window boxes or wooden chalets, but here it's always Berlin at her worst, doom and gloom." Vivi, leaning on the stove, could feel the chili steaming her back, a warm current rising up her spine to the nape of her neck. Martin rose and came close but did not touch her. He was waiting for an answer but she did not know what the question was.

On a Friday morning in February Vivi and Peter met in a pleasant square not far from the southwest corner of the wall. The sky was a dark and threatening gray, but the weather was a bit warmer than usual and there was no hint of a flurry or even a drop of rain. Vivi was wearing a new cloth coat she had bought with her dwindling savings, bright red and heavy and marvelously warm. She wore a small black knitted cap, her ears tucked inside. Peter wore his usual tiny blue parka.

"This is Rosengartenplatz," he told her. "I've been saving it until you were ready."

"Ready for what?" she asked.

"Ready to handle it." She did not ask what he meant and he stared up into her face for a long moment before continuing.

"A long time ago, probably two hundred and fifty years or so, a Jewish family lived on the top floor of that building." He was pointing to a narrow, well-preserved structure five stories high with a steep, tiled roof. "Burchardt was the name, he'd made his fortune in shipping on the Baltic and came to Berlin to set up a bank. He had a beautiful daughter, Mathilde, who studied piano and voice in that building over there, right across the piazza, with a German called Franz Huber. He raped her, that Franz Huber the music teacher, and she never set foot in his building again. She lay at home, despondent, and the family did not know what to do for her. There was no going to the authorities, this was still pre-Enlightenment Germany. Then, some months later, she was discovered to be with child. The despondency of this beautiful, talented young woman grew worse by the day so that a short while after giving birth, in fact in the first moment she was alone, she dragged herself to the window and threw herself into the street. And her father, agonizing over his daughter's death and unable to tolerate this unwanted child, took the newborn baby and threw it over the wall of a small church that stood over there"—he pointed to an ugly postwar apartment building—"but which burned down some years later.

"A woman passing by spotted him and set up a cry, 'Baby killers, the Jews are baby killers, they killed our Lord Jesus and now they need more blood!' You know, all the usual. And in minutes an angry mob had gathered, and someone brought the dead baby from the church garden and then all mayhem broke out. The rest of the Burchardt family was dragged into the street and stoned and clubbed by the mob, until all of them—Burchardt and his wife, the wife's sister,

and their other two children—all lay dead. Then people simmered down and went home to their families, to a hot meal and a warm bed." Peter was shaking his head. Vivi was numb, her breathing shallow; she felt herself to be on the edge of life, floating precariously.

"But that's not all. During World War Two a Jewish family by the name of Simon lived in the same apartment. The father was a doctor, he had a clinic on the ground floor and he was known as a compassionate and generous man. He took impressive sums from his richer clients and used them to cover free treatment for the poor of the neighborhood, who knew they could always pay him a visit if they really needed to.

"Dr. Simon didn't read the signs, or maybe it was his wife and mother-in-law who were certain no harm would come to them and preferred to ride out the Nazi storm. In any case, they stayed, through 1939 and 1940. They stayed through 1941, when they were made to wear the Star of David, and through 1942, when their home was marked as belonging to Jews. Then in June 1943, just before the very last Jews were deported from Berlin, Dr. Simon tried to arrange hiding places for his family with former patients of his. He approached this one and that, rich and poor, and not a one would help him. Maybe they were terrible people, maybe they were just frightened of the consequences, I can't tell you. But at night on the ninth of June, as Dr. Simon and his mother and mother-in-law sat down to dinner, the Gestapo pounded on the door. They ordered the doctor and his wife downstairs, into the street. When they were standing directly in front of their building a signal was given and the old mother-in-law was tossed headfirst from the window, landing precisely on her son-in-law and killing him. A Nazi shot Mrs. Simon in the neck just as she began to scream. The three bodies were carted away the next morning."

The day ended quickly for Vivi. She staggered homeward as though she had been delivered a hard blow. The pavement seemed to hang on a tilt and she could not regain her bearings. Each footfall was treacherous, as if she were stepping on writhing body parts or pools of blood. She walked the wrong way and wound up in an unfamiliar neighborhood. A woman hanging laundry on the upper floor of a five-story walk-up seemed to be calling her. Vivi listened more closely.

Swine. Murderer. Anti-Christ. Was she hearing her correctly? *Vermin. Blackmailer. Jew.* Was she really raining down these words on her, pelting Vivi with verbal rocks? She began to run, turning away from the laundry woman at the first corner, and knocked down an elderly man with glasses. She stopped to help him up, apologizing and gathering his groceries. The old man said nothing while Vivi blabbed as best she could in German. *Jew?* she thought she heard him ask quietly. Vivi ran until the streets looked familiar. Here was the greengrocer, and there the man who sold her newspapers. She began to run again, afraid she might hear words she could not bear to hear from them. She burst into a shop just around the corner from home, bought some supplies and headed home.

Two hours later, when Martin came home from the university, he found his apartment transformed. The lights were dimmed and two tall candles glimmered at the center of the makeshift table. The table was set for two, as elegantly as Vivi had been able to muster, and several pots and pans sat simmering on the stove. Vivi stood stooped in a corner of the room, her back to Martin. She was swaying and mumbling.

Martin said nothing, but crept up behind her. In her hands he could see a prayer book. He stood to her side and for several minutes watched her pray the Sabbath prayers, her eyes closed to him and all

the world. The words were a constant hum, indecipherable one from the other, but melodious. Finally Martin turned and went to wash up, splashing warm water on his face and neck.

At dinner he tried to be sympathetic, ask about her day, thank her for the lovely Sabbath meal. She was dispassionate. She looked at him like a stranger who had wandered in uninvited from the street, though they both knew the reality was that she, in fact, was the guest. After dinner she picked a fight.

"Am I here because of your guilt?" she asked him, two plates balanced midair.

"What guilt is that?" he asked, guilelessly.

"Germans and Jews, Germans and Jews, centuries of Germans and Jews." She was mumbling, but Martin could hear every word.

"I thought perhaps you meant last Passover. Jail."

Vivi stopped mumbling. "That'll do, too. Are you guilty? Do you feel bad that I am dead to my family, that I ran away from them for you? That my commanding officer thought I'd betrayed my country for you?" Martin backed away as though he feared she might hurl the plates if she got any more worked up. Were those flames dancing in Vivi's eyes, or merely a reflection of the candles?

"I thought we had something special, Vivi," he said, weighing his words carefully, "something that transcended our peoples and our histories. But this city's done something to you. The memories, the history, they're too much for you."

She cocked her head and stared into his eyes until he looked away.

Quietly she put the dishes in the sink and slipped into her red coat. Martin did not say a word. She left the warm flat and wandered the streets for hours singing Sabbath songs to herself, mumbling prayers, reciting psalms. She walked in circles and reached the wall several times without intending to. She passed a busy beer garden

where dozens of red-faced men sat noisily drinking. They called to her, they dared reach their hairy paws toward her, she who was deep inside the Sabbath behind a shimmering veil. They did not know she was untouchable, protected. *Liebchen*, they called. *Baby*, they crooned. She sang her Sabbath melodies louder, warmed herself in their fire.

It was nearly three o'clock in the morning when she returned to the flat. Martin was sleeping soundly when she lay down next to him on the mattress, next to him but apart. She thought about his hands, his shoulders, his uncircumcised penis and turned her back to him.

At precisely seven o'clock, before the sun had risen, a blackbird landed on the windowsill and Vivi snapped awake with the cold and certain knowledge that a baby was growing inside her.

That day she had no desire to walk. Her head was clear, her legs were tired, and she was afraid of the cold. But she did not wish to stay at home with Martin.

He would be on duty at the hospital that afternoon and the next, he told her, but offered to make them a big brunch in the morning. They ate eggs and toast and potatoes and read the newspaper. Martin did not ask when Vivi had returned. He was relieved to find her subdued but sane.

By Sunday, Vivi had her answers, knew her plan. Later that morning, when Martin had settled in for some studying before leaving for the hospital, Vivi left home and walked three blocks to a large cinema. She spent the afternoon and most of the evening watching one film after the next: martial arts and Westerns and science fiction and adventure movies, until her eyes glazed and her head pounded. When she was thoroughly exhausted she took herself home, walking in a roundabout way just to clear her head. She lay silently in bed

feigning sleep by the time Martin straggled in smelling of beer and cigarettes.

On Monday morning Vivi was waiting at the Lufthansa office when it opened. She bought a one-way ticket to Tel Aviv for Friday before dawn. Next she found Peter. "I need your help," she told him. Together they boarded a train and headed for a clinic in Zehlendorf. She lied when asked about having been tested. By afternoon her relief was so great that she would have floated all the way home had she not been weak and in pain. Peter helped her home, got her settled in bed and departed silently before Martin returned.

Vivi convalesced quickly, her mind running ahead to the packing—which would be little more than cramming all her belongings into any suitcase available—and to when and how she would tell Martin she was leaving. But no moment presented itself that week and so, with a taxi waiting downstairs, Vivi awakened Martin very late on Thursday, in the small hours that had in fact pushed the day to Friday, and, buttoned into her red coat, suitcase in hand, she said a hasty good-bye. Martin did not even stand from the bed as she left the flat, but she did see him step out shirtless into the cold night air on the verandah as the driver hurried her away.

It was an hour and a half before Sabbath by the time she passed through Israeli customs. Vivi reckoned the taxi would put her at her parents' doorstep just as her mother was lighting the Sabbath candles. It would take her mother and father more than a few days to forgive her, but she had no doubt they would be enormously, deeply relieved to have her home.

In Copenhagen Teodor settled in quickly, studying at the school of the Royal Danish Ballet and living with the Sonnenfelds, a family of Danish Jews whose prize possession, which hung at the entrance to their apartment, was a letter dated 1672 signed by King Christian V inviting a hallowed ancestor of theirs to settle and engage in trade in the Danish capital. Teodor shared a room with Peter, a year older than he, and six-year-old Bent, but he preferred the company of Peter's twin sister, Sofie. Their house at Danas Plads in Frederiksberg, a half-hour walk from the ballet school, was a cozy mess, a noisy, happy riot most hours of the day. It took Teodor no longer than a week, probably less, to feel absolutely comfortable and welcome, even without a common language. The children taught him Danish, played games with him, helped him with homework. He did chores and occasionally ran errands for Mrs. Sonnenfeld, but mostly he spent long days into the evening at the school. Still, he always managed to join the family on Friday nights, first in the synagogue and then around the table for a festive meal. The Sonnenfelds were more observant of Jewish customs than his own family, and he enjoyed their sense of fun and excitement about being Jewish.

In those days the school of the Royal Danish Ballet preferred to pay little attention to the scholastic successes and failures of its pu-

pils; if they could dance they could stay, if they stayed they would graduate to the level of *Aspiranter*, then to the corps de ballet, and once in the corps would probably stay for life. The ballet, and therefore the school, needed dancers, not intellectuals. Teodor studied Danish with a private tutor while his peers learned a bit of history and literature, math and science.

But since the major part of the day was spent in the dance studio, Teodor was just one among many. They had a pas de deux class, repertoire class and character class, but most of their time was spent in the Bournonville Daily Class. He had been warned his style would be different, he would have to learn and adapt to the Danish style, but he was surprised at how limited, how clipped it made him feel. Where Madame Valentina had taught him the long flow of lines, the expressive arm work, the powerful leaping jumps, here in Copenhagen his teachers hounded him on minutiae. "Once again, Mr. Levin, sixteen bars. Keep the arms down at your sides, it's the toes we need to notice." "Mr. Levin, spin with your head straight, as if it were merely the star on a Christmas tree." "Try, if you possibly can, Mr. Levin, to dance that without looking like a Russian soldier in battle."

Those first months at school were trying, especially on days when the entire school rehearsed according to the Bournonville system developed more than a century earlier. They had been learning it from the age of seven and knew every plié and sissonne battue and grande pirouette in its proper sequence, could start in the middle of Tuesday's lesson or at the end of Thursday's lesson without giving it a thought. It took Teodor long weeks and months to catch on. He followed along lesson after lesson, dazed and frustrated, until finally in January, after the brief Christmas holidays, he made it through a Monday lesson without a single fault. The dance mistress took note, and gave him a nod and a wink after the final tour en l'air.

After that, Teodor seemed to catch on to everything. Bournon-ville, pantomime lessons, making friends, the Danish language. He danced with joy and sparkle, he pushed himself, he enjoyed. The younger students looked up to him, the older ones included him in their activities, the staff felt he was making tremendous progress.

He stayed on in Denmark through the summer, unwilling to return to Poland. Rosa and Margot came to Copenhagen for a two-week holiday in August, but Teodor was often short-tempered and impatient with his mother and sister and the trip was difficult for them all. More than anything Teodor was anxious for school to resume. At the end of this school year, which would be his last, he would have the opportunity to audition for a position in the company, and he was terribly eager to stay.

In May of his second year in Copenhagen it was announced that the entire ballet company had been invited to perform a ballet from the Bournonville repertoire, *The Konservatoriet, or A Proposal of Marriage Through the Newspaper*, at a gala evening at the Berlin Staatsoper on the first night of September 1939. Students in the ballet school could audition for one of four roles, those of two boys and two girls enrolled in the ballet school of the Paris Conservatory and shown participating in a lesson. Teodor won a role by emulating flawlessly the Bournon-ville style with high, straight leaps and fluttering toes. A boy named Niels was selected for the other boy's role.

Considerable debate ensued in the press about sending the Danish troupe to Berlin. Hitler's Anschluss with Austria and the annexation of the Sudeten and then the whole of Czechoslovakia were noted with worry in Denmark, Germany's close northern neighbor, and the Danish public was repulsed by the racial laws enacted there years

earlier. But the Danish ballet master, in radio and newspaper interviews, stressed the apolitical, bridge-building nature of art, especially in the atmosphere of growing European belligerence, as well as the importance of bringing a thoroughly Danish ballet to the German capital, and so the public was appeased and rehearsals continued.

The dancers, for the most part, were absorbed in the perfect, stylized beauty of their ballet and paid little attention to the mounting tension around them. Teodor in particular was too excited about having landed his first role to consider the implications. But the Sonnenfeld parents would not let it go by so easily.

At dinner one evening Henrik Sonnenfeld said, "Teodor, Dina and I have been discussing this and we don't think you should travel with the troupe to Berlin."

Teodor stopped chewing and placed his fork on the plate.

"We are responsible for you, Teodor, and entering the Reich could be dangerous."

"I'll be traveling with the Danish ballet, I'll be perfectly safe," he said, as evenly as he could muster.

Now Henrik returned his fork to his plate.

"Teodor, German Jews have been leaving their homeland in a steady flow for years, especially now. You've seen how many have come to Denmark, the synagogue hasn't been this full for years. It's simply not safe for you. We've written to your parents on this matter and will act according to their wishes."

Teodor pouted but at the same time started to form a plan of action. Indeed his parents wrote back immediately with a plea for him to remain in Copenhagen, but before their letter arrived Teodor spoke with the ballet master. He was willing to assume full responsibility for Teodor's safety. Teodor, with the ballet master's backing, fought the Sonnenfelds and his parents for many weeks and contin-

ued attending rehearsals until it was simply too late for him to withdraw. He was immensely pleased at the fait accompli he had staged, relieved that he would, in fact, be performing with the company.

The Konservatoriet, an 1849 vaudeville-ballet in two acts, was a nostalgic look at Bournonville's own student days in Paris. The costumes and sets paid homage to Degas, the style graciously elegant with a touch of silly humor. Teodor loved the short white jacket and floppy black neck bow that were his costume, and was thankful he would be dancing in plain tights allowing freedom of movement. Much of his time on stage was spent loafing tastefully near the tall curtained windows or lifting one of the girls for low leaps. He also had a short mirror dance with Niels, in which they did some typically strong, low Bournonville leaps, and a pas de deux with a girl his age. And then there was his solo.

Barely three minutes long, it meant everything to Teodor and he worked on it incessantly. He understood the role as an audition of sorts, a young Parisian boy hoping desperately to impress the ballet master enough to give him a chance to join the corps de ballet, and the lesson for himself and his own career was not lost on him. The choreography, flashy for Bournonville, was still controlled and stylized. Dancing it was a matter of technical expertise, not emotion, so Teodor spent his time refining his tendu, sharpening the point of his toes, pulling his tailbone under his pelvis. He watched the mirror for perfectly curved fingers, the angle of the head, chest up but not thrust forward. Even his face he shaped into a look of courtly disdain.

In spite of all he had heard about Germany, Teodor could not help but feel excited as the Danish bus roared off the ferry onto the soil of a country he had never visited, his second, third if you counted a

short field trip across the Oresund to Malmö to catch a performance of the Royal Swedish Ballet. The dancers were abuzz as they passed through pastures and forests and into Berlin by nightfall.

The Adlon Hotel was a short walk to the Staatsoper and the troupe was too impatient to wait for a tour in the morning. En masse they flowed to the theater. Technicians working late to prepare the stage with sets shipped earlier were hard at work, clearly pleased to host the young and attractive Danish troupe. Several husky workers stopped their hammering to engage the ballerinas in conversation.

Tuesday, Wednesday and Thursday the troupe was engaged in final rehearsals from morning to night. Thanks to heavy promotion by the Nazi party the dancers learned that the performance had been sold out for at least a month. They worked harder than ever to smooth out every flaw, even the tiniest. The ballet master was unusually testy and the flight of weeping ballerinas in a rush to a quiet corner or the dressing room became more and more common with each passing day.

On Friday morning the troupe stretched, did a straight run-through with the full orchestra and conductor, and retired to the hotel for a light meal and some sleep. In Teodor's room, which he shared with Niels and with Lars, a member of the corps, there was too much excitement for slumber.

The troupe met in the hotel lobby at six and walked the three long blocks to the theater down the Unter den Linden. On the way Teodor spotted a small sign nailed to a tree that he had not noticed before, even though they had walked this way several times already. He thought he understood its meaning, but for confirmation he asked his dance partner—who read German well, thanks to her Austrian mother—to translate it. "The Unter den Linden," she intoned, "is forbidden to Jews." They stared at the sign while the troupe flowed

past them. Finally she grabbed his arm and pulled him toward the theater. "Forget it," she said, "the Germans are idiots." She kept her arm linked with his as they walked on. "Don't think about it. You've got a debut to worry about now." He was grateful for her arm and her smile, but was disturbed nonetheless.

At the Staatsoper the troupe limbered, applied makeup, dressed, peered through the curtains at the gathering audience. Every chandelier was lit. Teodor was quieter than the other dancers, pensive. He was thinking his dance through, his feet and hands twitching with movement, though sometimes he turned a pirouette much as a person alone might be talking to himself when suddenly, to his own surprise, he will say something out loud.

At five minutes to eight the dancers took their places. The audience was in place and precisely at eight the lights dimmed and the crowd fell silent.

A tall blond man in uniform pushed past Teodor, parted the curtain and disappeared into the lights. The dancers could hear his voice, slightly muffled, as he addressed the audience. "*Damen und Herrn*, good evening. As vice-minister of culture for the Third Reich I am pleased to welcome you tonight to an historic performance by our northern neighbors, whose long tradition of superb ballet is a source of pride not only to their own nation but to the Aryan races of every nation." Most of the troupe could understand the speech and several of the dancers smiled at one another at the minister's praise. Teodor's German was quite good enough to take offense.

"I am also here tonight in place of our beloved Führer, who planned to enjoy this performance but who was called away on urgent state business. He has asked me to inform you, his dearest and most beloved subjects, that today the Army of the Third Reich staged a major retaliation against our belligerent neighbor to the east, Po-

land, which was carried out to great success and with lightning speed and agility. We can expect our troops to reach Warsaw by the end of the week."

A burst of spontaneous applause exploded through the heavy curtain to the dancers. Now no one looked pleased, and several glanced toward Teodor. Teodor himself stood stunned, his mouth open and his head tilted slightly backward, his eyes focused on the top of the curtain where it met rows and rows of colored lights. But before he could think to react, the minister of culture was taking his leave.

"Let us now celebrate this momentous day with a lovely performance by our Danish friends. Please welcome the Royal Danish Ballet, in *The Konservatoriet!*"

The curtain rose and Teodor gathered himself quickly into position. He could see the ballet master in the wings, a wistful grin of sympathy on his lips. He put his hands together as if in prayer, but Teodor did not know whether the ballet master was wishing him a successful dance or safety for his family.

At first it was hard for Teodor to focus on the ballet and indeed the entire troupe took a few minutes to recover from the news. But the orchestra was outstanding, and the audience, exuding excitement, was supportive and uncritical, so the troupe warmed quickly and left the world behind.

Teodor jumped into position, moved away from the wall to lift a girl, then glided back to his spot. He sailed through his pas de deux with Niels in perfect synchronization, the best they had ever danced it. They smiled exuberantly at one another at its conclusion.

His partner was dancing her short solo now, and Teodor prepared to step into the spotlight once again, first to partner her and then for his own solo. He thought briefly of tanks and troops roaring over

bridges on the Vistula River and then pushed these visions from his head. He stepped forward.

She was slightly slippery in his hands, but he was accustomed to the nuances of her body and held her tightly. Arabesque, arabesque, glissade, glissade, she floated gracefully in his arms until, spent, she twirled away from him and out of his vision. Teodor was alone at center stage.

Behind him, without looking over his shoulder, he knew the corps de ballet stood posed in small, asymmetric groupings. Close ahead and below were the musicians, just completing the cadenzas that ushered him to this place at the center of the stage. And all around him and ahead, and above him as well, were two thousand faces, white, groomed and plumed, plucked and shaved and oiled. Men in uniform, women in feathers and fur, all sparkling with pleasure and confidence, their faces hungry with anticipation like baby birds.

For a small moment Teodor considered these faces, all assembled here to watch him spin and leap through three minutes of trifling Danish music. But as he planted his feet, as he pulled his torso high above his legs, as he rotated his head slowly, slowly to the left and floated his arms gently into place, the dancers and the musicians and the audience disappeared. Teodor was alone with his body, poised. He could hear the sound of his breathing, slow and deliberate, could feel the pulse of blood coursing to his toes and fingers.

The orchestra sounded the last chord to his introduction, the grand pause that would end only when Teodor broke the spell of silence. The conductor turned his attention to Teodor on stage. The hall fell completely silent in watchful anticipation, but Teodor was in no hurry.

Here it was, this moment. A moment of infinite space, as if he had squeezed his way through a tight, dark tunnel and found him-

self at this spot, unfurled. This moment of infinite possibility, too, of ways to travel, or not. He could stop right now, crawl back into his safe tunnel. He could freeze, fail to move, crumple. He could rotate his head straight forward, toward the musicians and the audience, and scream insults at them in Polish. Worst of all, he could dance badly.

The audience, the musicians, the dancers. They were waiting for him to move. He knew this moment had gone on too long. He must give the signal to the conductor, and he wished to, he was looking forward to his dance. But he was enjoying this moment of all possibilities too much. He had sensed what he would know to be true only many years hence: that this bubble of freedom and floating would be his last, that he would tumble headlong to one destiny, setting his future, one certain future, in motion. He knew that the moment he moved his foot something would have changed and there would be no return.

At the end of this moment, his moment and no one else's, as his right leg steeled itself to support his weight, as his head craned upward from his neck in a tiny, imperceptible gesture, as his toes strained the cloth of his slippers, as the audience and the musicians and the dancers breathed as one with him, Teodor understood, with great clarity, as if remembering, that he would dance without a flaw, knew this would be the most perfect dance of his life, in fact, its pinnacle. That at seventeen and a half, his body would spin, stretch and soar, that there was nothing he could not do. He was aware, too, of Madame Valentina and Sofie egging him on, daring him to dance unfettered. Now he was ready, and with a touch of melancholy mixed with the unbridled excitement of youth, he sent a wordless farewell to his moment, pointed the toes of his left foot as taut as a freshly sharpened pencil, and sailed into the music.

"To my great surprise," Vivi says with a smile as she places his usual repast in front of him, "you're not as different from other men as I'd originally thought."

Teo purses his lips and squints up at her. "I wouldn't even know where to begin to respond to that," he says. His right hand has been shaking terribly all morning. He will wait until she is no longer at his side before attempting to raise his coffee cup.

"Want to hear?" she asks.

"I'm sure I have no choice."

"That's right. You don't. So here goes," she says, and she takes an audible breath. "For the past week I've been doing everything I can to get you to invite me to see your ballet at the gala and you have thick-headedly failed to notice all my attempts. I've asked you who you're taking, I've hinted that I'm free on Saturday night, I've mentioned on three separate occasions how much I enjoyed watching the rehearsal and how I'd love to see the entire ballet performed. Nothing! Frankly, I would be happy to buy a ticket but of course the event's by invitation only so I can't. And now I've been reduced to begging you."

His gaze is sharp and mirthless when he responds. "And you, my dear, are proving yourself less different from other women than I'd originally thought."

She gestures for him to continue.

"First, that you tried all manner of wily approaches instead of confronting me man-to-man as it were. But mostly, because you believe that I failed to notice your attempts, instead of giving me credit for being an artful dodger."

"Oh," she says, "I had no idea—"

"Now don't get all offended on me, it has nothing to do with you. I would love nothing better than to spend an evening with you. But since I myself will not be attending the gala I cannot ask you to join me."

"Not attending the gala? What are you talking about?"

He rubs his temples. "It's complicated," he says.

"Everything's complicated," she says. "Just tell me why you can't make it to a gala that's staging what you consider to be your very best work. What could possibly be more important than that?"

"Look, Vivi—"

"Don't you dare tell me it's not my business. I won't take that for an answer."

He closes his eyes. "It's one thing for me to see the ballet in bits and pieces in rehearsal when I'm focusing on every finger and toe, every angle of every head, that sort of thing. It becomes just another dance. But watching *Obsession* on the stage, hearing the music . . . I just can't. It's too difficult . . ."

"I still don't understand. What's difficult? Because it was your best? Because the dancers don't do it exactly as you wish? Because you once danced it and now you can't anymore?"

"No. No. None of that." He does not meet her gaze. "It's too . . . personal. Painful, even though I hate to use that word. Watching this ballet makes me exceedingly uncomfortable. I've avoided it for a quarter century now."

"You certainly are a mystery sometimes. Your best work and you can't watch it. Don't you think it's time to change that?"

"Why should I?"

"For the same reason you've been trying to get me to be serious about my art: a person has to be able to look into himself and examine everything, learn from it, use it."

"I've already done that. *Obsession* is that precisely, a look into my own personal abyss."

"So if you did that in order to create that work then why should it be so hard to revisit?"

"I suppose it was a kind of purging, a once-in-a-lifetime act meant to solve something. Something internal."

"Well, excuse me for saying so, but if you can't watch this ballet being performed then it seems to me you haven't solved anything at all."

He smiles wryly.

She says, "Come on, you know I've won this argument. Just say yes and I'll dress up nicely and you and I will sit next to one another in the theater and I won't ask you all sorts of questions if you don't want me to. But you've got to attend. And if you're attending, it may as well be with me."

"Where did you learn to argue like that?"

"I've told you: my mother."

"There's a reception beforehand that I should attend. If you will agree to be my date for that and if you will agree to escape the theater the very moment the ballet ends, then I'll go. I don't want to talk to a soul about it afterward."

"Agreed."

"And you must be willing to come out for dinner following the ballet. Just the two of us. And I may be sad and speechless."

"So I'll be happy and talkative. And hungry."

"I hope I won't regret this."

"There's nothing to regret. Didn't you once tell me we regret what we haven't done, not what we've done and failed at?"

"Touché, my dear. You're a quick study."

"I'll be ready at seven." She leans over and kisses his forehead before she walks away.

The first time Vivi came to this building she expected it to have some special aura, but even the apartment itself gave nothing away: no beaded curtains, no incense, no Eastern music. The front door was decorated with children's drawings and the doorbell chimed a tune Vivi thought might be a Christmas carol.

By now, perhaps her sixth time, she knows it is not the building or the apartment that is special but Daniella Klein-Paz, the occupant, herself. Her insights into Vivi's past, her psyche, even—frighteningly—her future, are uncanny and inspired. Whether she reads the coffee grounds, scrutinizes the palm of her hand or studies tarot cards, she is always accurate. After the first several meetings Vivi overcame her shock and was more attentive and better able to make use of these sessions in her daily life.

Daniella ushers Vivi into the little room just to the left of the apartment door, brings a pot of tea and a plate with homemade biscuits, and sits down so that the two women are facing one another. She has a pad in front of her with handwritten notes.

"Is this usual?" Vivi asks. "I mean, getting a reading for someone else?"

"Oh sure, people do it all the time."

"Because it almost seems . . . unethical. Like I'm going to know things I shouldn't. Private things."

"That's precisely why people do it. There are things they often need to know but have no way of discovering." Daniella pours them each a cup of tea from the pot.

"So, what did you find out about him?" Vivi asks as she takes a sip of her tea.

"Well, first of all you were of course right that all the twos in his birthday are quite significant. I can tell you that this man has had a difficult life filled with enormous changes. He may have had a twin sister who died at birth. He is very brave and very opinionated. He comes from a closed family and he himself is very closed to others, even though he is loving, gentle and extremely sensitive. He was very close to his mother, and family life was absolutely holy to him. In fact, I would say his biggest regret is the fact that he never built a family environment as he wishes he could have. He feels terribly unfulfilled, and that would be the greatest source of his frustration."

"Fascinating," Vivi says, already engaged.

"He is a man understood by very few people. He is brilliant, highly original and afraid to find his true self. He comes from a good family, well educated but not wealthy. Eastern Europe, I think, Russia or Poland."

"Yes, he was born in Warsaw."

"He is not assertive. He lost his mother too early in life. He trusts few people and is most fearful of manipulative, powerful men. On the surface he seems calm but inside he is very tense."

"I should be taking notes," Vivi says, fishing in her purse.

"I've prepared a copy for you, Vivi," Daniella says, "there's no need."

"Okay. Go on."

"As a child this man possessed an exceptional beauty that attracted quite a bit of attention. His eyes were particularly arresting."

"Yes, yes," Vivi says with fervor. "He's got one blue eye and one green one. It's a bit spooky but really lovely."

But Daniella is not looking for confirmation. She pushes ahead. "He also possessed an understanding of the world, highly unusual for a child. His mother, who may have been called Anna or Hanna, loved him very much."

"Okay. Anything else?"

"Your friend should have been born a woman, he has a strong feminine side, he learned to appreciate beauty from his mother, he works from emotion and not from logic. He is honest but secretive. He could have been a Buddhist master, but as a Jew he is undeveloped. He is not in good health."

"Anything about relationships?"

"His wife—something with an L, Lily perhaps—she is closest to him, but still distant. He should have one child, a son, born late in life."

"No," Vivi says, almost disappointed. "He's never married or had children."

"You might want to check that," Daniella says vaguely. "He is full of mystery, and layers. Contradictions. Things you feel absolutely certain about could prove to be dead wrong. Assume nothing about this man."

Vivi nods, contemplative. A question percolates. "And what," she asks, "is his role in my life?"

Daniella Klein-Paz looks squarely into Vivi's eyes for the first time. "What *is* his role in your life?"

They stare at one another until Vivi looks away.

Daniella says, "Let's get started on you, now, shall we?"

Vivi downs the last sip of her tea, places the cup in its saucer, and looks expectantly at Daniella across from her. But all the while she is thinking of Teo and his life of duality.

H e is standing at the window watching Nelly down in the garden pulling weeds that sprouted after a recent cloudburst. She spends hours there every day, planting flowers or harvesting the vegetables they dine on. He marvels at her patience. Of all the Hebrew she has learned in her twenty-odd years in Israel, he figures the overwhelming majority has to do with food and gardening.

A bird flutters at the window, hovers there as if asking to enter, and Teo raises his face to watch. His left arm rises, too, as he imitates the bird; his upper arm is all grace and elegance, a long fluid motion, while his hand down to the fingertips quivers in tiny, rapid jerks. Teo's eyes fall shut as his right arm rises, too, his back extends and his neck climbs higher and higher. He is floating now, beating his wings, lifting himself, strong and unimpeded, high above this building, this neighborhood, this city. He extends a hand to a partner just a short reach away and pulls her close, only to discover Vivi suddenly in his arms. They move in perfect silent unison until a large truck, bouncing noisily through the neighborhood, causes Teo's eyes to flutter open and his arms to drop to his sides.

When the telephone first rings he makes no move to answer it. He has never enjoyed speaking on the phone, does not own a mobile, and often simply refuses to pick up when it rings. But it is Saturday

morning, an odd time for a call, and he is mildly intrigued. When the caller speaks to him in Danish, he knows who it is at once.

"Sofie, darling," he says. "What a pleasure!" They speak only rarely anymore, but he is always happy to hear her raspy voice. It is only after they hang up that he feels a deep sadness, a malaise of missed opportunity and loss.

"Happy birthday!" she enthuses.

"Oh dear Sofie, *plus ça change . . .*"

"What? Have I missed again this year?"

"Only by a month or so."

"But isn't your birthday the twenty-second?"

"Yes. Of *February*. So I am still officially only eighty-four and would ask that you not rush me."

Sofie laughs her deep smoker's laugh until she coughs. He worries about making her laugh, which she loves to do, simply because it nearly always brings her to asphyxiation. "Did I have the date right last year?" she asks between spasms.

"Last year you forgot entirely, then wrote me a card in May or June. It is still on top of the piano."

"So I'd better send something really special for your eighty-fifth."

"Good health is all I really need."

"Yes, that makes two of us. I seem to be the only unhealthy Sonnenfeld, you know. My brothers are the picture of health, not a single thing wrong with either of them. This lung business makes me the black sheep."

"You always did have to be different."

"Hmmm. Teo, I don't know if you heard, but your old ballet partner, Kirsten, passed away last month."

"Kirsten? Oh, *Kirsten!*" He is at first grateful to recover the name, then sad to lose her so quickly. "Oh. Oh dear."

"Sorry, Teo."

"Lovely Kirsten." He can hear the allegretto music from their duet in *The Konservatoriet*. "Was she ill?"

"No, not at all. She was leading some master classes in Stockholm and didn't come down to breakfast one morning. They found her in her hotel bed, she simply never woke up. That's perfect, don't you think? She was still so elegant and good-looking. Anyway, I attended the funeral—I find funerals are wonderful for catching up with people you'd never see otherwise—and I met the young man who's now the artistic director at the ballet. Oh bother, I've forgotten his name again. Well, he knows that you and I keep in touch and he asked me to tell you that he'll be contacting you soon about permissions because the Royal Danish Ballet wants to perform several of your ballets in the coming seasons. Don't ask me which ones or when, I can barely remember my twin brother's name anymore. But I thought you'd like to know."

"Yes, thank you. I would love more than anything to see them danced well."

"So that means you'll come over here?"

He looks out the window. Nelly is lugging a large bundle of weeds to the garbage bin. "I doubt it," he sighs.

They both fall silent.

"Not likely I'd be here to greet you, anyway," she says, and they fall silent again. He thinks she may be weeping.

"Come, Sofie, let's not be morose. We've tried to live full and productive lives, haven't we? We've stuck around longer than most, too."

"I've done little more than having and raising two children who, I might brag, turned out to be rather wonderful. But you've done enough for ten people."

"Nonsense," he says, and then again, angrily: "Nonsense! I was meant to be a dancer but wound up on a small stage in a country that

despises ballet. I've taught several generations of middling dancers, choreographed a few decent ballets, even collected a prize or two. It all means nothing, though. Do you believe me, Sofie? Nothing. I should have married, had children."

"What? Teo, what are you talking about? You're one of the best choreographers of the century. And you were only thwarted in your dancing career by the bloody Second World War! Anyway, since when have you wanted a wife and children? That's news to me."

"It's been on my mind lately. Do you never think about what we leave behind, eventually? Our legacy?"

"Not really. I'm content with thinking about how I've lived, what people have meant to me and what I've meant to them."

"Even worse," he says, "never to have felt that. I have been a dance teacher to hundreds but I've never meant to any of them what you mean to your small circle of family and friends."

Sofie sighs deeply into the phone. "Do you really regret it all, Teo?"

Teo feels as if something is pressing down on him, his arms like anchors. He can barely hold the telephone anymore. "I just, well, I've missed a few things, Sofie. A few important things."

When they say good-bye he places the receiver lightly in its cradle and lifts his fingers to his nose, straining for just the tiniest whiff of her scent. It was early evening in August 1939, just one week before the ballet's departure for Berlin. The long northern summer had trapped the sun high in the sky and the day gave no indication that it would ever capitulate. Teodor was alone in the studio; Sofie appeared in the doorway as he positioned himself before the mirrors for yet another go at his solo. He caught her reflection just as he raised his arms. Tall and fair in a soft flowery skirt. Teodor was happy to see her.

"Sofie, hullo, how long have you been standing there?" He let his arms drop but talked to her reflection in the mirror.

"Just got here," she said, taking a few steps onto the wooden dance floor. "Mother sent me to call you home, she wants to get one good meal into you today."

"She sent you all the way down here just for that?"

"Teodor, you've been working on this performance like a madman for weeks. I think she's worried you'll exhaust yourself."

"I just want to get it right, that's all. This is very, very important to me."

"Of course it is. Come, show me a little."

Teodor needed no further prompting. He turned to face her. "Well, you know, the scene takes place in the dance school of the Paris Conservatory. My role is that of a ballet student desperate for attention, out to prove himself. Well, that's the way I see him, anyway." He moved to the phonograph and lifted the needle, but did not place it on the record yet. "I do a few lifts with this girl Kirsten, really just a crossover from her solo to mine, in fact. Then I dance for three minutes on my own. My big solo," he said, attempting to laugh it off.

He placed the needle carefully on the record and moved quickly to the center of the room. "I'll do the end of our duet straight into my solo," he told Sofie as she folded herself into a sitting position on the floor in the middle of room, directly in front of him.

The music, scratchy on the phonograph, picked up in a few seconds. Teodor was aware of all the elements merging in him, he had control of all the pieces of this dance as he performed leaps and jumps, pirouettes and arabesques.

Sofie leaned back on the heels of her hands and spoke up the moment he finished dancing. "Your style has changed, my friend. You're a real Danish dancer now, aren't you, like all the other boys?"

Teodor frowned. "Do you really think I dance like all the others?"

She widened her eyes and turned up her palms in a look of calculated innocence. "Well, that was the point, wasn't it? You were too much the Russian dancer when you came here. Now in less than two years they've got you dancing Danish. The real thing, Bournonville would have loved you."

"It's how I got the role, Sofie. And it *is* a Bournonville ballet."

"Oh I'm sure, I'm sure it's just the thing. Never mind. Why don't you teach me the pas de deux. I still remember a thing or two about ballet."

She rose to join Teodor. He dropped the needle to the gramophone, then approached Sofie, whom he turned around so that her back was to him. He placed his left hand on her left hip, and slid his right arm under hers into a long stretch. "It's simple, really," he said, "just two arabesques en l'air, one to the left and one to the right, then a set of glissades, and finally a pirouette. Then you twirl out of the way, upstage left, so that I can dance alone."

Sofie felt different in his arms than Kirsten. She was taller, nearly as tall as he, and her limbs were longer, her arabesques rather low and lacking grace, but she was warm to his touch. When he lifted her he felt her thigh, softer than Kirsten's hardened muscles, and he caught her scent, a mix of lavender and roses and something earthy and pungent, like forest mushrooms. Her skirt fluttered in his face and he breathed her in deeply. When he returned her to the floor he did not continue with the glissades; instead, he held her waist.

"What happens now?" she asked quietly.

He was uncertain. All he knew for sure was that it no longer had anything to do with dance. Her back was to him, and he slipped his arms around her and pulled her close so that she pressed into

his body from shoulder to heel. They stood like that for a moment, breathing in rhythm. The needle skipped and the music evaporated.

He kissed her ear, soft and hesitant.

She tilted her head, exposing her long neck. His mouth moved downward while his hands roamed, first hovering then caressing. When his lips reached her shoulders he turned her around slowly to face him. A boy and a girl in their late teens in the center of a large, airy room filled with summery yellow light, their arms at their sides, their bodies leaning toward one another, their faces nearly touching. A lock of her fine hair fell loose over one eye; tiny freckles he had never noticed dotted her cheeks. They continued to breathe in rhythm. His body felt as though it were pulling toward her, as though gravity itself had shifted directions. He thought his heart might burst through bone and skin to fly to her. They watched one another in silence.

After a very long moment, Teodor held out his hands, palms up. "Dance with me," he said, and she stepped into his arms. There was nothing to this ancient dance. No choreography. No flash and sparkle. No moves to learn. Just two bodies speaking to one another. The gramophone scratched out a tuneless love song.

She pressed her ear to his cheek. "We have to go," she said without conviction.

He moved his head so that they both nodded.

After another moment he said, his voice gravelly with desire, "You shouldn't have stopped dancing, you know. You could be really good. I wish we could dance together."

She pulled her head away so that she could look into his face. "Don't mind what I said before," she told him. "Your dancing is tremendous. I can see how far you've come here. You'll really be a dancer one day, won't you?"

"Yes," he said, "I will be a dancer one day."

During the busy week that followed before the troupe left for Berlin, Teodor and Sofie had barely a moment alone together. Then, while Teodor spent the war languishing in Berlin, Sofie, along with her family and most of the Jewish community of Copenhagen, fled to neutral Sweden in 1943. After the war Teo found the Sonnenfelds back in Copenhagen, intact and healthy, cheerful even, and thrilled to see him. They were careful not to ask too many questions about his survival, and he volunteered little information. But he was devastated to learn that Sofie had stayed in Malmö, married to a Swede. She was expecting a baby.

Teo and Vivi make their way from the theater quickly, shunning well-wishers, sycophants and journalists. He leans heavily on her arm, slightly dragging one foot. They emerge from the front of the Suzanne Dellal Center, skirt the diamond-shaped fountain, and navigate the stone walkway carefully, turning left when they reach the street and ducking into the new restaurant that has just opened there. The foyer is crowded, and their reserved table is not quite ready. A sympathetic hostess provides a chair for Teo, which he lowers himself into with caution. He is flushed and slightly rumpled, but on their way out of the theater, when Vivi asked if he preferred to go straight home, he refused, insisting that they keep their dinner plans in spite of proving himself to be "sad and speechless" as predicted.

Eventually they are seated in two plush velvet armchairs facing one another over a shiny gold table toward the back of the restaurant. The lighting is low, the music is a little loud and the conversation around them a lot louder, but it is the best that can be expected on a busy Saturday night in the Neve Tzedek section of Tel Aviv. Teo does not open his menu. Vivi tries to catch his gaze, to ask him what he might like, but she sees he is elsewhere in his thoughts. When the waiter arrives, she has barely managed to read through the appetiz-

ers, so she orders a bottle of the house red and the pâté de campagne for starters and randomly, halfheartedly, agrees to two of the evening's special dishes rattled off by the waiter and prepared with a whole slew of ingredients she has never heard of.

Teo makes several stabs at conversation, gets as far as clearing his throat, but says nothing. Vivi makes encouraging faces, unsure whether to carry the conversation on her own or let them be silent together. When the wine arrives it revives Teo and he is finally able to speak.

"Did I mention how ravishingly beautiful you look this evening?" he says, his voice deep and clouded from disuse.

"You did!" she says, nearly barking from relief that he has returned from wherever his mind had led him. "You made quite a fuss when the taxi picked me up." Indeed, she is wearing a new and elegant little black dress with a cinched waist, and heels higher than she is accustomed to, and a gold chain with a simple diamond pendant. She bought makeup to replace the caked and dried receptacles she found in her bathroom and washed her hair and left it down so that it hangs to the middle of her back, thick and glossy. His own dapper appearance has not escaped her attention, either: the pressed suit and tie, the starched shirt, the shiny shoes and the wild white hair tamed for once into submission.

"Yes, of course. Of course I did." He fumbles with his napkin. "Well, just so. You still look lovely, just as radiant at the end of the evening as the beginning."

A different server brings their appetizer and sets it in the middle of the table. When she has left, Vivi says, "For me, this has been a very special evening. I . . . you may not want to talk about it, but I thought the performance was astonishing. The ballet itself was astonishing, and the dancers did a phenomenal job with it."

He nods, first lightly then with vigor. "They did a very fine job with it indeed," he says.

"Did you . . . were you watching? I mean, I noticed you had your eyes closed for, well, a good part of the time."

He smiles for the first time this evening. "You don't miss much, do you?"

"Ah, but you already know that about me."

"Yes, I do."

"So?"

"From what I saw, they were just fine. But I told you, I can't really watch that ballet."

"I still don't understand. You created it."

He does not touch the pâté but after a long, slow slip of his wine he levels his gaze at her. "What do you think that ballet is . . . about?"

She sets her own wineglass on the table. "I was hoping . . . we could talk about that," she says. "I've been thinking about it ever since I saw the rehearsal. And now of course I've seen the whole ballet." She shakes her head. "Look, I don't really understand how it all works. I mean, there are ballets with clear stories, like *Swan Lake*, so the dancers' movements have something to do with the progression of the story itself. That much is clear. But with a ballet like *Obsession*, I'm just not sure. I did some homework, I read a few reviews that appeared when the ballet premiered, and one of them said it 'dispenses with narration while at the same time evoking it.' Tonight I was watching to see if I could find a story there."

"And did you?"

Two couples at an adjacent table burst into laughter at a joke one of the men has just told. Teo and Vivi shrug off the interruption.

"Well," she says, sitting up a little higher in her chair, "what I understood was that the beautiful young male dancer was kind of a

rising star. He seems to be featured or favored from among the dancers of the corps de ballet. You certainly gave him the most exciting choreography."

"Go on," he says.

"And then when the older male dancer appears I guess he's jealous and tries to ruin him. His dance is full of anger, even though he's quite tender toward the younger dancer at the beginning. Almost like an older brother."

"For years critics wrote that the ballet was about me," he says, "bitter that my career as a dancer was over. Some reviewer even came up with a theory that I was depicting Nureyev and some young Swedish dancer whose career he was thought to have destroyed."

There is a constant flow of traffic next to their table, but Vivi and Teo are pleasantly unaware of it. They have barely touched their appetizer and the waiter stops by twice to make sure they are satisfied.

"But that's not it," she says.

"If it were, I should have called the ballet *Jealousy* and the whole work would have been obvious and dull."

There is a sharp, bitter tone to his voice now. She has heard this tone before, though only briefly.

"Obsession," he continues, "is so much subtler than jealousy, so much more complex. And so much more interesting. You know, the origin of the word is Latin, it means 'siege' or 'blockade.' As if one's senses are besieged by the object of one's desires."

"So an obsession can be destructive or constructive," she says.

"Exactly. The dancers in my ballet strive obsessively for perfection."

"Ah, that explains the repetitive movements at the beginning . . ."

"Mmmm, yes. What you saw me working on at rehearsal that day was exactly those subtleties of movement and stance, how in the

early stages of learning a dance a dancer can simply perform what he is supposed to without thinking too much about all the little touches that will make it perfect. But those touches gain importance, in fact they make the difference between a mediocre performance and a superb one. And the only way to get from one to the other is by obsessively focusing on every tiny little aspect."

"So that's the positive side of obsession," she says. "But the older dancer in your ballet—he's the negative, isn't he?"

Teo nods. The waiter appears with two large plates filled with artful, unidentifiable food. Vivi indicates that he can place them wherever he wishes.

"Sometimes," Teo says, more to the plate than to Vivi, "someone can think so highly of your talents that instead of nurturing them he destroys them."

For a few moments they pick at their food in silence. While he is lost in unshared reveries, she imagines tapping his head like a coconut so that the memories will gush forth, a river of milk that would douse them both. There are so many things to ask now, but it is clear that anything too direct will be rebuffed. The waiter comes by to refill their wineglasses. The noisy couples at the next table knock into them as they sling coats and purses over their arms on their way to the door.

Vivi lays down her knife and fork and looks up at Teo as he slowly chews. "If obsession can be plotted on a continuum, like we've said, between positive effects and negative, what role do you think it has played in your own life?"

He looks past her, then responds. "Working obsessively has enabled me to create ballets and train dancers to a highly professional degree. At the same time, it's kept me from enjoying some of the simpler pleasures of life. So there's no clear answer to your question. Which makes it a damned good metaphor for life in general."

She nods, eager to add something, but she sees something brewing in his eyes and remains silent.

"You know, this continuum you just mentioned. It makes me think. I've been telling whole generations of dancers to reach for the stars, which would mean pushing to the very end of that continuum. But if I am completely honest with myself I can't say that's what I myself have done."

"How not? Haven't you sacrificed everything for dance?"

"That's what I like to believe. And certainly that's what a lot of people believe about me. But ultimately, it isn't true. Those years in New York . . . I came back to Israel because I just couldn't share Mr. Balanchine's religiosity about ballet, not after living through the war in Europe. Ballet, which is all order and precision, was my answer to the chaos that was Europe. But it still didn't provide all the answers. That's why my ballets are more chaotic than his. Less generous of spirit. They contain evil and treachery."

"Which makes them more true to life."

"Perhaps."

The two fall silent, each in contemplation.

Finally Teo says, "Here is the truth for you: I wish I could go back to a time before language, when I was one with my surroundings. That business about color and heat I was telling you about, when my body could absorb everything around me and turn it into something beautiful. When I could *feel* the bright pink of a falling leaf or the flow of the Vistula or the hiss of the radiator and I could express them through movement. When I could dance water, or heat, or even love."

He is wide-eyed now, as lucid as glass. "It was heaven. My body was heaven. It was omnipotent, with its own language. I would give anything to get back there. Just to feel the sensation again. Every-

thing I've done since, all this teaching and creating and dancing, they're all just approximations."

"You're lucky, even if you don't know it. At least you've experienced it. Most of us never get the chance."

He nods.

"I hope you don't mind me getting you to talk like this," she says. "It's partly to know you better, and partly to help me figure my own self out. I've always run away from obsession because my mother is obsessive and I didn't want to go that route, but these talks of ours make me realize I'm also missing something by not letting myself get fully absorbed. Without obsession, there's no passion. No getting carried away."

"Why do you call your mother obsessive?"

"She gets on kicks about things and can't let them go. Sometimes it's about my getting married and having children and sometimes it's about her experiences in the Holocaust, but everything she does or thinks she carries out with obsessive zeal. She was already a crusader in the fifties, even before the Eichmann trial woke everyone up. She ran around telling her story everywhere she could, to anyone who would listen. Now it seems wonderful and amazing, but believe me, it was freaky back then, as a child, to have a mother who could talk about the Nazi who—funny how this is still hard for me—the Nazi who stuck his fingers up inside her. My classmates couldn't look at me for days after hearing her tell that story. I was tainted, probably for years. Bizarre, no?"

"Not really. And it explains a lot about you. But I'm an artist, not a psychologist, so I'll spare you an analysis."

"I thank you for that," she says.

They eat in silence while life hums noisily around them. A middle-aged woman in a sequined jacket stops by the table to tell Teo

how much she enjoyed the performance. When he does not respond, Vivi thanks her, and the woman, flustered, teeters back to her waiting husband.

"I'm quite certain," he says, as if the disruption had never occurred, "that that is the last time I'll see *Obsession*." He cuts Vivi off with a wave of his hand before she can protest. "And that's perfectly fine with me. I have my own version of it in my head, so I can watch it whenever I like. What I'm more worried about is its legacy. What will become of it when I'm no longer around to grant or deny permission to stage it."

"I suppose you hand it over to someone you trust. Your lawyer or some such person, no? It can't be very complicated."

"On the contrary, it's exceedingly complicated. Dance is the most fragile of art forms. My ballet master, Tom—who has actually danced in earlier productions of *Obsession*—did a fine job of recreating the ballet you saw this evening. But already when I was invited in to polish it I found quite a few distortions and misinterpretations. I call it an erosion. An erosion of the original. And if there is such erosion when someone as close to the ballet as Tom directs it, what will be left of it when it's handed over to others? Do you see, Vivi? Do you understand? This is my legacy, it's all I have to hand on to the world. No canvases, no books, no sculptures. No buildings. No children. Just a series of poses and movements strung together and performed for others, where fragments may or may not remain for an hour or a lifetime."

Vivi fingers the gold chain around her neck. "Maybe it's not important. Compared to your legacy, mine's, well, nonexistent. But does it matter? Who says we have to leave something behind. Maybe we should exist, make the best of it, and bow out. *C'est tout*."

Teo's lips curl into a noiseless laugh, his old man's teeth yellow and decaying. "That's age talking. You're too young to worry about such things. But at my age, legacy is all that's left."

"I'm glad to see you laughing," she says. "You survived. The evening, I mean. The performance."

"I've survived it all," he says.

"You're not finished yet," she says with a decisiveness that surprises him. "There's more in store for you."

They drink bitter espresso, share a profiterole. He daubs the corner of his napkin in a glass of water and wipes a chocolate smudge from her chin, an intimacy they both enjoy.

He orders brandy, she takes a sip. Out on the street, neither is quite ready to head home. They stroll up Shabazi Street arm in arm, peering into shop windows and street-level dwellings. They point out Moorish door frames and wrought-iron balconies and rooftop gardens to one another, and they take great delight in finding *menschelach* on the walls, the small handcrafted iron sentries, no two pairs alike, that prop open the shutters. They circle around and wind up back in the plaza near the Suzanne Dellal Center, where they buy Italian ices.

Vivi pulls Teo across Chelouche Street to sit and enjoy their treats in what she calls her favorite small park in Tel Aviv.

"Once," she says, after they have settled on the low stone wall that borders the park, "you told me that you'd been in love two times in your life. Many years ago. I want to hear about these two."

"Now Vivi, why ruin my good mood."

"Did they both make you that miserable?" she asks.

"In one way or another," he says.

The night air and the frozen dessert make them both shiver and they reluctantly agree to end the evening. She hails a taxi.

When they reach her apartment she puts her arms around him and plants a lingering kiss on his neck. She gets out of the car but sticks her head back inside the window. "I haven't had a date that I enjoyed this much in years," she says. "You've inspired me."

"How so?"

"You've given me new ideas. I think I'm ready now. To create." She grins. "Maybe even obsessively."

She wastes no time. Alone in her empty flat—for once she is glad to be alone there—she changes clothes and gets right to work, sketching her ideas, crafting them into an organized plan. There is no tingle in her nose; instead, her whole body feels as though it is suffused with light. She has emerged from a long, long stupor and is as wide awake as she was in those early days with Martin down at the Dead Sea. Her plan takes shape on a dozen sheets of plain white paper and over the remaining hours of darkness. She rises from the floor, where she has been scribbling, only when the sky begins to lighten, but she knows she cannot possibly sleep. Instead, she flops back down to the floor and continues until it is time to head to the coffee bar for a day of work on her feet.

Nelly has long since gone to bed. The house is tranquil but Teo is not. His mind and body are full of energy; at first he thinks about creating a few steps to a tune that has been in his head lately, but instead he puts the Chopin *Barcarolle* on the phonograph and dances—with caution, slowly—around the living room. For the first time in years, nothing aches, no part of his body fails to comply.

He showers, lathers himself lavishly, is surprised to find himself aroused. After toweling himself dry he slips into a silk dressing gown and sits at his escritoire.

Dear Margot,

he writes,

We are enjoying a particularly mild winter here in Tel Aviv. Just this week I spied people swimming in the sea first thing in the morning. The days are filled with cool sunshine and it seems to rain only at night, inconveniencing no one.

This evening I did as you suggested and attended the gala performance of *Obsession* that we had been rehearsing these past weeks. I believe it came out well; I was satisfied, and the

audience seemed more so. The dancers gave their all and they managed to absorb some of the difficult lessons I tried to teach them. This month was one of no small amount of despair on my part, a period of wallowing that I cannot be sure did not surface in my letters to you, try as I did to hide it from you. At times I was overwhelmed at how much teaching and cajoling and stroking and prodding my dancers required of me, but I nonetheless found new strength and energy that carried me through. At any given time there are a few dancers, or maybe even just one, who understand what I am offering and are willing to grab it. Those are the dancers who will work terribly hard, bump up against high walls of frustration and, if they are not broken, will scale them and succeed. So long as I have at least a few of these, I keep sane and content.

However, I must admit that for once, dance is not my only source of pleasure. If I am not mistaken, I was actually out on a proper date this evening! Your nearly eighty-five-year-old brother spent a lovely evening with a very young woman (early forties). The food and conversation were pleasant—no, far more than that, they were thoroughly enjoyable, relaxing, especially after the relative trauma, for me, of watching my best ballet being performed. I daresay, though we were slightly awkward with one another at the beginning of the evening, we were quite comfortable by the end.

Now, don't get any wrong ideas here: Vivi is the sole waitress at the coffee bar I visit most mornings before going to the studio. We have been getting to know one another over the past few months. She calls herself an artist (though I have yet to see any of her work) and we often discuss the creative process. There is something fresh about this young woman, and sad as

well. She is clearly a good soul, but troubled, and I simply enjoy spending time with her. She is also pleasant to look at, especially this evening when for once she was dressed properly and had (subtly) made up her face.

I have a terrible confession to make. The ballet world, in which I have been immersed my entire life, is one of beauty, aesthetics, suppleness—in short, youth. As a man of great old age (have I ever admitted to that before?) I find I miss my own beauty and suppleness. And I was beautiful, was I not, Margot? Without my own beauty, I have no real credibility with the beautiful youths I teach. Even in this sense I am passé. You, my dear Margot, are lucky; your beloved sisters will never abandon you for want of interest, never cast you aside for being of no further use. I cultivated youth and beauty, ignored old age, and now, as is only fair, youth and beauty are ignoring me. So the attentions of this young waitress, this new friend, are so very, humiliatingly, welcome. This evening I felt proud to be seen with her. Vanity, I know, but it made me feel . . . alive. Like the blood is still coursing, the joints are still working, the mind is still full of imagination and yearning and hope.

Imagine, hope at eighty-five! I wouldn't have believed it possible.

It pleases me to imagine this letter reaching you on a sunny day and that you will read it with birdsong outside your window so that you may laugh at my foolishness. How liberating to be foolish again!

All *my* love,
Your Teodor

I couldn't resist," Vivi says when they meet next, on Monday morning.

She places his usual order on the table, but adds an almond croissant bought at a French bakery nearby.

Teo smiles. "You, mademoiselle, are most charming."

"I had a wonderful time the other night," she says.

"As did I."

"And I've been preoccupied with a project since then."

"Marvelous. I have been buzzing with ideas as well."

"So," she says, "it seems we are co-stimulants to one another!"

Yossi ambles up to the table. "Something you two want to share with me? You're having too good a time," he says.

They laugh like conspirators. When Yossi and Vivi leave his side, Teo cuts a slice of the croissant and slips it into his mouth. The almond paste melts on his tongue and he closes his eyes to enjoy the pleasure.

Over the coming weeks, Teo arrives at the coffee bar earlier and stays longer. He and Vivi dine out once a week, usually Thursdays, at different places they both wish to try. She invites him for a home-

cooked meal. They tell one another stories, though each shies away from his and her most painful memories.

Vivi rushes home each day to resume work on her project. Many nights she sleeps only a few hours, or not at all.

Teo has an idea for a new ballet, his first in more than twenty-five years.

Y a'allah, Vivi. You're crazy. It's four in the morning. Don't you sleep anymore?"

Pincho has just come home from work at Indigo to find Vivi hard at work on the living room floor. She is surrounded by photographs, tools, a sewing kit, glue and sequins, picture frames, magazine clippings, and various bits and pieces of junk she has collected over the past few weeks.

"Who needs sleep?" she says, a big, crazed smile on her face. "I'm loving this, feeling so . . . engaged all the time. You know, I don't even have time for cigarettes anymore. I think I've just given them up without ever meaning to. Anyway, my mother always says there's plenty of time for sleeping in the grave."

"I've heard that joke," he says, trying to clear a place to sit on the armrest of the sofa. "But seriously, when's our apartment going to turn back into a place where two people live?"

Vivi looks up at Pincho. There is glitter in his hair and his trousers look newly pressed, but his beautiful face lacks luster, his eyes are dull. She puts down the photos she is holding. "You are such a dear for putting up with me," she says. "How did I ever get so lucky?"

"Yeah, yeah, kiss my ass," he says with a laugh. "You think if you're nice to me I won't complain?"

Vivi stands up, stretches. "How about if I give you a tour, show you what I'm working on."

"You've been so secretive, I've been afraid to ask."

"Silly, isn't it? I guess I just . . . I don't know, I want this to work out. I really want to get this right."

"All right, come on. Show me around my own apartment."

Vivi takes Pincho by the wrist and leads him to the upended cable spool that serves as their dining room table. "I dug out all my old woodcarving tools," she says as she lifts a small figurine into her hand and passes it to Pincho. "I didn't even think I'd find them."

Pincho handles the polished wood likeness of a male dancer with great care and runs a finger down one smooth thigh then the other. "How . . . ?" He stops mid-thought, entranced. "It's just beautiful, Viv. I . . ."

She smiles proudly. "You didn't know I could do this."

"It's not that I . . . I know you're really talented but . . ."

She plucks the statue from his hand. "I did it from a photograph of him. Something from the fifties."

"What's this?" he asks, lifting a jumble of cloth from the back of a chair.

"Oh, wait!" she says. He freezes while she gingerly lifts it from his hands. "It's full of pins."

Carefully she holds up a not-yet-finished white bolero jacket with brass buttons and presses it onto Pincho's body: "It'll be on a mannequin, you see, black tights on the legs, a white shirt on top and this jacket over the shirt." She leans her shoulder into Pincho's torso to hold the jacket in place and reaches to the table for a floppy black bow, which she hangs from the jacket, just under his chin. "It's an exact copy of the costume he wore for this ballet he danced at the Royal Danish Ballet. Don't you love it?"

"You're . . . you're crazy!" Pincho says with a laugh. "I can't believe you've managed all this."

As she drapes the jacket over the chair, taking care with the pins, she says, "I've got a few amazing recordings, too. Music from his ballets, even a dance lesson he gave once. The sound isn't spectacular but you can hear that it's him. The accented Hebrew, the way he kind of barks when he's peeved."

"You've really taken this all so seriously," Pincho says. "Taken *him* seriously. Shit, Vivi, is there anything you don't know about the guy by this point?"

She looks aimlessly out the window. "Lots. He's still a mystery, even with all this unearthing. I have to admit I feel kind of like an archaeologist, dredging up layers and layers of him. Hang on a minute," she says, ducking into her bedroom, then reemerging with a stack of photos. "This is really the crux of it all."

Together they gaze at one photo after the next. First there is a black and white series that she herself has created: the old man reading his mail, sipping his coffee, walking past the coffee shop, chatting with Yossi. He is never caught gazing into the camera, in fact seems not to sense its presence. The photographs then push back in time, through his six decades of dance in Tel Aviv, and earlier.

"Where did you get these?" Pincho asks, all the while staring at the photographs.

"Mostly from the dance archive at Beit Ariella," she says.

He gives her a horrified look.

"You monster, I didn't steal them! They're prints, anyone can get copies. I got his secretary at the ballet and even his housekeeper to cough up some things, too. That one's no pushover—talk about loyalty to her boss!"

"Wow," he says, holding up a prewar family portrait.

"Wait," she says. "The best one's at the bottom of the stack."

They scrutinize a few more photos before they reach the last one. In it, an impossibly young Teo Levin, wearing the very costume Vivi has been sewing, stands holding a barely drunk glass of champagne. To his left and slightly behind is a strikingly handsome and well-groomed man in uniform. His gaze is on Teo.

"Who is this?" Pincho asks.

"No idea. It's from the archive of a Jewish photographer who came to Israel from Germany in the late 1930s. She died pretty young. Her photos wound up at Beit Ariella and I was lucky enough to stumble onto this gorgeous portrait. I might not have noticed it was him, but then there was the costume. I'd seen it in another photograph."

"The other guy's an officer," Pincho says. "High-ranking. German, of course."

"Bizarre, isn't it? I wish I could ask him . . ."

"Does he know about all this?"

"Who, Teo?"

"Of course Teo."

"He knows I'm working on something but he doesn't know what."

"And you think he's going to be okay with this surprise?"

"Hard to tell. Yes. I mean, eventually. Anyway, nobody may ever be interested in showing it as an exhibition. So he'd never know. But if so, I'll find a way to break it to him. I think he'll like it. Ultimately."

"Well, you know the guy, I don't. I hope you're right. But from what I can see, you're really on to something. This thing's a winner. So you'd better start thinking how you're going to handle it."

They are quiet for a moment as they stare at the photograph.

"Look at this guy's eyes," Pincho says, pointing to the German officer. "I know this look."

"I'm sure you do. Men fall in love with you every day."

"That's not love, Vivi," he says, a trace of bitterness in his voice. "You think that's a look of love?"

She takes the photo from his hands, studies it. "What do you think it is?"

"Desire. Hunger. He's looking at Teo like he's prey."

"That's all? Nothing more?"

Pincho pulls the photo away from her and looks at it again. "I don't know," he says, a quiet admission. And then: "You can never know, can you? Not really."

Vivi puts her arm around Pincho's waist and squeezes. They breathe in unison, his eyes still on the photograph, hers on him.

"Pinch," Vivi says, after a few long moments, "what do you think about me having a baby?"

He drops his gaze from the photograph and turns his whole body toward her. "Are you pregnant?"

"No, I mean, what if I decide to become a single mother?"

"I'd say you'd better get this apartment cleaned up before you bring a baby here. You'll never find him."

"Really, Pincho, what do you think?"

"It's hard work, Vivi. I have six little sibs, I know what it's all about. You'd be spending your whole salary on day care. How would you manage?"

"Oof, you're so practical."

"Look, you'd make a great mom, that's for sure. But maybe the timing isn't right."

"Timing? I don't have much time left. Maybe it's even too late."

"You really want a kid, huh?"

"I do. I've been thinking about it a lot."

"I would help. Our schedules are so different, I could probably be here to take over from you a lot of hours."

"Are you crazy? You're supposed to be working hard, studying and trying to find the perfect man. Being stuck at home with a baby is not in the plans!"

"I'd do it for you, babe."

"Thanks, Pinch. I appreciate it. But if I make up my mind it will be because I think I can handle it on my own. Or nearly on my own."

"You know what?" he says. "I just realized something: you're happier than I've ever seen you. Is this about the project? Or maybe having a baby? Or is it something else?"

She laughs, clearly delighted. "You're lovely," she says. "Absolutely lovely. Now let's see if we can find our way to our beds."

They hug for a moment. Still smiling, Vivi presses her ear to his chest. She can hear his heartbeat, solid and steady.

On an impulse she takes the phone with her to bed and drifts in and out of sleep waiting for the sky to lighten. She dials her mother from under her comforter. "Are you terribly disappointed not to have any grandchildren?" she asks when her mother answers on the second ring, Leah's voice only slightly groggy.

Leah used to tease Vivi and her brother, Assaf, gently about this, but with a daughter-in-law unable to conceive and an unmarried forty-two-year-old daughter, she dropped this sport long ago. "I can live without grandchildren, but I'm sorry you and Assaf haven't had the experience of raising children. It's like nothing else I know."

"But as a Holocaust survivor . . ."

"Ah, that." Leah sighs. "The war produced so many ironies and incomprehensible situations, it's just one more on the heap. I'm pleased to have raised two healthy and intelligent and caring children. That was my mission. But why are you asking me about this now?"

"It's been on my mind a lot lately, that's all."

Both women know there is more to say, both remain silent.

"Mother?"

"Yes, Vivi."

"What do you think about these women who have babies by themselves? Career women, I mean, who get pregnant through a sperm bank or a friend?"

"Hmmm."

Vivi waits patiently, surprised. Her mother is always so sure of herself; she has always been able to answer any question without hesitation. And here she is contemplative, for once weighing her words with true care and attention.

"Yes," she says suddenly. "I think you should do it."

"Just like that?!"

"No, not just like that. I've been thinking about discussing it with you."

"Really, you have? You think it's a good idea?"

"In your case I do. And I'd be willing to give you all the help I can."

"You don't think it's terribly selfish of me, without a husband and all?"

"I've come to think that husbands are a highly overrated commodity."

"You certainly didn't feel that way about Father , . ."

Leah is silent for a moment. Vivi waits, quiet. Two crows clamor on the sill outside her window. "It was certainly *useful* having Amatzia around, at least some of the time, that is . . ."

"That's all? Just useful?"

"Well, in the beginning it was more than that. But—maybe we should be having this conversation in person, not over the phone . . ."

"No, Mother, don't stop now, please . . ."

Vivi recognizes the sound of her mother's morning coffee mug meeting the Formica tabletop. She is clearly steadying herself for whatever comes next. "Well, it didn't take me long to figure out that he wasn't for me. His interests weren't mine, his culture wasn't mine, and eventually his body wasn't mine, either. You remember the little hotel we ran back then on Ben Gurion Street?"

"Yes, of course."

Leah takes a deep breath. "Well, room number six was his, and he did no small amount of entertaining there. Sometimes I saw the girls coming or going, they wouldn't have known I was his wife."

"What? Mother!"

"Oh, it was hurtful in the beginning. I wanted a divorce. But life was hard enough and I knew he'd make it harder for me, so I just swallowed it all and went on raising you and running the hotel and talking publicly about my Holocaust experiences and lobbying or protesting for good causes. I had enough to keep me satisfied and busy. And eventually, when he gave up all that skirt-chasing, we got along all right. Relatively." She sighs deeply. "So that's why," she continues slowly, "I think it's wonderful that women have the option these days to have babies without having to hitch themselves to some man who may hamper them or make them miserable, that's all."

"Mother, I don't know what to say." She feels oddly detached at this momentous news, as though her budding happiness has provided an extra layer of protection against sadness, anger and loneliness.

"Let's talk about it when you come to visit. You haven't been up here in a while, you know."

Vivi clears her throat. "Do you think . . . do you think I'll make a good mother?"

"An excellent mother," Leah replies soberly. "And I'll be a first-rate granny."

"I'm busy now, a new project," Vivi tells her mother. "But when I finish—"

"All right, we'll talk more about it. Do you have an idea who you want for the baby's father?"

Vivi stares up at the ceiling, then pulls the blanket up to her chin. "An idea? Maybe," she says. They both sense the conversation should end here and they ring off simultaneously without another word.

These past weeks have been strange for him. He has been full of restless energy that he had hoped to channel into some new choreography, but he cannot settle on any music and the moves in his mind are muddled, too. No clear ideas come to him. And then there was the letter from Margot, a letter like none other in their correspondence. He has read and reread it many times but for the time being has penned no response.

> Teodor—
> How glorious to rediscover hope (and perhaps love?) at
> your age, our age! How exquisite to move beyond the dictates
> of youth and beauty to something so much richer, or, if we will
> not delude ourselves, a late-blooming find far more cherished
> than any gifts received in youth. In my own great old age I
> have become skeptical of youth's exuberance—the postulant
> enamored of Christ, the artist pouring herself onto one canvas
> after another, the breathlessness of a girl who mistakes snaking
> limbs and sweaty loins for love—and appreciative of the pleas-
> antly rich surprises of twilight.
> Just yesterday, for example, Sister Agnes asked me to
> accompany her past the vegetable gardens to the small shed

where most of our gardening tools are stored. Together we rounded the shed, stealthy and quiet, and she pointed to a low branch in the rare flowering dogwood tree there, where a family of hummingbirds had built an elaborate home for themselves. A mother and her chicks peered at us from within while another bird—which Agnes informed me was a second mature female—hovered just outside the opening, aloft with concern and what seemed to be a sense of duty. We stood watching, Agnes and I, arms round one another, for quite some time, and there was such beauty in those moments, such tranquillity, such a sense of rightness that I tremble at the mere memory of them, saddened only not to be living and reliving them as I write this (though writing is of course a form of reliving). Agnes's troublesome left eye did not twitch and my own flighty heart was still. As a young woman I could never have appreciated the simple pleasure of it all—the angle of the sun cutting through the branches, the whirring bird, the warmth of Agnes's work-roughened hands, the smell of mulching leaves and the rotting wood of the shed—would, in fact, have chided myself for taking time for such earthly distractions instead of praying harder or studying another text—but now, old and stunned by life's daily miracles, I could appreciate the very beingness of everything I was experiencing.

Teodor, I think I am writing this simply to say: allow it. No matter what comes of it or what does not. We must grab these gifts of grace with two hands and pull them close.

—*Your loving sister*

He has been seeing Vivi with regularity, and he looks forward to their evenings out. She is warm when they are together, but she has

become singularly preoccupied with this project she is working on, about which she has been unwilling to divulge a single word. A friend of a friend of hers offered his gallery space for ten days between several scheduled exhibitions and so she has been working maniacally to finish on time. This past week she has not come to work at the coffee bar even once. The days seem longer than ever to him.

He has explained to her that due to a late-running Tel Aviv Ballet board of directors meeting he will arrive at the opening of her exhibit toward the end rather than the beginning of the evening. He returns from the studio, showers, has a light meal with Nelly (whom he invited but, as always, she declined) and changes his clothes several times before phoning for a taxi to the gallery.

Aware of the energy and devotion that Vivi has invested in her project, Teo has reached the decision to be gentle in his criticism. While he does not expect to love what he sees, he also does not wish to discourage her. In the taxi, he practices several lines that will not compromise his integrity and will allow her the praise she so desperately needs. *What an accomplishment,* he says to himself. *What a stunning use of color. You have absolutely outdone yourself.*

The taxi pulls up to the address on the invitation and both Teo and the driver stare at the door in disbelief. In the middle of a street filled with auto repair shops it seems deserted. While there are cars parked up and down the street, the doorway itself is lit by a single bare bulb, and no light can be seen within. But a small sign for the gallery, nearly invisible, stands by a potted plant, so Teo alights from the taxi and makes his way carefully into the building.

Within, another sign leads him down a twisting corridor, at the end of which he sees light and hears noise. The tiny steps he has been taking, for fear of tripping in the gloom, expand and quicken. Several paces before the doorway, he stops. Like a dancer approach-

ing the stage, he prepares himself: he stabilizes his breathing, pulls his neck higher and shoulders lower, extends his hands and wiggles his fingers. He gives his head a slow turn in one direction and then the other. He pulls his stomach in, pushes back his pelvis. Just as he has finished righting himself, he hears music from within, familiar music. He turns his head so that his good ear, the right, will catch it more clearly. He hums along for a second, unable to give it a name, but steps forward anyway into the room.

A throng of people and a blast of noise flatten him against the wall. They seem to be shouting, and it feels as though the whole room is looking at him. He smiles, bewildered, looking for Vivi. He does not see her but does see quite a few familiar faces, all smiling crazily at him. Dancers young and old, the studio administrator, a few colleagues. The woman who writes dance reviews for *Haaretz*. A movie star who once came to him for help with a role. They are shaking his hand, embracing him, patting his shoulder. But how did all these colleagues of his learn about Vivi's show? Through the tumult and din, he finally makes out, in its final bars, the chorus of a song being sung for him, the same one sung at nursery schools and kindergartens all around Israel for birthday girls and boys. He notices a large cake in the middle of a table of refreshments in the corner.

Once he realizes he has been duped into attending a surprise party for himself, he makes the quick decision to be gracious, though his impulse is to bolt. His mind darts wistfully to the dark taxi ride home, the end of the hubbub, but he knows he will have to bear this. Still, he wonders at Vivi. Why would she have spent so much time arranging such an event? He has always abhorred marking the passage of time, which stampedes ahead heedless of whether we are ready or not. Such commemorations are to him merely stones on our graves, reminders of our mortality, our encroaching demise. He

has shunned birthdays, anniversaries of any kind—like the founding of the Tel Aviv Ballet, which his administrator insisted on fêting royally for its fiftieth in 1998—for these, more than conjuring pleasant memories, only serve to remind him how little he has accomplished, how much more there was to do and how little time is left to do it. They remind him of friends lost, opportunities botched. Where others see a string of opening nights and excellent reviews, he sees only waste and loss.

The din is nearly unbearable. If he could he would cover his ears, close his eyes, drop into a chair and wait for it all to subside. His cheeks ache from too much smiling, his forehead feels as if it will crack. Who is this man pressing his fleshy face into his own? Who is this woman with expensive jewelry and bad teeth? These are all people glimpsed once or often in the past, some intimately and some superficially, now gone old like himself, their skin blotched and sagging. He does not try to recall names or shared memories, he merely presses their hands in return, kisses their cheeks in reciprocation. He laughs at whatever they are saying, he cannot make out a word. It is all gibberish, noise.

Suddenly, at last, here is Vivi, flushed and lovely. She has taken his hands in her own, is smiling the smile he thought was for him alone. The din subsides and he can hear her, speaking only to him. "Come," she says, "I'll show you around," and it is only then that he notices, not two paces from where he has been standing the whole time at the entrance to the gallery, the sign: TEO LEVIN: A LIFE IN ART. He stares at it for a long moment. A flashbulb pops in his face, people are gawking, smiling, someone shoves a glass of champagne into his hand. All at once he recognizes the music, the music from his dance in Berlin from the Danish ballet, *The Konservatoriet*. In a flash, the entire room comes into focus for the first time. He no longer sees the people, it

is the walls that paralyze him. Here he is in black and white photographs taken recently in his studio, on the street, or at the coffee bar, as he pores over magazines or ponders his coffee; here is a polished wood statue of him, clearly it is he, poised to pirouette, every sinew properly sculpted; here he is in a charcoal etching, here is an old pair of his ballet slippers, now encrusted in a glittery work of art complete with a blown-glass bauble; here is the costume he wore in Berlin, a replica of the very bow tie; here is a monitor screening dances of his, some of them starring people standing in this very room; here is a map of north central Europe, the cities of his youth singled out, the route he journeyed from Warsaw to Copenhagen to Berlin clearly marked. There is more, so much more. She has drawn and sculpted and etched and woven and beaded and photographed his life. His voice, scratchy with time and almost unrecognizable to him, gives instructions in a ballet lesson from fifty years earlier. More original art, posters for his various ballets, artifacts, shards, objets d'art. Archaeology, his own. Finally, in the far corner, nearly hidden by a curtain, a trio of photos. He is stupefied by the shot of his parents, a portrait he has never before seen, probably snapped before he was born, his father trying to be serious beside his sparkling young bride. Then a photo of himself with Margot, probably their last, taken at the party their parents threw before he left Warsaw for Copenhagen. He marvels at the smooth skin and the eyes that knew nothing of what lay ahead. But then the third photo. It is he, young—a boy!— with a glass of champagne in his hand, still in costume, at the afterparty for his dance at the Berlin Staatsoper. And there next to him, in full uniform, dashing and confident, is none other than Freddy. The face he has not glimpsed in sixty years is here, now, pressing down on him more than all the bodies and memories in this room.

Teo pushes Vivi's arm away, stumbles backward as if blasted from

the photo, is righted by one of the party guests standing behind him. He teeters toward the doorway, grabs the doorpost to steady himself. He shuns all the hands and words trying to prop him up and coax him back into the room, and he flees down the dark hallway as quickly as his legs will allow, out of the building, out into the air, into a taxi that has just disgorged several more guests stunned to see the guest of honor dropping into the car, panting. "Away," he cries to the driver, his first words since arriving. "Away! Away! Away!" Sobbing now—an old man's cry, bitter, disillusioned, disappointed, frightened—they drive aimlessly for fifteen minutes before he is able to tell the driver where he must go to take him home.

There is a new girl at the coffee bar. Her name may be Sivan. Or Moran. She lasts only four days before she is replaced by another one. This one probably has a name, too, but no one bothers to learn it.

Vivi is busy. Her show proved to be so popular that the gallery owner extended it, then extended it again. He is in contact with several galleries in other countries that are interested in hosting it. And a number of prominent Israelis have already turned to her. They want their lives done in art as well. A new career is born.

Teo stays home. He tries writing Margot but no words flow from his pen. He dials Sofie's phone in Copenhagen but hangs up before it rings. Nelly prepares his favorite dishes; he eats less and less every day, and she grows frantic.

Vivi comes by each day, sometimes twice, and knocks at the door. Teo will not see her and will not allow Nelly to open the door. Yossi roars up once on his motorcycle, a noisy emissary, but he, too, is ignored.

Then one morning, spring comes to Tel Aviv. The winter rains, such as they were, have ended and the sun has not yet scorched the heavens dry. A bird lands on Teo's windowsill and warbles there at length, singing him a story. Teo eats a large breakfast, returns to the

studio. When he sees there is a new girl instead of Vivi at the coffee bar he decides to sit there. Yossi brings him his coffee, his steamed milk, his water with ice and lemon. He asks no questions, does not say, It is nice to see you. Teo stares blank-faced at passersby in the shopping arcade, but it is good to sit at this table again. He holds his nose over the cup and inhales deeply the rich, bitter aroma.

The dancers are pleased at his return. Tomorrow he will start to push them again. Today, while it is still spring (and who knows how long that will last), he has other plans.

In the late afternoon he taxis to Vivi's apartment.

She recovers in an instant, squelching her surprise. She has moved her materials and equipment to a newly rented studio and has been working on turning the flat back into an abode. It is unusually tidy and serene, though he has never seen it otherwise.

She ushers him in. He stands in the middle of the room looking lost. He is pale, and not quite steady on his feet.

"You stole my life," he says.

"I gave you your life," she says.

"You took bits and pieces without asking. That's thievery."

She shakes her head. "I'm sorry you see it that way. That wasn't my intention."

"Why didn't you ask me?"

"Because you would never have agreed. And I knew I had to do this."

"So you turned it into a birthday party?"

"I knew I wanted to do something special for you, for your eighty-fifth. It was a fairly simple idea when I first came up with it, but it kept growing while I worked. And then the gallery offered me space and things sort of . . . came together."

"You mean they got out of hand."

"Look, the only reason it turned into a real undertaking is that your life has been so full."

"Don't flatter me," he says dully.

"Hey, can we sit down? Can I pour us something to drink?"

He glares at her for a moment, but the newborn springtime floats the scent of orange blossoms in through the open window and the anger in him does not stand a chance. He collapses into the nearest armchair.

She sits facing him. Neither speaks for five minutes, ten.

He mumbles something she does not catch. "Sorry?" she says.

"I said it was good. Your show."

"Good?"

"Excellent. It was clever. And comprehensive."

She waits.

"It was my life, more than if someone had written a book with all the facts. Those impressions of yours told more. And you proved me wrong about dabbling in art. It turns out that you were able to use all those arts and crafts you've been teaching yourself for years, to great effect."

She smiles wanly.

He says, "I should see it again but I don't think I can."

"Why not?"

Now, in a rush, it is clear why he has come here. "That photograph," he says.

"The one with you in costume, next to a German officer."

"Yes. Where did you find it?"

"In the archives at Beit Ariella," she says. "The photographer was a German Jew who bequeathed her life's work to the archives. I chose it because of the expression on your face, that look of absolute wonder. It's nothing like any other of your photos."

He shakes his head slowly. "I never knew there were any photographs of us at all."

"Us?"

"There is a piece of my personal history that you missed in your Life of Teo Levin. His name was Freddy."

She tucks her legs under her, settles deeply into the sofa. "Tell me," she says.

And he does.

The dancers jostled one another genially as they made their way from a last curtain call to the Staatsoper dressing rooms. A general consensus of having staged an outstanding performance well received by an appreciative audience floated above them, through them, like a light, lacy cloud. Teodor was not part of the happy bustle; he was still, intensely, back in the dance, in his small solo, surprised to find that he could not recall how he had danced. He could only remember the moment before he began, and the roar of the audience at the end of his last tour en l'air, which, he now recalled, was a triple turn and not the single he had rehearsed. This startling recollection made him feel anxious. What had he done? How else had he exaggerated his tiny role, his three minutes of dance? And what would the ballet master think, and his fellow dancers? Would he be branded an unreliable and selfish dancer? Would they despise him, punish or even banish him from the corps? He was, after all, not a Dane, dancing with the Danish ballet only thanks to the goodwill of one or two of its directors. Perhaps, he pondered sadly, this would be his demise.

He stood away from his fellow dancers, stepped out of line and let them pass on without him. Not a one caught his eye, not a one insisted that he continue with them. That's it then, he thought, they

despise me. And rightly so for trying to steal the show. He tried again to recall how he had danced, but it was, mysteriously, nearly a complete blank, as though someone else had pushed up from within him and performed in his place.

The stage was silent now, bereft of dancers and stagehands. He could hear the scuffle of his ballet slippers as he made his way down the hall to the dressing room. He would slip in as quietly as possible, he would find a way to apologize, first to the ballet master and then to the company, perhaps even publicly. He had not meant to dance with such abandon, certainly had not planned such an extravagant debut, and he hoped they would believe his sincerity and give him another chance as a dancer and as a friend.

He pushed his way through the dressing room door. The company, and quite a number of well-wishers, a few in the uniform of the Third Reich, stood crowded together. They were listening to the ballet master, who was addressing them in German for the benefit of their hosts. Aproned maids were passing out small glasses of champagne among the dancers and the assembled guests.

"Mr. Levin, won't you come here, please?" Teodor felt one hundred eyes upon him as he made his way to the ballet master for what he knew was to be a public upbraiding. He stood long-faced and miserable beside his teacher.

"I wish to compliment you all, my dear dancers and pupils, on an exceptional performance. You were on a whole polished and professional, and I am proud of your poise and your technical excellence."

The ballet master motioned to a young German soldier, who stepped forward. "Corporal Brendel has been sent with a message from Herr Hitler himself. Please give him your attention." The soldier read a pompous trumpeting of the Danish ballet company that praised Germany's Aryan neighbors for their physical beauty, skill

and endurance. The members of the troupe listened patiently, then turned their attention back to the ballet master.

"Before we raise our glasses in a toast, I would like to say a word about our young Mr. Teodor Levin, who stands here to my right. As you dancers know, and our dear guests may have sensed, Mr. Levin, himself a guest in our company from Poland, did not comport himself according to plan. In his two years with us he has clearly learned and mastered the meticulous and energetic footing in the Danish fashion and can leap with the best of our dancers. But here tonight you saw his Russian training shine through our Scandinavian style. And while there is no denying the fact that young Teodor will have to learn not to surprise his fellow dancers and his teachers with an unrehearsed bravado performance, there is also no denying that what we saw here this evening, and what we all must know, is that Mr. Levin is a dancer of rare quality, of outstanding talent and sensitivity, and that this, his debut, will be remembered by all who witnessed it as a magical experience. It serves to remind us how beautiful, how demanding and courageous, how inspiring the ballet is. Mark my words, ladies and gentlemen, this is the beginning of a brilliant career for our Mr. Teodor Levin.

"Now let us raise our glasses in friendship and camaraderie, let us toast beauty and excellence, let us thank our gracious hosts, and let us drink to the new star born in our presence, this evening. *Skål! Prost!*"

"*Prost!*" the crowd responded in unison.

Teodor stood, glass in hand, too shocked to drink. In an instant they were upon him, his confreres, with congratulations and hugs, with pats on the back and kisses on the cheek.

Still barely able to speak, he muttered thanks and appreciation under his breath. When the general excitement died down and many

of the dancers had moved off to begin removing their costumes, the lone remaining German in uniform approached Teodor, standing close in front of him.

"Your first champagne?" he asked gently, gesturing to Teodor's still untouched glass.

Teodor nodded.

The German touched his glass lightly to Teodor's. "To perfection," he said quietly. He did not smile when he said this.

The German was only half a head taller than Teodor, but he seemed massive to Teodor in his smart uniform, gold epaulets gleaming. Teodor felt himself awakening, finally, from his performance, and took notice of the man standing squarely in front of him. His fair hair was thin, the color of honey in sunlight, and his eyes a pale blue, too pale, almost translucent.

"*Danke schön, Herr . . .*" Teodor tried unsuccessfully to read the name on the German's chest.

"Von Edelwald. Baron Friedrich Sebastien Amadeus von Edelwald, at your service." He clicked his boots and gave a slight nod to his head. "My friends call me Freddy." Now he was smiling in a friendly way, which Teodor found charming. "And you, perhaps, are Teo?"

Teodor laughed. "No one has ever called me that before. Always Teodor."

"Teodor, 'a gift from God' according to the Greeks. But I think Teo suits you best." Freddy stared into Teodor's eyes too long. Almost to himself he said, "One blue eye and one green. Extraordinary. As unsettling as a Modigliani." Teodor took a small sip from his champagne. "Drink up young man, you must be parched. You danced as if you were on fire, as if you were fire itself."

A photographer with a swirl of dark hair pinned into a neat chignon appeared from nowhere and snapped several shots of Freddy

and Teo chatting and sipping champagne. *"Genug!"* Freddy said sharply to her after the third blinding flashbulb. He waved her away, then leaned in even closer to Teodor, to whisper into the young man's ear. Teodor could smell him, a mixture of expensive cologne and tobacco. He felt wide awake now.

"I am a *Kunstsachverständiger*, an officer whose job is to advise Herr Hitler on matters of art and culture. He has asked me to join the dancers at the postperformance party at the hotel this evening as his emissary. I should like to invite you, afterward, to a small, private midnight supper. You needn't worry about your curfew, I shall take care of all arrangements."

Freddy's voice resonated richly in his ear. Or perhaps it was the cologne or the pipe tobacco, or the champagne, of which Teodor had by now drunk nearly to the bottom of his glass, or the gleaming epaulets or quite likely the headiness of the dance and the praise from the ballet master. Whatever it was, Teodor was swooning, overwhelmed and dazzled. He nodded his consent, but in that same instant knew it would not have mattered a bit.

The party was bright and loud, held in a plush reception hall. Teodor was fêted lavishly, plied with questions and champagne. Freddy largely ignored him, engaging in long conversations with the ballet master, the producer and several elegant guests, though Teodor did catch him watching him from across the room several times. There was a seriousness in his gaze he found both a fright and a thrill. Freddy unsettled him, but he could not tell why.

At half past eleven Freddy approached Teodor in a throng of dancers, who parted when the German officer came near. He took Teodor's hand and said, "Mr. Levin, I wish you all the best in what

will surely be a brilliant career and I look forward to seeing you dance again soon." Into Teodor's ear he whispered, "Front steps of the hotel at midnight," and took his leave. Teodor and the other dancers silently watched the soldier-aristocrat shake hands with the few remaining dignitaries and then depart.

As they made their way to their hotel room, Lars and Niels were in high spirits, reliving the excitement of the evening, while Teodor was pensive. He was aware of each step his feet took, the taste of champagne on his lips. Mostly he was thinking about Freddy. What would they talk about at the table?

At midnight he left the room as the other boys prepared for sleep, on the pretense that he wished to send a telegram to his parents in Warsaw. The front desk clerk was busy with an arriving guest and did not notice as Teodor glided silently across the carpeted lobby and out a set of heavy revolving doors. Freddy was waiting for him on the pavement, and when Teodor first caught sight of him he was framed by the Brandenburg Gate, which stood across the square. Freddy was wearing street clothes and seemed to Teodor to be slightly closer to his own height.

"Come, my friend, we'll walk."

A long evening of drizzle had turned into a soft haze lit up from within by light from the streetlamps. They strolled leisurely while Freddy talked. "Berlin is not a beautiful city, never has been. Massive, yes, even overwhelming, but never beautiful. It was built more to impress than to please." Freddy had come to Berlin from southern Bavaria, way down near the Austrian border, where his family had been the local royalty for more than five hundred years. His mother and his wife and three children were installed there, in the family castle.

"You see that building across the street, those round corners? That's a nice example of Bauhaus architecture, which lends a little

more character to our oppressive city. A Jew by the name of Mendelsohn designed it, talented fellow. He's gone now, left for Palestine I think." Freddy stopped walking and so did Teodor, several paces later.

"Say, Teo, I know you can dance, but can't you talk, too?"

Teodor smiled but said nothing. They turned a corner and continued to walk. The buildings were smaller here, clustered together haphazardly. They turned a few more corners and the streets were darker. At the entrance to a courtyard between two buildings Freddy took Teodor's elbow and directed him toward a staircase that led below street level. The stairs were dark, and Freddy kept his hand firmly on Teodor's arm until they reached the bottom. He gave two quick raps on a heavy door, waited, and rapped four more times slowly. A tall black man, taller and blacker than anyone Teodor had ever seen, opened the door. A cloud of noise and smoke accosted them. The black man smiled when he saw Freddy, pulling him ahead of Teodor through the doorway. He was an American, this black man, and Freddy spoke to him in English. Teodor understood nothing.

Through the smoky darkness Teodor could see that the room was vast, and filled with the most colorful, fanciful people he could imagine. This crowd was nothing like the dignitaries he had danced for at the Staatsoper, and certainly nothing like their usual audiences in Copenhagen. These Germans wore bold and revealing costumes, shiny and full of glitter; they were laughing and howling and drinking and petting one another with abandon. A jazz band of American Negroes performed on a small stage in the center of the room while couples and trios danced in wild gyrations. The general atmosphere was that of a circus, and Teodor, barely more than a child himself, was enthralled. The music was fabulous, and Teodor the dancer could scarcely contain his impulse to spin out onto the dance floor.

When they were seated side by side at a table clearly saved for them near the jazz band, Freddy stuffed a pipe with cherry tobacco and, gesturing to the crowd, leaned close to Teodor and spoke into his ear, over the noise. "All of Berlin looked like this a few years ago. Noisy, colorful. Unusual, original, artistic behavior was an asset during Weimar. Until the Nazis came in and cleaned everything up. Now you practically can't hear good jazz anywhere anymore." He lit the pipe and breathed in deeply, a look of serious concentration on his face.

To speak to Freddy, Teodor had to lean into his body, his chin grazing Freddy's shoulder. "I thought *you* were a Nazi."

"I am, officially. It's like this: the Nazis as a rule hate people like me from old, titled families. But privately they're enchanted by our blue blood. Hitler is only too happy to spend time with the von Edelwalds, and frankly, my family tolerates him because we want to hang on to our castle and our lands. But when Adolf showed interest in my sister, my mother married her off quickly and quashed a family alliance. As for me, he knows I'm a useful source of information about the arts, and culture in general, so he's given me a plummy job and even put aside a bit of state money to renovate our family home." A waiter put two beers, a basket of deep-fried chicken wings and several ears of corn on the cob on the table in front of them. "First time for American food?"

Teodor peered into the basket and nodded. Freddy showed him how to eat the wings with his fingers, a fairly shocking enterprise for Teodor, but a welcome relief from the usual decorum. Teodor took a sip from his beer and began to relax.

Freddy, too, unwound, drinking copiously and eating with gusto. "These Nazis," he said over a buttery yellow ear of corn, "they may have bad taste but they're very art- and culture-conscious. Adolf

draws, Baldur von Schirach and Hans Frank write poetry, Goebbels has published a novel. They profess to hate modernism, what they call degenerate art, the stuff that takes a good, hard look at who and what we really are. But it makes them so didactic." He looked carefully into Teodor's eyes. "I've seen some of Adolf's drawings," he says, scrunching up his face and shaking his head emphatically from side to side.

Freddy jabbered on about Hitler, Berlin, the war, art, his castle, the Alps. He talked at length about Weimar Berlin, about clubs with names like the Zauberflöte and Cosy-Corner, places he had frequented a decade earlier as a student. He talked about American jazz and sang along with the band through many of their songs, his hand on Teodor's thigh, or wrapped around his shoulders. He seemed to know the words to every song, in English, and translated some of the choice lyrics. When a certain Jimmie Lunceford song was announced, Freddy pulled Teodor close and crooned in his ear.

[lyrics to "The First Time I Saw You" TK]

He could not understand it all, but Teodor was fascinated, had never met anyone remotely as interesting as this German nobleman and soldier. He held his ear close to Freddy's mouth, trying to absorb and remember all the stories and information flowing his way. Once, at the end of a melancholy story about an American jazz singer whose name Teodor did not catch, Freddy leaned a tad closer, pressing himself into Teodor and planting a small kiss on his ear. "You are a charming and lovely boy," he said in a tone so low and close that shivers ran up and down Teodor's neck. Nobody around them seemed to care or even notice. Teodor wished to think quietly about Sofie, but there were so many distractions that each time he conjured her face she disappeared.

Later in the evening, when nighttime threatened to turn to day-light and the music had reached a frenzied pitch and beat, Freddy suddenly stood up straight and pulled Teodor to his feet. "How fool-ish of me!" he shouted. "All this wonderful music and I've kept you sitting next to me all evening, telling you stories. It's time for you to dance."

Teodor was intrigued but perplexed. For all his training, he knew no moves appropriate to this extraordinary music, and politely de-murred. But Freddy was insistent, and Teodor was curious, so when Freddy pushed him a few meters away from the table to where couples had broken into a throng of soloists, and then sat back down to watch, he did not protest. He stood still and alone for a moment in the sea of whirling humans, looked around at what some of his fellow dancers were doing, and slowly, subtly, began to move. To their low and slinky moves he added Danish ballet turns, Russian arms, the Charleston that a friend in Copenhagen had taught him, and then whatever else seemed right and natural with this music. In minutes he was swinging, swaying, spinning and strutting with the rest of them and the crowd began to make way for the lithe young man all on his own. Occasionally he turned toward Freddy, who was watching him intently. The serious look on his face caused Teodor's chest to tighten each time he saw it, but he kept on dancing, finally losing himself in the music, losing all track of time or the people around him.

He did not know how long he had been dancing when Freddy was suddenly there with him in the center of the circle of dancers, standing completely still. He held out his hand to Teodor. "I've come to take you home," he said. Teodor gave him his hand and let Freddy pull him from the dance floor.

The morning came far too quickly for Teodor, who had a difficult time waking up. His roommates asked him where he had been, and Teodor conjured a weak excuse, but the clothes next to his bed stank of beer and smoke and he doubted anyone believed him. They ate a quick breakfast in the hotel dining room then returned to their room. They would be traveling back to Stettin, where they would catch an afternoon ferry to Copenhagen. While he packed, Teodor thought about jazz and corn on the cob, and quite a bit about Freddy. After walking him to the hotel, Freddy had embraced him on the stairs of the hotel, but only briefly. He said he would come to say an official good-bye before the troupe left in the morning, and Teodor wanted to be ready in time.

There was a knock at the door just as Teodor laid his ballet slippers on the top of his valise. Niels answered the door. Two German policemen stood outside. "Mr. Teodor Levin, please," said one.

The boy stood aside and motioned to Teodor to come to the door. "We have orders to bring you to headquarters immediately," said the policeman. Teodor looked to Niels, who shrugged his shoulders.

"Why?" he asked simply.

"Security clearance for departure. Your papers are Polish, not Danish, and we need to ask you a few questions, that's all." The second policeman coughed and looked down the hall.

"I'm not permitted to go anywhere outside the hotel without my ballet master's knowledge," he said, hoping his ballet companions would not betray his late-night absence.

"You, boy," said one of the policemen to Niels. "Fetch the ballet master right away." Niels darted down the hall. In the meantime, Teodor stretched the bedspread over his bed and fastened the latch on his valise. Niels returned with the ballet master very quickly.

"What's all this about, gentlemen?" he asked with some irritation. The policeman again explained his mission.

The ballet master listened politely. "I'm certain this is a mistake," he said. "Mr. Levin's papers did not draw any attention on our way in to Germany."

"The situation between Germany and Poland has changed since then," the policeman said by way of explanation. "He is now a *feindliche Ausländer*."

After several long minutes of argument, the ballet master turned to Teodor. "They say you're an enemy alien now that Germany is fighting with Poland. This is certainly an unnecessary and untimely diversion, but perhaps you'd simply better go with these gentlemen to the station, clear up the matter and return as quickly as possible so that we shall not miss our ferry."

Teodor nodded his agreement but did not like the idea of setting out accompanied only by these two policemen. Still, he did as told, gathering up his papers and heading down the hall in between them.

It was a short ride to headquarters. He was shuffled from one desk to another, asked the same questions again and again and made to wait. After two hours the ballet master arrived, in the company of Freddy.

"Teodor, I have good news for you. When Baron von Edelwald came to say good-bye and learned you'd been temporarily detained, he offered his help. I'm afraid it's going to take just a little while longer and the troupe cannot imaginably stay, but I have the baron's assurances that he will see to it personally that you are released as quickly as possible and on the first train and ferry back to Denmark." He patted Teodor on the shoulder. "You are in very, very good hands."

Teodor glanced at Freddy. Today Freddy was all business, though for Teodor's eyes only he managed a small, secret smile. "Thank you, baron," Teodor said. He did not smile in return.

Two hours more passed, then three and four and five. Teodor was mostly alone during this time, though Freddy would occasionally pop into the office where he was waiting to say, "Only a little longer" or "This bureaucracy has become unmanageable" or "I am outraged and will be filing a complaint about this." It was seven in the evening by the time he was released to Freddy's custody.

Teodor was hugely relieved to be leaving the police station, and thanked Freddy for rescuing him. Freddy's car and driver whisked them away from the center of town. "My poor dear boy, you must be completely distraught. And certainly quite hungry and tired. I'll take you to my home in Grunewald, where Cook will feed you a nice soup, draw a bath for you, and we'll put you up in a guest bedroom for the night. Then tomorrow morning we'll have you on an early northbound train." Teodor laid his head back on the soft leather of Freddy's Mercedes and closed his eyes.

He awakened from a short sleep just in time to notice the car turn onto quiet, leafy Erbacherstrasse. They stopped in front of a heavy iron gate that looked like a row of medieval spears. It was opened immediately by a waiting servant, and they drove up to the grand front door of a large, square villa flanked by two smaller buildings, which Teodor guessed to be stables or servants' quarters. The house had a tall, sloping tiled roof and a balcony over the front door. Immense trees secluded the villa behind a wall of greenery, and no other house stood close on either side. A well-tended garden stood between the front gate and the door to the villa.

Cook was barely cordial to him when he sat at the dining room table, clearly hostile to his presence in the house. She did not seem to believe her master's story about the boy's origins, the scion of a noble Danish family. As soon as she placed a hot potato soup and thick brown bread with butter in front of him she announced she

would be leaving for the night. Teodor ate greedily, his first food since breakfast. The smell of nutmeg reminded him of his mother's own potato soup. He wished he could see her just then.

Freddy sat watching him in silence. When he finished eating, Freddy led him upstairs, to the bath. Steam rose from the scented, foamy water and the room was warm and cozy. "You may undress here and use these pajamas and the robe hanging on the back of the door," Freddy told him. He stood as if waiting for Teodor to begin removing his clothing. Teodor did not move, however, and after a moment Freddy left the bathroom, closing the door behind him. When he was sure Freddy had gone back down the stairs, Teodor locked the bathroom door.

He soaked for a long time, at once relieved to be free and at the same time apprehensive. He was sorry the troupe had not waited for him. He was grateful to Freddy and wondered how much longer he might have been trapped there were it not for him. Where, he wondered, would he have gone when released, alone in this foreign city?

The pajamas were silk, a deep red and sensuous to his skin. He wrapped himself tightly in the matching robe and descended the stairs. He found Freddy in a small study off the living room, poring over several full-color reproductions of paintings. When he noticed Teodor he returned the pages to a manila envelope.

"Ah, there you are, all fresh and rosy from your bath!"

Teodor smiled slightly, shifting his weight from one foot to the other.

"Come to the kitchen. Cook has left us some chocolate cake, and I'll put on a pot of tea."

Teodor plodded after Freddy toward the kitchen. Several bright watercolors and gouaches on the walls of the hallway caught his eye as he walked past, but he did not stop to inspect any of them.

Freddy bustled about the kitchen, though he did not always know where to find what he needed. Sometimes he yanked open the same drawer three times before he found whatever spoon or tea sieve he was looking for. Teodor waited patiently at the table, warm and comfortable after his bath.

After several minutes of banging around the kitchen and cursing the cook, Freddy managed to get the tea to the table. He added brandy to each cup. "This will warm up your insides and make you properly sleepy before bedtime," he told Teodor.

Freddy was unusually silent as they sipped the tea and nibbled the cake. After a long silence Teodor asked, "What time will I be leaving in the morning?"

Freddy stopped chewing the cake in his mouth and put his teacup down on the saucer. He stared at Teodor. "Are you uncomfortable?" he asked sharply. "Are you lacking something? Have my cook or chauffeur somehow disappointed you? Or is it my company that is not to your taste?" His voice was tight, as though his teeth were a dam holding back an angry flood.

"I'm sorry," Teodor interjected, cowed, "I just thought I . . ."

"You did not think at all. You did not think what an inconvenience it was for me to spend my day working for your release. You did not think about all the more important matters I could be tending to. You are a Pole and you are a Jew, two points against you. Do you have any idea how many strings I had to pull, how many VIPs I had to call today to be able to free you immediately? No, of course you don't. And now you sit in my kitchen, wearing my pajamas and enjoying my hospitality and all you can think about is when you can leave this horrible little house."

He snatched away the cups and saucers and plates, banging them into the sink. One saucer smashed to the floor, but Freddy ignored it.

Teodor remained at the table for a while after Freddy had thundered his way out of the kitchen and down the hall. There were no sounds at all anywhere in the house. He did not know if he should wait for Freddy to return, to show him where to sleep, or whether perhaps he was now meant to put his head down on the kitchen table and sleep right there, as punishment for having insulted his host. He wondered whether his faltering attempts at German had been too abrupt, or whether his manners had been inappropriate.

After a while Teodor stood up from the table and, with a sigh, collected the broken china from the floor. There were shards everywhere, a few crunched under his knees as he slid along the floor hoping to find every last piece. When he was certain he had gathered them all, he stood up and paced the kitchen, inspecting Cook's utensils, her cookbooks, her collection of aprons. As he was peering through beveled panes of glass into the darkened back garden, but catching mostly his own reflection and that of the room behind him, the kitchen door suddenly flew open and he spun around.

Freddy's face was flushed and his eyes red. He looked disheveled, hardly reminiscent, in fact, of the neat and polished officer Teodor had met only the night before. He was breathing hard, and seemed to be weighing something in his mind as he stared across the room at Teodor. He straightened himself before speaking, checking his posture and pushing a hand through his mussed hair. "You must be exhausted. I'll show you to your room." His voice was level, with effort.

Teodor followed him through the hallway and up the stairs, at a distance. The room was a bit musty, small but pleasant. His valise stood in a corner, and the bed had been turned down for him. An open door led out to a verandah, which Freddy instructed him to

leave open to continue airing the stuffy room. He was cordial, controlled, and after these brief explanations he left Teodor alone.

Teodor removed his bathrobe and climbed into the low bed. It was comfortable, deep and plush. Cold night air from the verandah made him burrow under the heavy quilts, but this was something he had always loved to do, especially on winter evenings in Warsaw. His mother would come to kiss him good night and there ensued a mild game of hide-and-seek, as Teodor would tunnel deeper and deeper into the wilds of his bed. He thought about his mother now, and Margot and his father, too, what they might be doing, whether they were thinking of him. Too bad he had not really sent that telegram, they knew he was due to perform and were undoubtedly wondering how he had fared. And what about them? Did they know the German army was on its way toward them? Were they making preparations to pick up and leave?

He thought, too, about his new family, the Sonnenfelds, in Copenhagen. Little Bent would be asleep by now, the older children would have finished washing the dishes, their parents would be settled into their armchairs for a long evening of reading. Peter would be in their shared bedroom sketching airplanes in his notebook. And what about Sofie? Would she be dreaming of him now as he was of her? He wished he had kissed her full on the mouth that day in the dance studio.

Suddenly from the edge of wakefulness he leapt from the bed and ran to the door. He turned the lock, in absolute silence, and crept noiselessly back to bed. In no time he fell into a deep sleep.

It could have been minutes later, or hours, he did not know. He was aware first of the cold, but when he reached to pull the covers back into place he met with Freddy's head on his belly, his face turned away from him, toward his legs. Teodor gasped, and Freddy,

who was kneeling on the floor, reached his left hand backward, caressing first Teodor's cheek, then his hair. They remained like this for several minutes, Teodor too frightened to move or protest. Presently Freddy raised his head from Teodor's belly, unbuttoned the boy's pajama tops and grazed his lips up and down his flat white stomach. Teodor could feel the tickle and scratch of whiskers. At the same time, Freddy's hand was gently probing his face, passing lightly over his eyes, brushing his forehead, a finger tapping delicately at his lips. When his other hand reached down into his pajama bottoms Teodor began to shudder, his whole body wracked by jolts large and small. Freddy removed that hand but continued stroking his face gently with the other, like a father comforting his son.

Freddy raised his head and for the first time looked at Teodor. "Are you hurt?" he asked quietly. "Are you suffering?"

Teodor hesitated briefly, then shook his head slowly from side to side. Indeed, he was neither of those, really, just terrified.

"Good," Freddy said. "Relax." He laid his head down again, and this time both hands were at work fondling and stroking Teodor's body. The boy did not resist when Freddy's fingers crept beneath the waistband of his pajamas, nor did he shake when the man took hold of his penis, which was now hard as a dancer's barre. Freddy rubbed his hands down the shaft two times, maybe three, when Teodor erupted and sat bolt upright, gasping and squirming.

Freddy pushed Teodor back down on his pillow, then climbed on top of him, releasing the sash on his bathrobe as he did. Teodor could feel his nakedness, the tautness of his body, the thrust of his penis as it pushed heavily back and forth in the small puddle on his belly. Teodor turned his head sideways to avoid Freddy's panting mouth; a drop of his saliva dripped into Teodor's ear and, with a deep moan, Freddy clutched the boy's shoulders and slammed his groin down

hard. Teodor could feel the man's body relax, gradually, before he pushed himself up and off of him. Wordlessly Freddy retied the sash on his bathrobe, tossed a hand towel to Teodor, unbolted the lock on the door and closed it behind him silently.

In the morning Teodor roused himself with difficulty, confused. The door to the verandah was still open, bright sunlight deluging the room. When he sat up he thought he could see a small lake glistening through the thick trees at the back of the garden. He washed his face and his chest and stomach at the bathroom sink, and ran a wet cloth over his privates before dressing. Outside he could hear a train pulling into a station, but the inside of the house was, as the night before, silent. He found Cook pulling a tin of muffins from the oven. "Out in the garden," she said brusquely.

Freddy was seated, in uniform, at a small table of glass and wrought iron, reading a newspaper. Several plates lay in front of him littered with scraps of food. He made a great show of welcome when Teodor approached. Cook was washing the muffin tin in the sink behind them, with one eye to the table in the garden.

"Well, good morning my young and sleepy friend," he said, folding the newspaper and setting it aside. "In this house we are usually up bright and early on weekday mornings. Are you aware that this is not a holiday?" he said with a laugh to his voice. He winked at Teodor, causing Cook to frown.

"What time is it?" Teodor asked, taking a seat across from Freddy.

"Nearly nine o'clock, and I've got a mountain of work to do, so I will have to leave you now in the good care of my trusty staff." He swilled down the last of his coffee as he stood from his chair. "Cook," he called, "bring young Teo a breakfast fit for a growing young man who worked hard yesterday." Another wink for Teodor. He was gone before Teodor could ask about departure.

The day passed slowly. Cook ignored him, and the chauffeur, an old uncle named Albert, was gone most of the day. Teodor would have liked to write a letter to his family or take a walk or read one of the books in Freddy's locked study, but all these required Cook's permission and assistance, so he contented himself, just barely, with exercises in the garden, some dancing in a corner of the salon, and hours of watching the occasional passerby from the second-floor balcony. Twice he dragged his valise down the stairs and set it by the front door, twice he lugged it back upstairs, worried that its presence might irk Cook. He was careful to avoid thinking about what had happened in his bed the night before, and by late afternoon was not entirely sure he had not dreamt it.

The light in the sky was nearly gone when Cook called Teodor to the kitchen. "The baron will be late, he says you're to take your supper alone right here." A plate of sausages and potatoes lay steaming on the table. "I hope those Danes taught you to wash your own dishes," she called over her shoulder as she let herself out the back door.

He ate carefully, slowly, but did not have the appetite to finish everything on his plate. He scraped the remainder into the rubbish bin and washed his dishes with caution, in hot water. Alone in the house now, he wished to pick up the phone and place a call, but to whom? Anyway, the only telephone was in Freddy's locked study.

Teodor meandered around the house a while longer, this time daring to enter Freddy's bedroom. He opened his closets and drawers and found racks and piles of the most beautiful sweaters and shirts and trousers and suits. He found cuff links and medals, he found photographs from Paris and London and a big gleaming city of skyscrapers, probably New York, but he could not be sure. He found a charcoal drawing of a young boy, yellowing at the edges, and by tilt-

ing the page this way and that Teodor thought he could see a young Freddy. In a drawer in the night table next to the bed, he found a stack of postcards, naked boys and girls frolicking in nature. *Licht-Luft-Leben* it said on the back of each one, Light-Air-Life. None of these fair and healthy children appeared to be Freddy.

The hour had grown quite late by the time he put everything back in its place and turned out the lights. He washed up and, before changing into Freddy's silk pajamas again, he ran his hand over the crotch and sniffed the fabric for signs of a scene he now barely believed had actually occurred. He checked the verandah door for a lock and bolt but there was none, so neither did he bother to lock the door to his room.

This time he was awake when Freddy staggered in. Teodor could see from his silhouette in the doorway that he was still in uniform, the square epaulets pointed at perfect right angles. Freddy flung his cap on the dresser, struggled to pull off his boots, and climbed in next to Teodor in his low, narrow bed. He reeked of alcohol and cigarettes and his skin was damp with sweat. He lay motionless next to him for several minutes, his breathing slowing down by the minute until Teodor thought he might have fallen asleep.

But he had not fallen asleep, as Teodor, in his heart of hearts, knew. And any doubts he might still have been harboring about the previous night disappeared. By the time Freddy left his bed, Teodor lay curled in a tight ball, sore and raw, feeling stunned and ashamed and despoiled, under the heavy comforter.

Two more days and two more nights passed thus. On the fourth day in Freddy's house neither Cook nor the chauffeur was in residence. Teodor spent the morning rattling the garden gates, looking for a route of escape, then poking through drawers for a set of keys. He could not even gain access to the cellar, where he thought

he might find a ladder tall enough to scale the gate of spears. After a lunch of bread and cheeses he stood at the edge of the garden trying to glimpse the train station he could hear off to the right. When a man or woman walked by, he searched their faces for sympathy to his plight, but found not one he dared signal for help.

Freddy pulled up at the gate, driving the Mercedes himself. "In the house," he ordered Teodor, "I won't have you standing out here like some waif." Once inside the front door Freddy grabbed hold of his waist from behind. But Teodor broke away and ran down the hallway, Freddy in close pursuit. He ran up the stairs but Freddy took them two at a time, overtaking the boy at the top landing. Freddy did not smell of alcohol this time, nor was he disheveled or threatening. He was rough with Teodor, tearing off his clothes with abandon. When he tried to enter him from behind, the boy began to whimper and Freddy stopped.

He lay down next to Teodor, who, though relieved at the reprieve, was now sobbing quietly. Freddy stroked his naked back, kissed his ear. He pulled the boy close and held him, but Teodor continued to cry. Freddy turned the boy's face to his own and kissed him on the mouth, running his tongue over Teodor's lips. Teodor stopped crying and felt himself kissing Freddy back, grateful for kisses instead of something worse. Freddy held him now in a tight embrace, kissing him deeply. Teodor put his arms around Freddy, pressing himself into the man. Frightened and confused, he nuzzled his cheek, his neck, while Freddy sang softly in his ear:

[lyrics to "I Call You Sugar" TK]

Then, almost as a coda, he whispered, "We're at war, Teo." Teodor at first thought he was referring to the two of them. "All borders have been sealed and passage in and out of Germany is impossible right

now." He tried to pull away from Freddy. "I'll take care of you here until we can figure a way to get you back to Denmark." Teodor's arms slackened their grip, but Freddy still clutched him tightly. "You're safe with me," he said.

Y ou're safe with me," he repeats. He seems to be looking right through her.

Only when he stops speaking can she pull herself back to the present, to Tel Aviv. Their Berlins—hers and his—are separated by forty years and a war, but with this telling she finds herself back there, wandering. Martin, Hans-Peter, the wall. And now this Freddy. That city, that street, that villa: they are her story as well.

She staggers into the kitchen, returns with a pitcher of tap water and two glasses. She pours water into each, puts them on the table. He is still staring at the spot where she had been sitting.

She holds one glass in front of him, lifts one of his hands and then the other and curls them around it. Only then does he notice her.

"He told me I was safe with him," he says, looking into her face. His magnificent eyes are asking her a question she cannot answer.

He does not drink from the glass of water.

She folds herself back into a corner of the sofa and waits for him to continue.

For the first month, and the second and third, as he grew accustomed to his metamorphosis from Teodor to Teo, to his new, altered life, little changed in their routines. He made himself scarce during the days, wandering the wooded back garden, reading the art books Freddy set aside for him, writing in his journal. Freddy made a makeshift studio for him in the salon, complete with mirrors, a barre and a phonograph, and Teo did practice most days, but could not maintain the dancer's schedule he needed to keep in shape. He stayed clear of Cook and rarely ran into Albert.

Freddy was never home before dark, but always visited him in his bed at whatever hour he arrived. Quickly, Teo learned to absent himself from these situations, flying off in his mind to sunny afternoons in one dance studio or another or back to his fateful dance at the Staatsoper.

On occasion he found himself trying to explain this new life of his to Sofie; she would float before him, her face blankly impassive, as he told her that what was rightfully hers was being taken from him by force. And yet, he could not deny, to her or to himself, the terrible, bewildering arousal that Freddy provoked in him. After a while his shame was too great, so that when she came to him in daydreams or night dreams he had to push her away. Soon he could no longer recall what it had felt like to hold her in his arms.

Sunday became Teo's favorite day of the week, when Cook and Albert were off and Freddy was home. In the morning Freddy would spend hours showing him his newest acquisitions, works of art he had generously—he said—purchased for the Reich from departing Jews only too happy to rid themselves of unwanted baggage in exchange for much-needed cash. Freddy told him stories about the artists, how their lives crisscrossed their art, how it was the insane or the depraved or the debauched who produced the freshest, most startling work. He explained paint, he explained canvas, he explained light and shadow, perspective and palette, with extraordinary patience and boyish enthusiasm. He shared his secrets about how to judge a fake from the real thing, gave Teo books and articles to study. Teo saw Freddy was in love with the paintings, there was no other way to describe it. He found himself waiting with a conflicting sense of dread and guilty impatience for the moment when Freddy would turn that same proud, amorous gaze on him. Teo worked hard to remember his lessons, to prove a worthy pupil, and with time these oeuvres and their creators became his best friends, his companions through long, dreary days alone.

In good weather they might amble, after a languorous brunch in the enclosed garden, toward the edge of the property, to Freddy's tiny dock on the Halensee, the blue-black lake that lapped at their corner of Berlin. Here he would draw Teo: backed up against a mossy rock, or prone in the grass, or legs dangling in the inky water. Teo posed shirtless, or fully clothed, or in the nude when Freddy could be certain no neighbors were watching them from their own docks. Sometimes he dashed off sharp, angular pencil drawings and other times he lingered, using oil paints he would mix and mix until the soft hues were exactly as he desired. Once he used a huge canvas—the length of Teo's body—rendering him life-size, sprawled lazily

among rows of pink cyclamen Freddy had planted especially for this purpose. At these times he doted on Teo, was his mentor, and the boy was enthralled almost to the point of forgetting the man's other, malevolent, side.

Teo never saw what Freddy did with those drawings and paintings, where he stored them, nor did he ever glimpse them again.

When it was too cold or dreary for drawing they would stay in the house, where Freddy would place a record on the phonograph for Teo to dance. Mostly he selected French or Russian composers, as romantic and airy as possible, and Teo would fit them with some routine he had once learned to other music. Sometimes he simply danced a Bournonville lesson, since Freddy would never know he was watching a Danish dance class, and it felt good to Teo to remember what he had been taught. Freddy was invariably enraptured, his hand often hiding much of his face: his teary eyes, his panting mouth. Later in the afternoon, if there was still enough light in the sky and if Freddy was not aroused, he might unlock the gates and drive Teo to the Tiergarten or Charlotten-Schlossgarten for a stroll, or to Café Kranzler or the Breitscheidplatz for coffee and a cream cake, safe in the knowledge that without the forged certificates and papers he had had prepared for the boy by a Jew living underground in the Kreuzberg district, Teo would never try to escape. In public, when he thought no one was looking, Freddy would rub his hand on the front of Teo's trousers or plant a sharp kiss on his lips. Once or twice they were nearly caught, but Freddy merely laughed off these close calls. Teo prayed these moments would end quickly and without incident.

Just before Christmas Freddy announced he would be going home to his family for the holidays. At first the plan was to leave Teo alone in Berlin, but this worried Freddy for reasons he did not share with Teo. And besides, he told him one evening in his study while

making Teo stand naked in front of him as he drank and sketched and drank some more, he would go mad without touching the boy's smooth thighs, he would fall ill if he could not taste his lips every day.

In the week before their departure Teo saw more of Berlin than he had for all these long months. Freddy took him to buy clothing, had his hair cut and lightened. He took Teo to hear Hitler speak at a rally in the sports stadium, but he became excited groping Teo under a coat placed strategically over their laps and they left early, Freddy racing the car home and pouncing on Teo when they had barely gotten through the front door.

During that week Freddy brought home for Teo a thigh-length *Waffenrock* military coat with braided silver belt, piped *steingrau* trousers and a pair of white gloves. He taught him about his family's Christmas traditions and rituals, and coached him on the few remaining sounds he made that were not perfectly German in their enunciation. "Make your h's softer and all your other consonants harsher," he scolded him. "You Poles sound like you're mashing your food when you talk."

Two days before Christmas they left Berlin, both Freddy and Teo in full-dress uniform, the Mercedes piled high with gifts for his family and their own luggage.

They drove south past Leipzig, stopping twice at roadblocks at which Freddy instructed Teo to speak as little as possible. Each time, as their papers were being scrutinized nearby, Freddy rubbed his hand between Teo's thighs with one hand and squeezed his own member with the other while Teo gazed listlessly out the window, silently willing the guards to send them on their way quickly. Back on the road, Freddy opened the windows to the cold air, banging the steering wheel jubilantly, shout-singing an odd mixture of nursery rhymes and songs the enlisted men sang. He glanced at Teo during

one particularly raunchy ditty and laughed. "So grave, *Liebchen*," he said, tousling his hair. "We're having fun. Stop looking so serious!"

They stayed overnight at a small inn east of Regensburg, at the edge of the Bohemian Forest. While Freddy slept deeply atop a pile of down comforters, Teo threw open the wooden shutters and swallowed the cold air deep into his lungs. He heard music from somewhere in the village, something he had once danced to back in Poland, and thoughts of escape entered his head. Freddy had locked them in and pocketed the key, but perhaps he could climb out onto the low roof and jump to the terrace of another suite. In uniform and with exquisitely forged papers, he thought he might just get somewhere. He looked at Freddy sleeping innocently, glanced outside to the quiet village below. He lifted the poker from the fireplace, tested the sharpness of the tip; would it penetrate Freddy's temple, bore through his brain? Freddy stirred and Teo returned the poker to its place, choosing, instead, to strip to his underwear and dance to the music, unable to leap in that tiny German inn but following the dance through nonetheless, flying and twirling in his mind. His body ached to move to its fullest, to push through gravity to the other side of movement. But the walls and the roof and the furniture—and the man sleeping soundly on a bed of comforters—had caged him in. Eventually he dressed, curled up on a small sofa under a window, covered himself with a heavy curtain, and slept.

Teo was awakened by Freddy before dawn for a rough and numbing hour on a thick rug in front of a hot fire. In the small breakfast room below they were served eggs and sausages by the fat, smiling, innkeeper's wife, who praised their bravery and kept up a continuous rant about the Jews. Freddy found this highly amusing and goaded her into telling one venomous story after the next, tossing laughing winks all the while to his young companion.

By late morning they were climbing into the mountains. "Fresh air at last," Freddy said with a smile. A while later he pointed to a snowy peak straight ahead of the car. "Look a bit down and to the right," he instructed Teo. "That's Schloss Edelwald." It was a fairy-tale castle of turrets and ramparts. Teo wondered where he would be sleeping.

Another hour passed as Freddy sped recklessly around bend after bend before they reached the castle. He tooted the horn loudly as they entered the cobblestone courtyard. A young boy, eight or nine, emerged first from the castle doorway, but a girl with a small bou-quet of flowers clutched in her hand pushed past him and jumped into her father's arms. Presently, Freddy's wife and mother appeared with a toddler and several servants. Teo watched the boy, dressed in lederhosen and a Tyrolean jacket, as he stopped halfway to the car and stood waiting to be summoned, while his sister was still enjoying a big, hearty hug from her father.

Teo thought about his own sister, Margot, who would be ten now. He tried to imagine her taller and older than he had last seen her, but he could conjure no clear picture of her. Nor could he precisely remember his parents' faces. He sat watching this family's reunion from the car, his throat clogged with sadness.

Freddy embraced his plain wife perfunctorily, and made the baby cry when he wrenched him from his mother's arms. Teo stepped slowly from the car and marched across the courtyard past the curi-ous children to the arched doorway. "Pleased to make your acquain-tances, your ladyships," he pronounced carefully, as Freddy had instructed him. "Heil Hitler," responded Freddy's wife, and Teo was not certain whether this were not a reproach.

"Teo," Freddy was shouting, "meet my son Leopold. Leo—Teo, Teo—Leo!" Freddy and his little girl laughed heartily at the silly

rhyme. The boy eyed Teo with suspicion, his face grave, but he bowed politely.

Freddy had Teo assigned to a large circular room in the castle's highest turret, despite the protestations of the baronesses von Edelwald, who had planned for him to occupy a more central wing of the house. Freddy was adamant, however, insisting on the spectacular view for this guest who, he explained to the ladies, was from flat Schleswig-Holstein, up near the Danish border, and should take full advantage of the mountain view. More importantly, the stairs to the turret were accessible by a passage that lay hidden behind a bookcase in Freddy's study.

Here in the south, in his ancestral home, Freddy was bolder than ever. He visited Teo's bed every night full of mountain air and ardor. The weather in the valleys was particularly mild, so during the day he took the boy on drives to secluded forests where they hiked and picnicked and he could find more opportunities for reckless sex. If the children were permitted to accompany them, Freddy would tease them into a game of hide-and-seek in order to steal a few orgiastic moments with Teo, or send them on missions to find wildflowers or berries. Once, as Freddy smothered him in a field of purple and yellow loosestrife, Teo thought for one sickening moment that he spied Leopold glowering at them from behind a spindly birch.

Just after the new year, Freddy announced a family ski trip on a nearby mountain slope. The next morning they set out, with Freddy and Teo up front and the rest of the family in the back. A servant had driven up the mountain earlier with their ski equipment and food. By eleven o'clock they were on the slopes. The baroness stayed with the children on the easier slopes, while Freddy insisted that Teo join him on one of the higher slopes. "You'll learn to ski quickly when there's no way but down."

After a brief lesson at the top of the mountain, Teo took to skiing with ease. Freddy brought him down the slope in stages. When they reached the bottom Freddy threw his arms around Teo and lifted him in the air. A few other skiers took note.

The next time, Freddy led Teo to the back side of the same mountain, a steeper run on the shaded side of the hill. Here it was colder, gray and bleak. Teo saw few skiers below them.

They skied quickly this time, Teo trying to keep pace with Freddy without tumbling dangerously. Several times Freddy got far ahead and Teo lost sight of him. He nearly ran into Freddy in a long arcing curve, surprised to find him waiting in a grove of three or four tall firs off to the side of the piste. From here, the lower hills were just barely visible. Teo thought he could see the baroness and the children skiing slowly down a nearby slope.

Freddy pulled him in close, their woolen snow jackets hissing as they slid together. He kissed Teo roughly on the mouth and plunged his tongue deep into his throat until he nearly choked. Teo's eyes were open, he could still see skiers on other hills careening silently down the slopes.

Freddy had his hands around Teo's neck now, mashing their faces together. He maneuvered his right ski between Teo's so that the boy's leg stood squarely against his groin, then leaned in to ensure that Teo would feel his hardness through bone and flesh, through lined gabardine ski pants and thick underwear. Freddy's eyes stayed closed as he rubbed himself slowly on Teo's leg, pulling the boy closer all the time and smothering him with kisses from his warm, pink mouth.

Freddy pushed Teo away from him, just slightly, and Teo thought this crazy moment on a ski slope in gray daylight was over and they could continue down the mountain. Freddy took a brief look around, then pushed Teo to his knees. With his right hand he unbuttoned his

ski pants and fumbled through his underwear, while with his left he held on to Teo's hair, a tinted blond tuft caught neatly between his long, thin fingers.

Teo was frantic to find a way for Freddy to finish quickly. He was pulling too hard on his hair, smashing his nose into his groin, and the cold snow was beginning to seep through his trousers to his knees. Freddy was at a steady rhythm, plunging himself deeply into Teo's throat, when suddenly he released his grip on the boy's hair and stopped pumping. He pulled Teo to a standing position. Freddy's face was wild, his mouth a crooked frown. "Step out of your skis and your snow boots," he ordered. "Now, quickly!" he added, in the moment that Teo hesitated.

While Teo did as told, settling his stocking feet gingerly onto the freezing snow, Freddy yanked the boy's ski clothing and underclothes away from his body and pointed to his socks. "Take those off, too," he said brusquely. Again, Teo did as ordered and stood, finally, bare and shivering in front of Freddy.

Freddy rubbed his hands up and down Teo's chest, tweaked his erect nipples and gave a tug to Teo's limp penis. He pulled him close again, at first in an embrace that Teo mistook for a kind gesture, Freddy wanting to warm up his freezing body. But Freddy was groping for his buttocks, the buttons on his ski jacket boring small circles of freezing pain into the skin up and down the boy's chest.

Freddy turned him around, spit into his hand, made an initial stab at forcing his way in. Teo stood frozen and raw, stunned and numb, too shocked to plead or argue. He no longer cared whether another skier would catch them there; in fact he no longer felt guiltily complicit in this horrible act, but, finally, a victim. And although he knew that if caught and brought before the authorities it would be he who would be punished and not Freddy the aristocrat and

high-ranking officer, Teo nevertheless prayed for someone, anyone, to come close enough to them to interrupt Freddy and make him realize the madness of his obsession. But the slopes were eerily silent, deserted, and Teo could imagine Freddy having bribed some ski patrolman above to keep skiers off their slope for an hour. He was devastated to realize that in this horrifying moment, as always, no one would come to his rescue.

A raven cawed noisily overhead and for a brief second Teo thought the bird had pulled Freddy back to his senses. Instead, Freddy pushed him roughly to the snow, flat out on his belly, and was immediately on top of him, tearing at him with more ferocity than he ever had before. He clawed and pawed and humped him, mashed his face and body into the snow thrusting himself deep, deeper, without compassion or mercy. Finally, after several terrible minutes, when Teo could no longer contain his shivering pain, he began to scream and sob. Freddy, hearing Teo, increased his pace and his ferocity, pushed harder and harder and, much too late for Teo, released himself in a raging gush. Teo was by this time barely conscious, no longer moving, and so he pulled himself off the boy, roused him, and dressed his raw, bluish body, talking the whole time to revive him. He put him on his own skis but then moved him down the hill pressed up against his back, until they reached the lodge a difficult twenty minutes later.

"He fell behind and I didn't realize he'd taken a spill," Freddy told the startled attendants. "He must have lain in the snow for half an hour before I reached him." They covered Teo with blankets and plied him with hot chocolate, but his fever was climbing and he could not stomach the drink.

Back at the castle, Teo remained bedridden and delirious with fever for days. A nurse was brought in to care for him, but Freddy

himself insisted on doing most of the nursing, ignoring the comments made by his wife and his mother. He ladled warm broth into Teo's mouth, kissing away the droplets that remained on his lips. He carried the boy tenderly to the toilet, cooled his forehead with dampened cloths and lay next to him on the bed, holding him tight to keep him from shivering. He sang to him:

[lyrics to "One Look at You" TK]

He read to him of Alexander the Great, and of the Emperor Hadrian, whose love for the dark and lithe lad Antinous he claimed was the greatest love the world had ever known. He begged Teo to get well quickly, promised him they would leave the south just as soon as he could travel. He was oblivious to Leopold who, silent and stealthy, crept up the secret stairway to spy on them. They needed to return to Berlin, Freddy told Teo, where they could continue their life together. He knelt next to Teo's bed. "I love you," he told him as Teo drifted off to sleep, his fingers tangled lightly in his beloved's hair.

But Teo thrashed in his bed, finding himself back on the Staatsoper stage, poised to begin his solo. He could hear the boots of the German vice-minister receding into the darkness backstage, could see the NO JEWS sign on the Unter den Linden; he was staring into the faces of two thousand rapturous Germans—suddenly his official enemies—awash with the excitement of an impending victory and conquest. He could also now, with a clarity of vision he had not experienced since leaving home, see his family: his sister, Margot, her weak eye and black, kinky hair, her shy and lovely smile; his father, Oskar, wiping his eyes and waving from the pier in Danzig; and mostly his mother, Rosa, at his side for every adventure and every disappointment. Anger rushed up from the floorboards through his body so violently that it nearly threw him from the bed. In wakeful

dreams his legs shot up from the floor, his arms flung out from his shoulders. He felt out of control of his own body. He was suddenly a bloodred demon spinning across the stage, setting the floor beneath him on fire with each pirouette. His skin was burning, his fingers and toes were stilettos, each movement was razor-sharp, each breath fire. Kill, slash, burn. The music was faster than he had ever heard it, the sweet melodies gave way to leering violins and mocking clarinets; or maybe there was no music at all, maybe the musicians had caught fire and imploded, maybe, too, the audience had burned up, the hall smoky with the scent of singed fur and silk and human hair. He did not know what had happened to them all for sure, he could see and hear only red, a screaming, howling, throbbing, fuming red. He was no longer dancing: he was hurtling, flying, flailing; he was a tornado, a tidal wave, an earthquake, a volcano. His body was a devil's chorus of shouts and groans, a cacophony of pain. And then, after one final tremendous leaping spin in the air—around and around and around so many times, too many times—he landed, and there was a tiny moment of complete silence before sound erupted and washed over him and he was aware of the musicians stomping their feet and tapping their bows to their instruments, the audience jumping from their seats to shout *Bravo! Bravissimo!* Up to the highest balcony he could see them, their hands raw from clapping, their mouths open and red, barking praises. Every last one of them, save one officer, so close by at the edge of the first balcony, simply staring at him.

He took it all in, rooted. He did not smile, nor would he bow down before them. The audience was still applauding with ecstatic energy when he dashed from the stage and vomited noisily into a pail of water holding dozens upon dozens of perfect white roses.

Teo opened his eyes to find Freddy wiping his brow.

Several weeks passed before Teo was fully well enough to make the trip to Berlin. Freddy remained solicitous, and although he resumed his sexual demands before Teo's fever had completely waned, he was gentler than before, cautious and tender with his depleted boy. He kissed Teo more than he had before, held him for long hours in his arms, told him he loved him and needed him. Once, as they lay together, he asked the boy whether he loved him in return.

Teo held his breath until a small bird trilled outside the window. Freddy did not ask him again.

It was nearly February by the time they returned to Berlin. Germany's war was clearly going well; the city was full of bunting and flags and cheering crowds. At home, Freddy felt it would be a danger for Teo to be around Cook any longer; she had been suspicious from the start about his origins and Freddy worried she might turn them both in. He installed Teo in an old servant's bedroom at the back of the cellar, where he remained motionless and silent during daylight hours; Cook was informed that their guest had at long last returned to Denmark. Then, after a week, he fired both Cook and Albert on the pretense that he would be closing the Berlin house until further notice.

It then became Teo's job to cook and keep house, which he did without interest. Day after day, locked in the gated house and forbidden even from strolling in the garden, he made simple meals, washed and ironed Freddy's clothes, made the beds and swept the floors and all the while dreamt his dreams: of his family, of returning to Denmark to dance, of simply walking out the front gate and into a park, where he could watch the swans bathe and squabble. He dreamt of Madame Valentina, his ballet teacher in Warsaw, who (he had no way of knowing) had been killed as the small airplane ferrying her and her diplomat husband to a new posting in the Congo had sputtered and swooped, plunging with grace into a cool lake at the edge of the jungle.

Freddy became more and more busy as the war blazed on. He was up early, gone before Teo could climb from their bed and home often past midnight. Occasionally he would be away for several days, after which he would return with a new painting or sculpture. He had less time and less patience to explain these works to Teo now.

On a crisp Sunday morning in autumn 1941, more than two years after Teo had come to Berlin, Freddy announced an outing. "Pack us a picnic lunch, we're taking a drive." Teo was glad for the diversion, but surprised to see that Freddy was taking his leather bag of magnifying glasses, solvents, brushes, tweezers and chisels with them, as if going to work. On the way out of town Teo spotted passersby with yellow Stars of David pinned to their coats. He swiveled his head to get a better look, which Freddy noticed. "New regulations," he explained. "Can't leave the house without them. I understand Jews in other parts of the Reich have been wearing them for a while already." Teo could see that Freddy was bothered by this medieval form of ostracism, but his mood was too jubilant to ruin.

"Why do they stand for it, why didn't they leave?" Teo asked, his gaze fixed on a young Jewess just passing in front of the car.

"They can't anymore, Teo, but even when they had the chance they stayed, always thinking the situation would improve." Teo thought about all those clever Jews on the ship bound for America, and his own parents probably still in Warsaw.

"You know," Freddy said in a matter-of-fact voice, "a frog will leap out of his pond if you pour a lot of hot water in all at once. But if you add it slowly, gradually, the frog will remain through discomfort, then danger, then death. He never figures out it's time to jump, and then it's too late."

"Some frogs," Teo said quietly, "don't have a choice."

They headed west in the Mercedes, toward Brandenburg, but turned off at an estate on the Havel River. As they entered a huge park of forests and ponds with an enormous home set at the river's edge, Teo read the name Himmel-an-der-Havel—Heaven on the Havel—on the stone portals.

They pulled up in front of the house, where the door was opened by a thin and sallow man in an elegant suit. Freddy bounded up the stairs and shook hands warmly with the man. "Teo, come meet Ernst Halberstadt, Berlin's foremost collector of art and my most esteemed teacher. Ernst, this is my assistant, Teo." Teo was surprised by the thin man's strong and bony grip on his hand. "Please, do come in," he told them both.

Inside, the house was nearly denuded of furniture, and what remained was covered in cloth. Halberstadt was clearly planning an imminent departure. "My apologies for the state of affairs here," he told his guests as they passed through the kitchen to a hidden stairway that led down to a secret room underneath the house. Here it was cozy if crowded, obviously the room to which Halberstadt had removed all his most essential belongings. There was a bed, a desk, several chairs, neat piles of clothing on a bureau and a large bookcase built into the stone walls. A fire glowed in the hearth. Herr Halberstadt invited them to be seated while he poured three snifters of brandy.

"Ernst, you'd be proud of your pupil," Freddy said as he stuffed and lit his pipe. "I picked up an exquisite van Gogh and discovered a brilliantly forged Brueghel last week, both in the same collection. Stein family, you know them, they love anything Dutch. I don't believe they knew what they had, the old wheezer blanched and almost fainted when I showed him the worthless Brueghel. Must have paid a fortune for that one, though I had the feeling he'd gotten the van Gogh for a song."

Herr Halberstadt was mainly quiet, nodding occasionally or asking a question when Freddy's prattle slowed. He had a neatly trimmed mustache that twitched and bobbed and seemed to have a life of its own. Several times Teo caught Halberstadt peering over his snifter at him.

After a refill of brandy Freddy sat up higher in his chair. "Well, now, Teo, we've come to help our dear friend Ernst here with a problem he's having. You see, like yourself, Ernst is of the Jewish persuasion and should have left Germany long ago." Teo and Ernst exchanged glances, each quite astonished. "But he could not part with his art, and couldn't get it out of Germany, either, so he stayed. Now we're going to help him escape."

Ernst stood, pulled a book from the shelf on the wall, reached his hand into the empty space and then stepped back from the shelf. The entire bookshelf spun slowly sideways, revealing another room behind the cozy sitting room. "Ah, the good stuff!" Freddy said as he tapped the remaining tobacco leaves from his pipe and put it in his pocket. The three of them passed by the bookshelf and into the room.

Even Freddy was silent as they stood on the threshold peering in. It was a large room, perhaps the size of the entire floor above them, and it was completely full of the most sumptuous works of art. Teo could identify many, had seen a number of them in Freddy's art books. But there were others, new and raw and exciting, that he did not yet know.

Freddy pointed to one canvas standing nearby. "That Soutine," he said, breaking the silence. "I'm sure I saw it at the firefighters' headquarters before the war, when they burned all those priceless works of 'degenerate' art. You managed to salvage it," he said with awe.

Halberstadt nodded. Then he turned toward Teo and raised his

hand feebly in the general direction of the crowded room. "My life's work," he said with a sigh.

"Your obsession," Freddy said offhandedly.

"My passion," Ernst corrected him.

Freddy shrugged. "What's the difference?"

"Oh," Ernst said, turning to face him, "the ancient Romans could tell you. Passion means suffering, the suffering of intense desire that remains unfulfilled. So Toulouse-Lautrec had an insatiable passion for shady women that never dissipated. Gustav Mahler for Alma, Kafka for Milená Jesenská; how about our own marvelous Else Lasker-Schüler, with her poems full of strange, protean passions? I could name scores of the greatest artists and writers and composers, all of whom were driven by this wonderful, terrible, consuming passion that, in the best of cases, erupts like lava into the most beautiful works man has ever created, or for the less artistically inclined among us, into new inventions, the massing of wealth or technology."

Freddy smiled broadly. "Then I am a man of passion."

Ernst seemed to weigh his words before letting them out. "I hope for your sake it's passion and not obsession. Passion creates, but obsession destroys. Your Mr. Hitler, for example, has his obsessions and I am about to pay for them with my own life's passion, these most astonishing works of beauty."

"You shall be reunited with them after the war, I'm certain of it," said Freddy.

"Which will you be taking with you?" Ernst asked.

"Well, first we need to work from your catalogue. You do, I assume, have a complete catalogue?"

Ernst nodded.

"From that we'll create a new catalogue for my department. Teo here has a lovely handwriting, we'll ask him to record our selections.

That's what I'll be working from when I come with my team to remove them. As for my own selections, I have a few ideas, but let's get to work and make those decisions later."

For hours the three of them created a new catalogue and hauled each selected artwork upstairs to what had been the library. Ernst seemed to mourn each selection, though some caused him more grief than others. When they had finished, the library was filled with twenty-two paintings and six sculptures. The secret room underneath the house still contained at least eighty paintings as far as Teo could tell, and perhaps two dozen sculptures.

On their last trip downstairs Freddy stood looking at the remaining works and, hands on hips, said, "Ernst, you know my tastes. I can't leave without that exquisite Monet and the boy dancer by Degas. I thought he'd only sculpted girls."

"That's the only one," Ernst said evenly.

"Now I know I should be happy with those two, but, well, there's just one more I'd like, and I know it's being selfish but I can't resist."

"She'll bring you trouble," Ernst said.

"I know. The best things always do."

"Leave her here Freddy, come visit. She'll be safer at Himmel-an-der-Havel than in the middle of Berlin."

"I can't Ernst, I have to have her. I've always wanted her, you know that."

Ernst sighed heavily. "You haven't changed, young Baron von Edelwald. You are talented and clever, but you let your obsessions blind you, you do not know when to stop."

Teo expected him to take offense, but Freddy laughed loud and hard. "Right you are!" he said cheerfully. "You know my motto, Ernst: *Ad astra*. There's no stopping until you've gone all the way to the stars." He pushed past them to the back of the

deep room, returning a moment later with a smallish portrait, one that Teo had not noticed before. He placed it on an easel and flicked on an overhead lamp. The three men stood in front of the painting, silent.

It was, Teo could see for himself instantly, glorious. A pale young woman in a butter-yellow ermine-trimmed cloak, her gathered hair the color of sun-baked wheat, stands fiddling with a pearl necklace around her neck. She is gazing at herself in a small mirror on the wall, or perhaps she is enraptured by whatever is taking place outside the window next to the mirror.

Teo was intrigued by the bland nonchalance of her expression, the simplicity of her gaze. She seemed completely self-absorbed, clearly unaware of the attention she was drawing. In fact, he suddenly realized, she reminded him of Sofie Sonnenfeld. He quietly revisited their pas de deux late that one afternoon in Copenhagen, and he wondered what had become of her and her family. Did she think of him sometimes, or did she presume him dead?

"She's more than two hundred and fifty years old, but she's sweet and pure as a fresh-cut flower," Freddy said with hushed passion. Teo turned to look briefly into Freddy's face; this was a voice he had heard Freddy use only when ardor and desire had taken over his senses.

"Look here, Teo," Freddy said, without taking his gaze from the painting. "Vermeer was a genius with light. Look how the room is flooded with it from the little window here, next to the mirror. Look how the light is refracted in the curtains, in the wall, and especially in her robe."

Teo, too, was captivated. Freddy instructed him, "Now tell Herr Halberstadt where the vanishing point of the painting is."

"Just above the tabletop," he answered dutifully.

"And what do you think this chair is doing in the foreground?"

"Perhaps it has something to do with depth? The chair seems to add space between the girl and us."

"Well said," Ernst remarked. Freddy beamed.

"And why do we think Mr. Vermeer chose to put pearls on his model?"

Teo thought for a moment. He could not recall any paintings with pearls in his apprenticeship with Freddy, or having learned anything about them. "Purity?" he ventured. "Perfection?" Teo glanced from Freddy to Ernst.

"In fact," Ernst answered, "we cannot truly know. To some painters pearls did symbolize virginity and purity. To others, pearls were a symbol of womanhood, or motherhood. And indeed, Vermeer's young lady, who may in fact be his niece, looks as though she might have been pregnant. Mostly, however, pearls were a symbol of vanity, and this was certainly an accepted theme among Dutch painters of the seventeenth century. The mirror, too, may be there to remind us of the worthlessness and transience of all things worldly." Ernst nodded to himself, and glanced around at the room still full of art.

"She is exquisite, one of a kind, Ernst," Freddy exclaimed, ignoring his quiet reverie. "You were a genius for getting her away from the Pergamon."

"Oh, but of course I had nothing to do with that. These are strange times, who better than you would know that, my friend. Everything is in flux. I was simply clever enough to recognize her when she was made available, and rich enough to give her a good home."

"But Ernst, I feel certain you will agree with me that there is still one work of art in this room even more beautiful than our exquisite *Frau mit Perlen*."

Ernst raised his eyebrows in surprise but said nothing. Freddy turned to Teo and kissed him full on the mouth. "This young man, of the mismatched eyes, is more perfect and quite a bit more responsive than anything here." To Teo he said, "Don't look so shocked. Ernst is a fellow connoisseur."

He hit Teo squarely on the bum and shepherded him up the stairs, his treasures in tow.

At the front door Freddy removed a small box and an envelope from his work bag and placed them in Ernst's hand. "The documentation and tickets should get you safely to Switzerland, where I suggest you wait until this madness is over." He opened the box for Ernst, and poked his finger into the contents. "You've got some larger ones and some smaller ones, should fetch almost one hundred thousand francs from the right people. This one little blue diamond is apparently worth half that alone." He plucked the stone from its bed with his thumb and forefinger, held it to the light and passed it to Teo. After inspecting it carefully, Teo offered it to Ernst, who declined. He laid it in the box next to the others, and Freddy replaced the lid.

"I hope you know something about sewing, you'll really have to hide those things carefully. But keep one or two for bribes if necessary. There's some cash, too, in the envelope," he said as he let himself out the front door and made his way to the car. He opened the door for Teo, then bounded back up the stairs.

"Good luck, old friend," he said with emotion as he embraced Ernst Halberstadt and raced back down the steps to the car. He did not look back as they sped out through the park, toward Berlin.

Freddy was brimming with excitement on the trip home. He turned his head frequently to catch a glimpse of the Vermeer on the back seat, and chatted loquaciously. "If I am correct, even our wise

friend Ernst does not know how valuable this painting really is. I believe that the *Woman with a Pearl Necklace* is the first in a series of five canvases Vermeer painted in this same room, this same corner, with the same young lady, most often in her glorious gold robe. The action from picture to picture tells a story, for sure, but on a deeper level may even hint at political and social developments in Holland at the time. I'm working on a theory right now."

The car was waved through a roadblock and Freddy continued.

"In the other paintings, our lady is involved in seemingly domestic occupations. But in ours she is preoccupied, not really paying attention to the necklace at her throat. It's the window that draws our attention, and hers, especially the light from outside. In fact, King Louis XIV of France had at that very time marched on Spanish Holland and the country was in turmoil. The letters our lady is seen writing in the other paintings may well have something to do with that, some sort of espionage. And in our painting there is no map on the wall. In *Woman Playing a Lute Near a Window*, for example, that same wall holds a huge map of Western Europe."

"Look at these," he said, fishing several sheets of folded paper from his breast pocket, reproductions of paintings. He tossed them onto Teo's lap. "*Woman Playing a Lute Near a Window, Lady Writing a Letter, Lady with Her Maidservant, The Guitar Player.* And now our lady of the pearl necklace. How grand to have found the fifth and last, or rather first, in the set. Do you see, Teo, do you see?"

Teo scrutinized them, then looked to Freddy's new painting on the back seat for some clues.

It was the same woman in each, indeed, in the same buttery cloak. Sometimes she wore her hair in ribbons, sometimes in long curls. Mostly she looked to the left—out a window, at her maid, at someone outside the frame of the painting—but once, taking a break

from writing, she gazed directly at the painter with a small smile of recognition. Maybe even complicity.

Teo, however, was not interested in Freddy's theory. In fact, since leaving Halberstadt, only one question had been on his mind. So when, on a particularly dangerous curve that shut Freddy up for a moment and forced him to drive with caution—more for Messieurs Vermeer, Degas and Monet than for their own safety, he knew—Teo turned in his seat to face Freddy and asked, "Were those diamonds real?"

Freddy frowned, and Teo noticed his knuckles, strained and white, on the steering wheel. Then suddenly a pleasant smile spread across his face and he reached to stroke Teo's cheek. Teo turned his head before Freddy's hand could touch him, swinging around in his seat to face the side window.

Later that evening, as Freddy lay deeply sleeping and Teo sat up in bed watching the pearl lady on her easel, Ernst Halberstadt, age fifty-six, art collector and lifelong bachelor, last in a line of four hundred years of German Jews, including a brother killed in the Emperor's service in the Great War, was stopped at Eisleben, not one hundred kilometers from his home on the Havel, and was divested of his diamonds, his tickets, his documents, his hat, his shoes and his clothes, then shot in the back of the head and hurled into a shallow grave with four other hapless travelers.

A garbage truck lumbers by. Though the sky is still black she realizes that a new day will be starting soon. The sun will rise again, miraculous and defiant. Pincho has not returned home.

Her body feels violated. Her knees are pressed together, an afghan from the back of the couch is wrapped round her and still she feels defiled. He has not stirred, not so much as crossed one leg over the other. At one point while he was talking she leaned toward him, removed the full glass of water from his cupped hands and placed it in front of him on the table.

She stands, stretches, moves to the window. Cool air enters her in shallow breaths and she wishes she were still smoking. Everything down in the street is as it was yesterday, and the day before.

He picks up his story before she has returned to her place on the sofa.

M onths passed, and years, and in spite of the escalating chaos of the world around him Teo's cloistered life was constant and unchanging. He grew accustomed to bombs that fell nightly, as close as Charlottenburg, rattling dishes and glasses and occasionally knocking a painting to the floor. Sometimes he dreamt of, and even prayed for, a bomb in Grunewald, one that would blast away the tall gate holding him captive. He would run down Erbacherstrasse to the Grunewald train station, but there the dream always ended; he had no papers, no money, and he knew his freedom was not good for more than a few hundred meters.

With the decreasing variety and quantity of food, he had less to prepare and with Freddy's more frequent absences, he had less house-keeping to account for. Freddy denied him access to the radio, he was forbidden contact with every human being and had to stay away from windows at all times. Sometimes, deep in the house where he could be certain no one would hear, he would put Lena Horne on the gramophone to recall what it was like to feel something, feel anything:

[lyrics to "Prisoner of Love" TK]

He was to leave no trace of his presence at any time, lest an impromptu search be conducted. He returned books to their places on the shelf

even if he was only walking down the hall to the kitchen for a few minutes. He shared a single toothbrush with Freddy, he dried droplets in the sink and hid the moistened hand towel from view. On one frightening occasion he had heard Freddy making a commotion at the front gate and looked out in time to see him entering noisily in the company of two uniformed officers. Freddy had fumbled long enough with the lock in the front door to enable Teo to shimmy into a tiny space behind the pantry, his appointed hiding place. The men stayed for an hour, in spite of Freddy's mixture of reassurances and outraged ranting, finding not a single clue that Freddy lived anything but the life of a faithful husband forced away from his family and castle.

Teo began to fancy himself a ghost. Where once his physical presence, his dancer's physique, had been the focus of his world, now he paid no attention to his body at all. His solid muscles slackened, his pliancy waned. He glided lightly from room to room, even dust lay undisturbed in his wake. He spoke rarely, either to himself or to Freddy, when he was around. He no longer fantasized or dreamed, elaborate plans to murder Freddy and escape the house in disguise drifted away like so much smoke. His expression carried the look of a man once stunned, now jaded.

For he was now, indeed, a man. He had passed eighteen, nineteen, twenty in this secluded villa in Berlin. Had Freddy not insisted, Teo would have let his hair grow long and unkempt, would not have bothered to shave the new whiskers that crowded his narrowing face. He was maturing, no longer the fawnlike boy who had come from Copenhagen to dance for the Führer. He was taller now, fully as tall as Freddy. Hair sprouted on his chest, but this, too, Freddy demanded he remove.

His twenty-first birthday passed but he could not recall ever having reached twenty. He barely remembered his family, now so many

years distant though really, he hoped, still only a pleasant day's drive over the wheat plains of northern Central Europe. The Sonnenfeld family had scattered from his mind like so much ash, though he could still picture Sofie's tapered fingers. His own fingers twitched as he imagined lifting her in the air, her thighs soft and buttery, her skirt fluttering in his face.

Never, ever, did he revisit the Berlin Staatsoper or his dance these days. He would have been unmoved to know that the theater, only a few kilometers to the east of him, was now an annex of Nazi head-quarters or that the stage on which he had danced the dance that had changed his life now held a printing press that printed many of the millions of flyers and manifestos that fluttered from German airplanes and rained down upon Paris, Prague, his own Warsaw. It wasn't that he had forgotten, it was that for Teo that evening, that theater, that dance no longer existed. Their memory had been ex-punged. Where once he had dreamt of escape, had imagined daily the scaling of the gate of his prison, the cool unobtrusive walk through the streets of Berlin, the slow hay wagons that would convey him to Warsaw or Copenhagen, now his imagination prevented him even from passing through the locked front door of this villa.

On his twenty-second birthday, a cold gray morning in the month of February 1944, in a small window of time between massive British air raids and massive American air raids on Berlin, Teo prized open the French doors to the small verandah over the front entrance to the house. He could smell Freddy on him, smeared across his skin like an ointment. Teo had not recognized the date until Freddy presented him with a tiny packet of chocolates wrapped in green tissue paper and tied with a bow, all hard to come by in Berlin, and a risk: what would Ober-stleutnant von Edelwald, whose wife was a world away in the moun-tains near Salzburg, need with a sentimental packet of sweets?

Teo held the packet of chocolates in his hand as he stepped onto the verandah in the cold daylight, dressed only in trousers and shirtsleeves. He unraveled the satin bow, let the tissue paper flutter in the wind, watched the leaf-green sheet lift high into the trees and catch on a thin twig. He lifted the lid of the box, selected a chocolate and sent it soaring over the gate into the street. Two boys running by noticed the chocolate as it landed, pounced to pick it up. "Idiot, you've smashed it," said one to the other. Teo threw another, which hit one of the boys on the side of his head. He stooped to retrieve the chocolate. Both boys looked up at Teo standing on the verandah.

He stared down at them, wordless. He threw another chocolate, then another, and several more boys appeared. By the time two more chocolates rained down on them, general mayhem had broken out, five boys were swinging fists at one another. A whistle sounded from up the street and two Freikorps officers appeared. They pulled the boys apart. They asked no questions, but the evidence of Teo's presence was long gone, the chocolates either consumed and digested or smashed into the sidewalk. The Freikorps men did not look up to discover Teo in his perch, but one of the boys peered at him over his shoulder as he was being dragged off.

Teo sat waiting all afternoon for a knock at his gate. He listened, that evening, for a pounding at the door. None came.

Freddy spoke rarely to Teo of the war; Teo was left to gather scattered crumbs of his conversation, collect hints dropped on the pillow as Freddy drifted off to troubled slumber. Sometimes he would tiptoe down the stairs once Freddy was sleeping soundly, on the off chance that Freddy had left a communiqué or even a newspaper on his desk.

The war had been raging for so long that sometimes Teo could not remember what peacetime was like, what it meant to cross a street or sip hot chocolate in a café. It seemed as though the war would last forever.

In bed one late August morning that year, nearly five years to the day since Teo had arrived in Berlin, Freddy told him that the German army had been forced out of Paris by the English and the Americans. "It's the beginning of the end," he said. He told him how Rome was now in Allied hands, how the Russians were advancing from the east, how Hitler had nearly been killed in an assassination attempt just one month earlier. "That may have sped up the inevitable." In a whisper he added, "It would have been a blessing. How could he think he could fight the whole world and carry out this ridiculous Final Solution at the same time? There simply aren't enough resources for everything all at once."

Teo turned on his side to face Freddy. "Final solution to what?" he asked.

Freddy tried to pull him in close, to gather him to his chest, but Teo resisted. "Final solution to what?" he asked again.

At first it seemed to Teo that Freddy was in pain; he had never seen his face contort in such a way. Then Freddy began to sob heavily, burying his face in Teo's neck. He cried and cried, his heaving body disconsolate. Teo lay still until the sobbing ended and Freddy was breathing normally.

"Final solution to what?" he said quietly to the ceiling.

Freddy lifted himself on one elbow in order to look into his face. "Teo, my teddy, my lovely boy. Tell me just once you love me. Tell me that when this awful, awful war has ended you will forgive me, tell me you won't leave me. I need you, Teo, I need you beside me. I can't imagine . . ." He began to cry again, collapsing onto Teo. Teo let him

spend his crying, then slipped out from under Freddy and away from him, as far away inside the house as he could possibly get.

After that, Teo was hungry for news and took every measure to wrest it away from Freddy. Once or twice he was raped for his efforts, but far more often he played on Freddy's fatigue and his desperate obsession and was successful at trading secrets for sex. That was how in September he learned of the liberation of Brussels, in October the Allied occupation of Athens, in November, the sinking of the *Tirpitz*, Germany's only surviving forty-two-thousand-ton battleship, which the Allies had been after continuously for eighteen months. He enjoyed this new power, felt good about being reciprocated for what he had been forced to give away for so long. He enjoyed, too, Freddy's self-loathing at paying for favors and his constant, painful turmoil.

Less than two weeks into 1945, Freddy came home early, just after dark, ripping off his uniform on the stairs as he sped Teo up to the bedroom. "You're mine tonight, my love. The Russians have captured Warsaw."

Teo stopped. "Warszawa?" he asked in Polish.

"Yes, yes, your Warsaw," Freddy said, now rapidly stripping to his underwear. "The Warsaw where you lost your first tooth and where you began to dance and where your body blossomed into ravishing adolescence." They tussled briefly as Teo resisted, but Freddy was aflame, strong and alert as he had not been in months. He twisted Teo's arm behind his back and pressed him roughly to the wall. "You wanted to play it this way, now pay up."

Teo reached blindly behind him, grabbed Freddy's flesh where he could and squeezed hard. "This may be your last chance," Teo spat through clenched teeth.

Teo saw little of Freddy after that. With constant bombing in Berlin and frontline officers falling regularly and being replaced by others, Freddy was promoted to more serious intelligence work, rapidly rising from Oberstleutnant to Oberst, Generalmajor and finally Generalleutnant in the Abwehr, German Military Intelligence. He was meant to sleep at headquarters but would bribe the guards, taking advantage of the general chaos that was descending on them all, and straggle into bed next to Teo at two or three in the morning, only to leave again before dawn. He no longer begged for sex, he just lay next to Teo and held him, wrapped himself around and over the young man as if trying to absorb him into his every pore. Sometimes Teo would awaken to the light of a lantern and find Freddy staring at him, not touching him at all. Freddy's eyes, full of tears, would plead with him then, but Teo would turn over and feign sleep. Once he heard Freddy singing, weakly, to himself: "*Who'll take my place in your heart when I'm gone? . . . There is no one who will love you like I do.*" Teo no longer worried that Freddy might harm him.

In mid-April Freddy wandered in late one evening looking dazed. He'd attended a concert of the Berlin Philharmonic playing Bruckner's Fourth Symphony. At the exits, members of the Hitlerjugend had handed out free cyanide capsules. "It's all so surreal," he told Teo, incredulous. "The Russians are closing in on Berlin, but my job now is to organize a wonderful party for the Führer's fifty-sixth birthday." He gazed at Teo wildly but did not seem to see him. "A party. With champagne and a cake. Hah! A celebration! And music! But who will play for us? All the best musicians were Jewish, but there are no Jews

in Berlin anymore, no Jews in Germany." Now he was looking at Teo, seeing him. "You, my friend, may be the last one for all we know. You've made it, you know, because I've kept you here safe with me. You can't ever forget that."

"I won't," said Teo coldly. "Ever."

On the day following Hitler's birthday, Berlin lost its gas and electricity. Freddy was only home for an hour or two each day. And then, on the night of April 25, Freddy did not come home at all. He flew into the house late the next morning, a warm and sunny Thursday, his shirttails loose and flapping from his trousers. "The Americans and the Russians have met, they're one hundred twenty kilometers south of here, at Torgau." He ran about the house collecting papers. "I'll be back for you in a few hours, we'll make a break for the north, try our chances outside Berlin. In the meantime, take as much of the art down to the room underneath the garden shed as you can. Just try to put the paintings on furniture, keep them off the ground." He was out the door before Teo could respond, then a second later barged back in. "Keep the Degas dancing boy and the Vermeer up here, we'll take them with us." He tossed the keys to the shed to Teo and was gone.

Teo spent several hours hauling and arranging the works of art, and his shoulders were sore from the effort. He packed what few clothes he owned and set his suitcase beside the door, but years of keeping himself hidden took their toll and he stashed the suitcase in a closet. He could hear commotion in the street, and sometimes passersby would shake the sturdy iron garden gates, but mostly Teo sat immobile, staring at the small statue of a boy dancing.

Teo awoke in his chair in the middle of the night, the house completely dark. He lit a lantern and walked from room to room. There was no sign that Freddy had been there. The noise in the streets grew louder the next day, and still Freddy failed to return. By Sunday Teo

knew Freddy would not be coming back. As the afternoon sun fell in the sky, Teo toured the perimeter of the house and scouted the garden shed for any implements that could help him. Back inside, waiting for dark, he collected portable valuables—Freddy's monogrammed cuff links, a gold cigarette lighter, a fountain pen, and on an impulse, his Bournonville ballet slippers; he did not look for money or his real documents, knowing he would find neither—then as soon as the city had sunk into darkness he dragged a stepladder, several planks and a thick rope out to the tall chestnut tree at the front corner of the garden, nearest the gate, and set to work. From the top of the stepladder he threw the rope over the lowest, sturdiest branch he could reach, then descended and moved the ladder up close to the gate and positioned a plank where he would be able to reach it when he swung from the tree; the idea was to lay the plank over the spearlike tips of the garden gate that would otherwise impale him. Even with occasional pauses as military vehicles lumbered past, the whole operation did not take long to arrange thanks to the extinguished streetlamps, but the execution was considerably more difficult. Teo spent hours swinging on the rope. His hands were raw from the rough hemp, he smashed himself repeatedly into the gate and was bruised on the right and left, and several times, after successfully scaling the top, setting the plank in place and attempting to climb onto it, the plank slipped and he caught the tip of the spear. At one o'clock he went back into the house to rest, since his arms were shaking so that he could no longer hold the rope. He did not awaken until after dawn and was forced to postpone his escape until that evening.

He had experience this time and so, on his third attempt on the evening of April 30, 1945, at just an hour before midnight, Teo left the house in Grunewald for the last time. He had not seen life beyond the gates in nearly three years.

Berlin was not at all as he recalled. Peaceful and gracious avenues were now overrun with rubble and litter and people running this way and that. White-paint messages shouted from every wall: *Every German will defend his capital! Victory or Siberia! Wir kapitulieren nie!* Just two blocks from the house a man ran past him screaming, "*Die Russen sind hier! Die Russen sind hier!*" and then around a corner came a Russian tank, aimed straight at him. Teo signaled to the tank, hoping to stop it, but the tank nearly ran him down and Teo was forced to jump to the side of the avenue, where he fell on the curb.

Suddenly he was being dragged from behind. "You fool," the voice behind him said, "what did you think you were doing?" Teo turned toward the middle-aged man who had just pulled him into a doorway. "That was a Russian tank, did you think he would stop to give you a ride? You're lucky he didn't shoot you or run you down! They've taken over the Reichstag, I saw the flag flying myself. The Reich is dead, some say Herr Hitler, too, long live the Führer! This is it, friend, our days of glory are over."

Teo threw back his head and with a violent heave, spat into the man's face. He dashed back into the street, running and running toward the center of the city, the rubble and madness increasing as he went. Traffic was streaming steadily in the opposite direction as German officers tried to flee and the conquering Russians tried to capture them, or chase them out, Teo was not sure which. There were no streetlights and movement was slow and dangerous.

Teo did not stop to ask himself where he was going; after hours of wandering, nearly run over on several occasions, after dodging stray bullets and falling repeatedly on bricks or bodies, he found himself at the entrance to the Tiergarten. Gone were the swans, gone were the animals in the zoo, gone were most of the trees; the park had been stripped for fuel, for food, for whatever besieged Berliners needed.

Here, on a low, grassy slope, Teo finally fell to the ground and slept until morning.

Teo roamed Berlin for two days, starved and parched. Sometimes he hid in abandoned buildings that looked as though they might fall on top of him, sometimes he returned to one park or another. A bomb fell half a block from him once and set his ears ringing for hours.

On his third morning of wandering about Berlin, two Russian soldiers lifted him off the ground from a deep sleep in a small grave-yard, just several hundred meters from the house that had been his prison and refuge for nearly six years. They brought him to an old stone church, one of the few buildings on the block left standing, and locked him up with twenty other men in a pen built for four or five. "*Ich bin ein Jude*," he protested first in German, then in Polish, but the soldiers were unimpressed. His cellmates eyed him warily, and one elbowed him in the stomach.

The next day Teo and several of his cellmates were called on to testify before being shipped out to a POW camp near Oranienburg. Teo answered all questions, explained his precarious imprisonment in a posh suburban villa, but could sense that his interrogators did not believe his story. Worse, one of the burly Russians seemed as though he might like to take advantage of Teo much like Freddy had.

For nearly a fortnight Teo was treated as a German prisoner of war, incarcerated with other males who had not been at the front: the lame, the insane, the elderly, the boys.

Finally, on his third appearance before the prison administration, he had a reprieve; a Polish Jew had been employed to interrogate the Polish speakers.

"What is your name?" he asked in Polish.

"Teodor Levin, sir. From Warsaw."

"I have heard this name before."

"You have? I was once a dancer . . ."

"Yes, precisely, that's it! I have a folder here somewhere," he said. He left his desk for only a few moments before returning with a dossier that he began to leaf through.

Teo was elated to meet someone who, for the first time in years, knew who he really was.

The man looked from the dossier to Teo and back to the dossier. "You don't look much like your photograph anymore," he said at last. He took Teo's chin in his hand, turned his head from side to side. "But your eyes match the description." He released Teo's face and shook his hand. "My name is Harry Cukier," he said in Polish. "I'd like you to answer a few questions for me."

In fact, it turned out that Cukier knew certain details of Teo's story even better than Teo did. He told Teo that it was Freddy himself who had had him detained and then released to his custody, that Teo could have returned to Copenhagen even in the first few weeks after the outbreak of war, despite what Freddy had told him. He told Teo that members of the Resistance had stopped looking for him years earlier, since a young man traveling under his name, with his identification papers, had boarded a northbound train in January 1940 but was stopped at the Danish border and sent to Sachsenhausen and later Auschwitz, where he perished. "Your baron dispatched some unlucky young man to certain capture and death just to keep you hidden and for himself," Cukier said, shaking his head. "But you are safe and in relatively good health, I see, so no matter what has happened to you, you are far luckier than most of our fellow Jews."

Teo looked down at himself, his body violated but whole. In the weeks following his escape from Grunewald he had been hearing stories of the concentration camps, of torture and deprivation, of beat-

ings and gassings, of mass extermination, the Final Solution Freddy had refused to explain. He had slept through the war on eiderdown in a villa filled with books. He had spent his days tracing the brush stroke of a Matisse or admiring the spectacular color of a Tahitian Gaugin. He closed his eyes tightly. "Do you have any word of my family?" he asked.

Cukier closed the dossier, sighed heavily. "Your parents and your Danish friends were frantic to find you, but Warsaw was under siege almost from the very day you arrived in Berlin. We lost contact with your parents shortly after they were moved into the Ghetto."

Teo held his breath and Cukier continued. "Your father, Oskar, fell ill and passed away there. Your mother, Rosa Levin, was deported to Treblinka in August 1942. She did not survive. Your sister, Margot, however, was not with them, and there is fair reason to believe she was hidden and may be alive today."

Teo's head suddenly felt too heavy for his body. He folded his arms and laid it on top of them, barely breathing. Cukier placed a knobby hand awkwardly on his own. Teo was grateful for this fatherly human touch, but he could muster no emotion. He wanted nothing more than the black obliteration of deep sleep.

They sat this way for several minutes, until Cukier said, "You obviously do not belong in this prison. I'll reassign you to the DP camp. The Sonnenfeld family were ferried to safety in Sweden several years ago, they'll probably already be back in Copenhagen so you may wish to consider relocating there." He stopped talking, and Teo lifted his head from the table. "I wouldn't return to Warsaw if I were you. The city's been razed, it's hard to believe you'll find anyone you know there. Besides, you left so many years ago . . ." Cukier could see that this was too overwhelming for Teo. "Anyway," he continued, "you'll have to think about all this. Try to remember that you've

been very lucky, that you have a new start in life now. Try to return to the living."

In July he returned to Copenhagen, calling himself Teo. The ballet master found him lodgings in an apartment building owned by the Royal Theater, just a small room under the eaves but a place for him to live free of charge. Teo tried working himself into shape, joined a few classes, but no longer possessed the stamina, the flexibility or the drive. Instead he was given a job working with the youngest dancers, and served as assistant rehearsal director and choreographer. Many of his classmates were now in the corps de ballet or even dancing as principals, including Niels. They were sympathetic toward him but kept their distance.

Two years passed thus. Teo's world was almost as narrow as his life in Berlin had been. He rarely socialized, spent his days at the theater and his nights alone at home. On Friday evenings he would eat a festive Sabbath meal with the Sonnenfelds, then escape as early as possible to his tiny apartment. He declined invitations and eventually the world complied and left him alone.

But a letter he received in his second Danish winter would change all that:

2 February 1947

Dear Mr. Levin,

 The Soviet sector of the Allied Control Council formally requests your participation at the trial of Friedrich Sebastien Amadeus von Edelwald, lieutenant-general in German Military Intelligence from 1939 to 1945. It is believed that your testi-

mony is crucial in the pursuit of justice and we thereby request
that you make every effort to be present. Your travel expenses
and accommodations will be provided by the Council.

The trial is scheduled to open 17 April. Please make plans to
be at the Allied Control Council headquarters in Berlin, at the
address below, several days prior.

Respectfully,

Ivan Poliakov

Presiding Judge, Soviet Military Tribunal

Teo moved the letter around his apartment for several days, reread-
ing it when he awoke each morning, when he returned from the bal-
let, before falling asleep. It brought him nightmares, and daymares
too. One morning he put the letter in the rubbish bin but by that
evening he had fished it out again.

On April 14 Teo packed a bag with his meager belongings. In an
inner pocket of his overcoat he placed Freddy's cuff links and foun-
tain pen and lighter, all of which he kept buried under a pile of hand-
kerchiefs in his bureau drawer. He locked the apartment and walked
to Copenhagen Central.

At passport control on the German border he began to shake
violently, but an aperitif back on board calmed his nerves enough to
complete the journey. The German countryside was quiet and pasto-
ral, a bright jeweled green in the spring sunshine.

Pockets of the city were still in ruins, but Berlin was already
showing signs of becoming the lively city it had once been. Teo found
the Allied Control Council headquarters easily and gave a deposition
on the morning following his arrival. He was surprised to learn that
Freddy was on trial for the murder of two Soviet soldiers who had
tried to detain him on the evening of April twenty-fifth, only two or

three hours after the last time Teo had seen him. On a break during Teo's deposition, a young German-speaking military adjudicator sidled up to him and whispered that this trial and the defendant's imprisonment in Germany and not the USSR were highly unusual and due to a combination of his high-ranking connections and money and certain facts that would come to light during the trial. Before Teo could ask what he meant, the break was over and the adjudicator had slipped from the room.

On the day of the trial, Teo arrived early and spent half an hour switching from seat to seat in the slowly filling courtroom. He settled, finally, on a spot close to the front but off to the side, from which he would have a clear view of the defendant's face but from which Freddy might not be able to see him well.

Shackled and gaunt in prison uniform, Freddy was led into the courtroom at just after ten o'clock, his eyes to the floor. Seeing him sent a jolt so great through Teo's entire body that for a moment he thought he had been shot or electrocuted, or that maybe his heart had burst open. He made a gasping noise that caused Freddy to look up, and when he saw Teo he stopped in his tracks. "Oh thank God, thank God," he cried in German. A guard shoved him into his seat, but Freddy stole glances at Teo when he could and continued weeping.

Teo sat doubled over in pain for the first part of the proceedings. He wished to bolt but felt as though he were riveted to his chair. It was all he could do to keep from tumbling sideways to the floor.

The charges against Freddy were read to the court in German and Russian. No mention was made of his art dealings, nothing was said about Ernst Halberstadt or the boy who had been sent to his death with Teodor Levin's documents. Freddy's statement was read before the court, and then Freddy himself was called to the stand.

From the moment he sat in the box, Freddy did not stop looking at Teo. Teo could only glance away. It came back to him in a flood now, the humiliation, the violence, the endless hours of servicing Freddy's obsession. He remembered, too, the tender moments, Freddy's proclamations of love and his own confused responses. He did not know which sickened him more.

"No," he heard Freddy saying. "It wasn't like that at all. It was completely unintentional. I was merely desperate to return to my home in Grunewald."

"But you did, in fact, murder two Soviet soldiers in cold blood, did you not?" said the Russian prosecutor, a bald man with an elaborate goatee. There were pauses in the proceedings as interpreters translated between languages. Teo wore a pair of headphones in order to make sure he could understand the questions, but Freddy's answers came to him unimpeded.

"I ran them over in a mad dash to reach home. I was terribly worried about the fate of someone in my care and so . . ."

" . . . and so you took the lives of two others in order to protect this person."

"I repeat, it was not intentional. They were there when I rounded a corner coming out of intelligence headquarters. I was speeding. I was hoping to save a Jew hidden in my household."

A murmur arose in the courtroom, which the judge quelled with his gavel.

"You expect the court to believe that you, a Generalleutnant, were harboring a Jew for his protection right in your home, just a few kilometers from Nazi headquarters?"

"Yes, he'd been safe there with me for six years, from the first day of the war."

The murmur was louder this time and the judge demanded order.

Teo, his head between his knees, heard this and understood why he had been summoned to Berlin. He understood that Freddy might be acquitted if the judge were to call the deaths of the Soviet soldiers an accident, and if he were further convinced of Freddy's humanitarianism by virtue of having harbored a Jew in secret for nearly six years.

Teo was called to the witness stand when Freddy had finished testifying. He scanned the room, taking in the judge, the guards, the grand architecture of the place, and, finally, Freddy himself, who looked far older than Teo remembered him. There seemed to be less of him, as though not only his body weight had shrunk but his very bones as well. For the first time in two years Teo felt ready to talk. A stockpile of words and images was pressing from behind his eyes and lips but he did his best to remain calm as the military prosecutor took him through the preliminaries: who he was, where he had been born, how he, a Jew, had come to live in the home of a high-ranking Nazi officer.

"And so," the prosecutor was saying, "he took you in. Befriended you."

"He kept me in his house under false pretenses. I was a prisoner there."

"A prisoner? The defendant has testified that he took you to museums and cafés, that he taught you about art. He even brought you to meet his family."

"That was all in the beginning—"

"Before there were restrictions against Jews in Berlin?"

"No, it had nothing to do with that. I was in hiding. I had no papers. Or rather, he had forged papers made for me but kept them in a safe, where I couldn't reach them."

"Mr. Levin, the defendant mowed down two Soviet soldiers in the last days of the war. This is not a crime we take lightly, even in the madness of those times and that place, but Soviet justice is fair

and we will not punish a man unduly if his crime can be proven an accident and his behavior, as in the case of harboring a Jew and endangering his own life, is otherwise exemplary. I wish to be very clear: if you have nothing to clarify or add then this tribunal will most likely release the defendant in a relatively short time, and he will—"

"I was his slave," Teo said in a clear voice, interrupting.

"Excuse me?"

"For nearly six years of my life I was that man's slave," he repeated, gesturing toward Freddy. "I was only seventeen when he lied to the police or bribed somebody and had me released to his custody and prevented me from returning to Denmark. I was a child. I didn't know anything of the world beyond dancing, but whatever I would have become, he took it away from me. Maybe it seems insignificant when you think about the unspeakable things that happened to people during the war, but in those six years I lost . . . everything. My freedom. My career. My personality. Even my . . . sexual identity." Teo turned to the judge, his voice rising. Bloodred panic was roiling inside him, a scarlet scrim between him and the world. "Do you know what that means? I never left the grounds of the house . . . I had to stay hidden from view all the time. Like a ghost. I had no . . . no power to make decisions about the most basic aspects of my own life." He stopped speaking to breathe, and to steel himself. "And . . . he raped me, almost daily. A week before I met him I was falling in love with a girl, back in Copenhagen . . . but then he took over my life and I stopped knowing who I was and what I desired. Who I desired. And I still don't know. I still don't know who I am."

With that, Teo gripped the arms of his chair and squeezed tight as a shout erupted from his gut through his lungs and out his throat, a sound more sharp and painful than any he had ever made, a growl

and a howl and a sob rolled into one. When it ended, there was silence in the courtroom but for Teo's panting and Freddy's weeping.

For the next hour the judge listened and the prosecutor listened and the courtroom listened as Teo told of his imprisonment. He shocked the court by describing the acts Freddy had forced him to perform, and detailed his obsession so thoroughly that no one in the courtroom could think Freddy incapable of murdering anyone who tried to prevent him from being with Teo.

Late in the afternoon Freddy was sentenced to life imprisonment. In Siberia. As the guards escorted him from the courtroom, Freddy stopped, wild-eyed, exuberant almost. "Jimmie Lunceford, remember?" he shouted, staring at Teo. The guards were pulling him as he sang, "*I'm so mad about you, say we'll never part! I can't live without you; you're the keeper of my heart. So if you love me, too, Honey, keep your mind on me!* Teo!" he yelled, jubilant, "with me, together, *ad astra!*" The last words reverberated as the guards wrestled Freddy out the door, but Teo sat motionless and winded.

Minutes later, back on his feet but dry-mouthed and shaky, Teo hurried to his hotel, fetched his small suitcase and ran the rest of the way to the train station. He had to get out of Germany, out of heartless Europe, tainted and barbarous. He would stop in Warsaw then leave the continent. America or Canada, Australia or New Zealand, these would be too difficult, he would have to wait too long for permission. He needed somewhere that would take him immediately, so he chose to leave for Palestine just as soon as he could ascertain what had become of his sister.

He settled in on the eastbound train, feeling more purposeful and even optimistic than he had in years.

Nothing in Warsaw was familiar to him, but he had left the city nearly a decade earlier, when he was only fifteen. Much of Warsaw

still lay in ruins; gaping pits or piles of rubble occupied space where buildings once stood. Apart from his brief interview with Cukier, he hadn't heard Polish spoken in so many years that he needed people to repeat themselves once or twice before he could understand them.

Reaching his old street by public transportation seemed nearly impossible, so he simply walked across Warsaw, arriving at Szara Street after two difficult hours. At first nothing made sense: the building on the corner was gone and so was the one next to it. His own building was still standing, but it looked so different—naked now, exposed—that he had trouble recognizing it. And then there were the holes, huge bullet holes running up the building nearly to the third floor. He approached slowly, wary.

He was trembling now, and stood looking up at the entryway for several long minutes before climbing the stairs into the building. Several of the names on the mailboxes were familiar to him; his own had been written over, rather sloppily, so that the L still showed through.

He climbed one flight of stairs, turned to the right and knocked. A young girl in braids opened the door and for a second Teo thought he had found Margot. Of course Margot would be a young woman now, he knew this, but for a brief moment he enjoyed the fantasy. Before he could speak, a woman loomed up behind the girl. "Yes?" she asked. "What is it?"

"I used to live here," Teo said, "I was wondering whether you know what became of my family, the Levins, especially my sister, Margot."

"Jew, go away," came a deep baritone from somewhere inside the house. "Maria, close the door."

"I'm sorry," the woman whispered, and closed the door in Teo's face.

Teo was stunned, but before he could knock again, a door opened behind him. "Please come in, Mr. Levin," said a thin young woman.

"I've been waiting for you."

Even more stunned now, Teo removed his cap and entered the house. It was a mirror image of his own family's apartment but shabbier. He tried to remember the family that had lived in this flat but could not recall a name or a face. The young woman disappeared to one of the back rooms for a moment, then returned with an envelope in her hand.

"Would you care for some tea?" she asked. Teo nodded. The young woman gave him the envelope and went to the kitchen.

The letter was addressed to Nelly Pukarski at this address. There was no return address. Teo's hands shook as he pulled the letter free from the envelope.

28 October 1940

Dear Nelly,

Greetings from the lovely south of our beautiful Poland! The weather is warm and pleasant here, the climate much more suited to me than Warsaw. The nuns are friendly and I have made many friends.

Please be sure to show this letter to my silly brother when he gets home today. Tell him I miss him and expect to see him soon. And remember: Make All Reasons You Know And Try Our Word In Christ Everlasting!

Your friend,

Kitty

Teo was reading the letter for the fourth time when the young woman came back with tea. He looked up from the letter, a quizzical look on his face.

"I am Nelly," the young woman said. "My family moved here shortly after you went to Denmark. Margot and I became best friends, we were together all the time. We used to prance about pretending we were ballerinas, too." Teo tried to smile but was not certain he had succeeded.

"That's a picture of my mother," she said, pointing to a blurry photograph on a small table next to Teo. "She starved to death during the war. We didn't know she was giving us all her food." She paused and there was an awkward silence until Teo said he was sorry.

"I live here with my father and my brother, they are working now." Teo lifted the letter in his hands.

"Yes, of course, Margot. I'm sorry, that's what you are here for." She sat down and motioned Teo to do the same. "Your parents arranged for Margot to be sent to a convent in the south. She was given a new name there, Katharina Lyczynski. This is the only letter I received from her during the war, but I believe she may still be at the convent."

"How can I find her?" Teo asked.

"Look at the last line of her letter. It's a code."

He glanced at it again but still did not understand.

"Make all reasons you know and try our word in Christ everlasting," Nelly quoted without reading it. "If you take just the first letter of each word you get 'Mary Katowice.' She's at Saint Mary's in Katowice."

Teo glanced again at the letter, his mouth open. He looked up at Nelly, nodding. Presently he stood up, and so did Nelly.

"Please write to me," she said.

"I will," he said as he moved to the door. Out in the hall he turned back toward her before descending. "Thank you," he said quietly.

"God bless," she answered, and she watched him as he ran quickly from the street of his childhood.

Teo had not slept in a bed for several days, but he did not care. He caught the next train to Katowice, down near the Hungarian border. The train was packed, so he stood in an aisle.

Sometime after dark, as he squatted dozing, he was awakened by shouts. A drunken Pole, red-faced and disheveled, was barreling down the aisle shouting. "Jews off the train, Jews off the train! This train is for Poles only!" He stepped on people in the aisle, poking his face into each visage to see if it belonged, perhaps, to a Jew. "Oswiecim, all Jews disembark at Oswiecim!" he ranted. Teo had not realized it but understood that this train would indeed pass by Auschwitz. Just before the drunken Pole reached Teo he found his victim. "A Jew, here, a Jew!" he shouted as he stood over an elderly man, stooped and disfigured. Teo was about to leap to the old man's defense when a whistle sounded behind him and two train guards apprehended the drunken Pole and led him away, cursing as he went.

Saint Mary's turned out to be several kilometers from the center of Katowice. Teo set out on foot from the train station, which he reached in the early morning, after splashing down a *paczek* with weak but steaming coffee. He had forgotten how tasty these doughnuts were, though there was less plum jam than he recalled from his childhood. Several trucks and buses passed him and one offered a ride, but Teo preferred to walk. He watched the Polish farmers till their land with great oxen and passed a village market with little to offer. His small suitcase had grown heavy in his arms but he walked on in the dust and sunshine.

At the gate of the convent he pulled a heavy bell and waited. A

wimpled nun greeted him.

"Good day, sister, I hope you can help me. I am here to see Katharina Lyczynski."

"What business would you have with Sister Katharina please?"

He was thrilled to learn she was still here, but surprised she would be called Sister.

"She is my sister, we were separated by the war."

"I see," said the nun. "What is your name?"

"Teodor L . . . Teodor," he said, unsure whether he would gain admittance with so Jewish a surname.

"Please wait here," she said.

Five minutes passed before she returned, during which time Teo, leaning on a stone wall clotted with moss, watched a dog chase a cat up a tall birch just inside the gate. The cat hissed from her perch while the dog barked crazily from below. "Please follow me," said the nun as she opened the locked gate.

Teo was made to wait in a small reception room just inside a stone courtyard. When Margot entered he did not know it was she and stood staring at this young woman in a simple habit. In fact, he may not have believed it was she at all if he had not noticed the lazy eyelid she was born with.

"I have prayed for this day to come," she said. "You must have found Nelly."

Teo nodded. They did not embrace.

"Margot," he said, in disbelief.

"Sister Katharina, now," she said with a smile.

"Come with me," he said. "I have come to take you away from here."

She stopped smiling, became earnest. "This is my home, Teodor. It is my life. I was brought here by Our Lord Jesus Christ and saved."

Teo sat down abruptly. A small porcelain Jesus with a forlorn expression stood in his direct line of vision. He caught the shape of a lamb in the stained-glass window on the wall next to him.

Margot sat next to him. "Are you still dancing?" she asked gently. He shook his head.

"One day you must tell me your story," she ventured.

He shook his head again. Then he stood to go.

"I am leaving Europe, I have no place on this continent any longer," he said. "I'm hoping to sail for Palestine in the next few days. May I write to you when I've gotten settled?"

"Of course, my dear brother. We must never lose contact again."

Teo stepped from the room and walked with his sister to the gate. "Go with God," she said as he departed, but he did not answer.

Four days later Teo boarded a Palestine-bound ship in Trieste with a visa issued in Budapest. The heaviness in his heart did not lift even when the ship was far out to sea, but he knew at least that at twenty-five he was sailing away to a chance for a new life.

This was a new story for Vivi. The themes are the same as the old stories—cruelty, lust, power, disenfranchisement, dignity, love and hate, obsession—but without the concentration camps, the dogs, the rampaging, murderous mobs. For the last hour of his tale she sat shivering; even the afghan pulled round her shoulders could not keep her warm.

She has too many questions but can only begin to formulate one: "Your sister . . ." she starts, then falls silent.

Unlike Vivi, Teo is sweating. His brow is damp, his shirt clingy. For the past few hours the words had come in a monotone, as if he were reciting, but it is clear to her this was a first telling that had been festering for more than sixty years. "She is still there, in the convent. The last time I saw her was in 1980, when I was invited to Warsaw to receive the White Eagle award. That's when I met up again with Nelly, too. Her father was dead and her brother simply hadn't returned from work one day. Poof, and he was gone. I married her to get her out of Poland and bring her back to Israel with me."

"She's your wife?" Vivi asks. She had thought nothing more could astonish her after this long, long night, and yet here she is, completely taken by surprise.

"In name only," he says. "A matter of convenience for us both."

"And what," she begins to ask, softening her voice, "what happened to Freddy?"

He glances up at her. At once she sees he is not really looking into her eyes but right through them. "I have no idea," he says. "I suppose he died out there in Siberia, most of them did." Quieter now, he adds, "The strange thing is that I feel a certain . . . ambiguity toward him. As a Pole, I may have been sent to a camp when the Germans entered Denmark, so maybe he really did save me. I even believe that he loved me. Well, at least until his love spilled over into obsession."

She takes a chance: "And you, in a fashion, loved him as well. In fact," she says, with a wakening sense of revelation, "I think he was one of the two people you loved. Freddy and Sofie."

He nods, abashed, as if he has been vanquished, as if he has given up his very last secret. "With Sofie, I never had a chance to find out. With Freddy, love was forced on me. He took so much away from me. But he . . . gave me something as well. In the midst of his obsession with me there was . . . I don't know. An iota of something pure and real. Beyond all his charm and culture and knowledge. Beyond the fact that he was a monster, that I was his prisoner. He could see past the beautiful dancer in me to the real person inside, and he loved that person as much as the dancer. Well, I responded to that. Maybe that's as close to love as I've come. I'm not sure, I've never managed to complete the equation. My life changed course in the muddle of all those gains and losses, and nothing adds up."

She thinks about gain and loss for a moment and wonders: have I exploited him? Did I really use the birthday party as an excuse? She believed she had meant it to be a gift, but now she is no longer certain. How much of what she did was for her own benefit?

And what about this next, final, part of her plan? She could ask herself these same questions about it, but she does not. She has let herself go free in the land of wanting and fulfillment and she cannot stop or even look back now. And anyway, wasn't it he himself who taught her to desire, to aspire? She is his protégée, his quick and eager student.

He is on fire, this ancient young man in the chair facing her. He is flushed and drenched. His body exudes the scent of cubbish maleness. He has finished speaking, but beneath his skin she sees he is smoldering; rather than depleting him, these hours of telling his story have inflamed him. There is more to this story, and it is about to happen. She rises from the sofa, shakes off the afghan, extends a hand. There are no more secrets at all as she leads him into the bedroom.

There is nothing new about their lovemaking. Men and women have been matching body part to body part since there were men and women. But for both, this is nonetheless a revelation.

Has she ever enjoyed herself in slow motion before, each movement a priceless gift?

Is this what his life has been lacking through long years of productivity, creativity, motion?

She feels his body was fashioned for this night, its muscles taut and hard. There is nothing old mannish about him—his scent, his ardor, his passion.

He drifts in pleasurable bewilderment over decades and continents. Could this be Sofie's soft skin he is possessing at last?

Long hours pass and his euphoria abates. He is being pulled down, the comforter weighs on him like a current of rushing water. He succumbs, finally, does not fight; he closes his eyes and lets himself slip beneath the surface of consciousness to a different kind of wakefulness. He is focused and ready for something, and even before that something happens he knows what it will be and so he settles back to enjoy, at long last, his dance.

He has just lowered Kirsten to the floor, the orchestra is making the transition from their duet music to his solo, and Teodor makes his way gracefully across the grand stage to stand in position. He can see everything now, all those details that have escaped him for the seven decades since he actually danced it at the Berlin Staatsoper: he sees the Danish ballet master in the wings; he sees the grand chandelier, the spotlights, the gold filigree on the balcony seats; he sees the festive audience, bright with the news of war and redemption, even picks out Freddy in the crowd. Yes, there he is, in a first-tier balcony seat, the closest one to the stage, next to him a pretty young man, really a boy, looking peeved.

As he stands in that great, long moment of silence before pivoting out to the left, Teodor makes his decision. It is born from the Nazi officer's announcement about Germany having attacked Poland that

very day, and from the NO JEWS signs on the Unter den Linden, and the looks and comments in the Adlon Hotel and maybe one hundred other resentments large and small tied in a bundle and thrown in with that other heavy bundle, the will and the desire to become a great dancer, the greatest; and since there are no bundles at all to tip the scales in the other direction, well, no decision really needed to be made; it is a fait accompli.

Yes, here it is at last, the juxtaposition of his Russian training on his acquired Danish style, the change from low leaps to high, dazzling ones, from single, slow pirouettes to frenzied turns, dozens of them. Take that! his body shouts. You are not superior, you are not wiser or stronger than we are, I'll show you what perfection is! Yes, he can see it now, feel every move exactly as he performed it; and more, as if detached he can see their faces, individually, following him in awe as he explodes across the stage. The woman in the third row, her hand over her mouth and tears in her eyes. The man on an aisle practically leaping from his seat in excitement. And Freddy, gripping the railing, perfectly still and watching with a crazed intensity. Yes, here it all is, the dance that shot his life in a new direction, up to the perfect triple tour en l'air that ends without so much as a quiver.

And with the roar of ecstatic applause in his ears, Teodor Levin leaves the stage forever.

Martin is gone. The coffee bar is gone. Twenty years of aimless ambling are gone. A new life has begun, here in this bed. There will be art and gurgling laughter. There will be fabrics and clay, scissors and secateurs, there will be a mad jumble of colors and music and movement and games and ideas, ideas, ideas are bubbling, percolating, foaming up like milk heated on a gas flame, they overflow, dousing the heat and finally, as light pierces the horizon, she sleeps.

Hours later, the sun rising high on a perfect spring day, she rolls onto her side and brushes against his arm. It is smooth and cold as marble. She jolts awake and finds him in poised repose, as if he has chosen his final resting position. His splendid eyes are wide open, but she knows right away that their blue-green gaze no longer sees anything at all.

She takes a deep, deep breath. Here, in her bed, an ending and a beginning.

EPILOGUE

"**C**an you hold him for a minute?" she asks.

"Come here, big guy," Pincho says, lifting the chubby toddler over his shoulder.

They have been promised the ceremony will be short, and she fed Nathaniel as soon as they were inside the President's Residence, but the president is tied up with a visiting dignitary and everything has been delayed. Nathaniel is growing restless.

Vivi may be the only person in the room more interested in the president than the visiting dignitary, for whom a phalanx of photographers stands waiting outside. The spry old president is a contemporary of Teo's, and she wishes to look into his face from up close, if for no other reason than to see if something there, anything, even the smallest flicker in his eyes, can bring back the tiniest piece of the man she misses so keenly.

She turns to her mother. Before embracing her from behind, she takes in Leah's careful coif only slightly flattened during the long drive from Haifa to Jerusalem, and the stiff new suit bought for this

occasion. Leah is scrutinizing *Berlin: Martin, Freddy*, the installation her daughter created and the reason they are here today.

Vivi hooks her chin over her mother's shoulder, snakes her arms around Leah's middle. At least there is nothing new about her scent, the same perfume she has been wearing for Vivi's whole life.

"I think I understand the meaning of the KaDeWe department store sign," Leah says with uncharacteristic equanimity, "but why the video with those old Dutch paintings by . . . what was his name?"

"Vermeer," says Vivi softly into her mother's ear.

"That's it, Vermeer. So what do they mean?"

Before Vivi can decide whether to answer her mother's question, a double door at the end of the large reception room opens and the president emerges arm in arm with an impressive middle-aged blonde whom Vivi, and everyone else, recognizes at once. On their way past tables laden with pastries and cold drinks, figs and watermelon, the visiting dignitary stops to coo at Nathaniel as he gurgles blissfully in Pincho's arms.

"What a beautiful, happy baby you have," she says in an American accent as flat as the plains from which she hails.

"Thank you," Vivi answers.

"What's his name?" the woman asks.

"Nathaniel. It's Hebrew for 'a gift from God.'"

"Well, he certainly is that, isn't he? Oh and look, one blue eye and one green. You're gorgeous, aren't you, little man!"

The president says, "His mother is about to receive a prize. She's a very talented artist, you know."

"You're a lucky woman," says the dignitary, her eyes sliding from Nathaniel to Pincho.

"Oh, don't I know it," says Vivi, a broad smile settling onto her face.